Karen Lee Sobol, an accompli
treatment for a rare life-threat
and occasional tears. She optec
leading cancer center, and combined it with a holistic approach to achieve wonderful results. Karen Lee's narrative is warm, insightful, inspirational and skillfully illustrated with her own artwork. *Twelve Weeks* is sure to benefit patients, family members, physicians, and nurses as it successfully conveys a message of healing, humanity, and hope.

Marvin J. Stone, MD
Baylor Sammons Cancer Center
Dallas, Texas

Twelve Weeks is a true account of the power of the mind-body connection and one artist's journey to become cancer-free. This is an amazing story of how the force of inner strength and belief in one's intention changes a person's physical being—one that validates the connection between our physical embodiment and the spirituality of life, willpower, courageous steadiness, and the commitment to self-care.

Karen Lee Sobol's journey will teach you to take charge of your own life... regardless of the obstacle.

Ellen Comerford
Reiki Master and Owner, Core de Vie Wellness Center
Boston, Massachusetts

Karen Lee Sobol's *Twelve Weeks* paints a vivid portrait of Karen Lee Sobol's journey into the world of cancer survivorship. Using elegant and at times humorous prose, not one to mince words or gloss over difficult and highly personal passages, Karen Lee's honest and heartfelt writing leads us through the symphony of emotions experienced by anyone who has ever received a diagnosis of cancer. Beginning with the somber sonata of disbelief and fear, followed by the slow but steady development of increased self-realization and courageous determination, and finally ending in victorious and joyous celebration—in this wonderful book of love and compassion, Karen Lee hits all the right notes!

Guy Sherwood, MD, FAACP, FCFP
IWMF Board of Directors Trustee,Cancer Survivor
Muncie, Indiana

Twelve Weeks is a must for all physicians, nurses, and other medical personnel. It places the reader in the "shoes" of the patient. One feels that he is with Karen Lee Sobol during the tests and treatments. Medical personnel must realize that most patients are unfamiliar with medical terminology and it must be "translated" for the patient. Diagnostic procedures, tests, and various treatments need to be explained to the patient so that they are understood. This would go a long way in reducing patients' anxiety and make diagnosis and treatment less frightening.

Robert A. Kyle, MD
Professor of Medicine, Laboratory Medicine & Pathology, Mayo Clinic
Rochester, Minnesota

When doctors care for patients, they learn from them. Karen Lee Sobol's story is personal, as well as an insight into Waldenstrom's Macroglobulinemia. It should be required reading for all doctors who listen to their patients.

Fred H. Hochberg, MD
Department of Neurology, Massachusetts General Hospital
Boston, Massachusetts

I stayed up all night making my way through the labyrinth of fears, questions, and resolve that Karen Lee Sobol's diagnosis occasioned, and then found myself following her (and her family's) brave journey through the underworld of treatment and its aftermath—and finally to the breathtaking clarity of 0.0.

As a fellow artist and teacher, I am so moved at the way Karen Lee chronicles her treatment and celebrates her recovery through her art. In an intense and accessible personal visual journey, she acknowledges and shares her fears and hurdles, as her brush and pen transform the "stuff of treatment" into a light at the end of the tunnel.

Annie Zeybekoglu, Artist
Senior Faculty in Visual Arts, Lexington High School,
Lexington, Massachusetts

When I read *Twelve Weeks* I could not put it down and read it in one seating. I laughed, I cried, I pitied, and I rejoiced with Karen Lee Sobol throughout the entire book. Her honesty in expressing her emotions was heart-felt. The artwork is part and parcel of the book. May Karen-Lee's life be filled with love, joy, and health!

Stephanie A. Gregory, MD
Professor of Medicine and Director, Section of Hematology
Rush University Medical Center, Chicago, Illinois

Twelve Weeks should be required reading for all medical students. Karen Lee Sobol has been able to share an experience that illustrates the significance of the patient-physician relationship and the importance of respect and communication between patients and healthcare providers. This is a book of trust, confidence, and respect. As a healthcare executive, I am impressed with Karen Lee's desire to explore every conceivable avenue in the treatment of what was initially characterized as an incurable disease. *Twelve Weeks* serves as a vision of hope for all patients, regardless of their diagnosis.

Thad Johnson
Executive Vice President (retired), All Saints Health System
Racine, Wisconsin

Working in diagnostics and research, it is very easy to become overly-focused on science. *Twelve Weeks* gives an enlightening view of diagnosis and treatment from a patient's perspective. The brave and frank discussion about the effects that diagnosis and treatment had on Karen Lee Sobol and her family are a powerful reminder that everything we do, no matter how insignificant it may seem to us, has an effect on the patient and their family. Keeping this in mind is powerful motivation indeed!

Ruth de Tute, Advanced Biomedical Scientist
Haematological Malignancy Diagnostic Service, St James Hospital
Leeds, England

As an oncologist, and having Waldenstrom's Macroglobulinemia myself, *Twelve Weeks* has been very interesting for me to read. Karen Lee Sobol appears as an extremely conscious and vivid person who managed to turn all her strength and mind into one purpose: fighting the cancer cells to become cancer-free. Her most important weapon was obviously to receive modern biomedical treatment by a highly professional medical team, but she also adopted alternative methods including regular meditation, positive thinking, and sound therapy. And she won!

Karen Lee's success increases my firm belief that the strong connection between body and mind is important in healing cancer. I recommend this wonderful book to cancer patients, their relatives, doctors, and healthcare personnel. They will recognize feelings and reactions beautifully described, and I am sure they will be inspired and encouraged in their fight against cancer.

Eva Hoff Wanderås, MD, PhD
Specialist in Oncology, Oslo University Hospital
Oslo, Norway

Karen Lee Sobol's *Twelve Weeks* combines western medicine with holistic alternative therapies. A synthesis of ancient wisdom and modern science resulted in her successful healing and freedom from a cancer considered to be incurable. Karen Lee's healing journey will inspire and bring the light of hope to the many who feel helpless and doomed with this disease. What a gift this book brings to the individuals and families facing life and death choices. Thank you Karen Lee, for writing and sharing your amazing experience.

Kathleen Krantz, MS
Reiki Master and Theta Healing Practitioner
Eugene, Oregon

Twelve Weeks

An Artist's Story of Cancer, Healing, and Hope

Karen Lee Sobol

A Note to the Reader
Every effort has been made to ensure that the information contained in this book is complete and accurate. However, neither the publisher nor the author is engaged in rendering professional advice or services to the individual reader. Nothing contained in this book, including ideas, suggestions and procedures is intended as a substitute for consulting with your physician. All matters regarding your health require medical supervision. Neither the author nor the publisher shall be liable or responsible for any loss, injury, or damage allegedly arising from any information or suggestion in this book.

All Artwork by Karen Lee Sobol
Photography by George Bouret
Design by Nick Stone

It is my heart's wish that my story will bring light to everyone who receives a diagnosis of cancer, or any grave disease, and to their families, friends and medical teams. The path need not be dark.

Some names have been changed to protect people's privacy.

To My Family
Our Friends
and
The Mighty Team

"The mind influences the chemistry of the body."

—Noah Sobol, my father

"The power of a vision is that it has to be ideal."

—Jeff Skoll, first president of Ebay.com
& founder of Participant Media

YEARLY CALENDARS

2005

january

s	m	t	w	t	f	s
						1
2	3	4	5	6	7	8
9	10	11	12	13	14	15
16	17	18	19	20	21	22
23	24	25	26	27	28	29
30	31					

february

s	m	t	w	t	f	s
		1	2	3	4	5
6	7	8	9	10	11	12
13	14	15	16	17	18	19
20	21	22	23	24	25	26
27	28					

march

s	m	t	w	t	f	s
		1	2	3	4	5
6	7	8	9	10	11	12
13	14	15	16	17	18	19
20	21	22	23	24	25	26
27	28	29	30	31		

april

s	m	t	w	t	f	s
					1	2
3	4	5	6	7	8	9
10	11	12	13	14	15	16
17	18	19	20	21	22	23
24	25	26	27	28	29	30

may

s	m	t	w	t	f	s
1	2	3	4	5	6	7
8	9	10	11	12	13	14
15	16	17	18	19	20	21
22	23	24	25	26	27	28
29	30	31				

june

s	m	t	w	t	f	s
			1	2	3	4
5	6	7	8	9	10	11
12	13	14	15	16	17	18
19	20	21	22	23	24	25
26	27	28	29	30		

+ CAT scan + EYES

16 ZACT

july

s	m	t	w	t	f	s
					1	2
3	4	5	6	7	8	9
10	11	12	13	14	15	16
17	18	19	20	21	22	23
24	25	26	27	28	29	30
31						

august

s	m	t	w	t	f	s
	1	2	3	4	5	6
7	8	9	10	11	12	13
14	15	16	17	18	19	20
21	22	23	24	25	26	27
28	29	30	31			

september

s	m	t	w	t	f	s
				1	2	3
4	5	6	7	8	9	10
11	12	13	14	15	16	17
18	19	20	21	22	23	24
25	26	27	28	29	30	

Plasma Feresis

Acyclovir + Bactrim

october

s	m	t	w	t	f	s
						1
2	3	4	5	6	7	8
9	10	11	12	13	14	15
16	17	18	19	20	21	22
23	24	25	26	27	28	29
30	31					

november

s	m	t	w	t	f	s
		1	2	3	4	5
6	7	8	9	10	11	12
13	14	15	16	17	18	19
20	21	22	23	24	25	26
27	28	29	30			

december

s	m	t	w	t	f	s
				1	2	3
4	5	6	7	8	9	10
11	12	13	14	15	16	17
18	19	20	21	22	23	24
25	26	27	28	29	30	31

Acyclovir + Bactrim

Dr Olstein

Acyclovir Levaquin

2006

january

s	m	t	w	t	f	s
1	2	3	4	5	6	7
8	9	10	11	12	13	14
15	16	17	18	19	20	21
22	23	24	25	26	27	28
29	30	31				

february

s	m	t	w	t	f	s
			1	2	3	4
5	6	7	8	9	10	11
12	13	14	15	16	17	18
19	20	21	22	23	24	25
26	27	28				

march

s	m	t	w	t	f	s
			1	2	3	4
5	6	7	8	9	10	11
12	13	14	15	16	17	18
19	20	21	22	23	24	25
26	27	28	29	30	31	

Prednisone/Prilosec

-P/P- -Rash

april

s	m	t	w	t	f	s
						1
2	3	4	5	6	7	8
9	10	11	12	13	14	15
16	17	18	19	20	21	22
23	24	25	26	27	28	29
30						

may

s	m	t	w	t	f	s
	1	2	3	4	5	6
7	8	9	10	11	12	13
14	15	16	17	18	19	20
21	22	23	24	25	26	27
28	29	30	31			

june

s	m	t	w	t	f	s
				1	2	3
4	5	6	7	8	9	10
11	12	13	14	15	16	17
18	19	20	21	22	23	24
25	26	27	28	29	30	

endo

prednisone

P/P: RASH

blood

Levaquin

CAT

allergy

DR HAYDEN

july

s	m	t	w	t	f	s
						1
2	3	4	5	6	7	8
9	10	11	12	13	14	15
16	17	18	19	20	21	22
23	24	25	26	27	28	29
30	31					

august

s	m	t	w	t	f	s
		1	2	3	4	5
6	7	8	9	10	11	12
13	14	15	16	17	18	19
20	21	22	23	24	25	26
27	28	29	30	31		

september

s	m	t	w	t	f	s
					1	2
3	4	5	6	7	8	9
10	11	12	13	14	15	16
17	18	19	20	21	22	23
24	25	26	27	28	29	30

PET CT

october

s	m	t	w	t	f	s
1	2	3	4	5	6	7
8	9	10	11	12	13	14
15	16	17	18	19	20	21
22	23	24	25	26	27	28
29	30	31				

november

s	m	t	w	t	f	s
			1	2	3	4
5	6	7	8	9	10	11
12	13	14	15	16	17	18
19	20	21	22	23	24	25
26	27	28	29	30		

december

s	m	t	w	t	f	s
					1	2
3	4	5	6	7	8	9
10	11	12	13	14	15	16
17	18	19	20	21	22	23
24	25	26	27	28	29	30
31						

BW WAO - Annual Physical

Symposium

Before

"The Healthiest Person We Know"

Remember the section in those high school yearbooks from the fifties and sixties, before the era of political correctness, when the senior class voted for kids in the categories of "Most Likely to Succeed," or "Most Likely to Be Famous?" On February 6th, 2004, my 56th birthday, I and everyone who knew me probably would have voted me "The Healthiest Person We Know."

I was the one who ate the right foods—if you allow chocolate and some wine on the list—exercised as part of my soul, and, except for an occasional antibiotic, never took a prescription drug. Genetics and metabolism seemed to keep me slender. I weighed 116 pounds, the same weight I'd been at forty, when I became pregnant with my daughter, Sara. Except for weakness in my legs, especially during the summer, and some progressing stiffness in my hands, it seemed I was totally healthy.

As for diet, I've never been a fan of "junk food" or soda. Organic foods, not much meat, and more fruits and vegetables than potatoes were my usual choices. After my daughter was born, a friend had observed my eating pattern—snacking all the time—and dubbed it "grazing." I needed to refuel often. As for cholesterol levels, mine were among the lowest my doctor had ever seen. "I want to frame your lipids," she said.

As a teenager growing up in suburban New Jersey, when most of my friends seized every opportunity to borrow the family car, I preferred taking solitary walks to the local shopping streets. Competitive in school, with no sports for girls and energy to burn, I needed some quiet time, and I needed to move.

Since graduating from high school, I've lived in cities. In Cambridge, Massachusetts, where I attended college and graduate school from 1966 to 1974, riding a bike was fun for a while. But my wandering, distracted mind made biking risky. Walking was slower, but safer, so my feet became my primary means of transportation.

With my Masters of Architecture degree in hand, I moved to New York City. For fourteen years, I practiced architecture, walked wherever I could, rode the subways and busses, and hailed an occasional taxi.

I met my future husband Bill in graduate school; we pursued separate careers in separate cities. In 1985, we re-met by chance. When we married in 1988, I sold my architecture firm and moved to Boston to live with Bill.

Walking remained my favorite way to get around town. Eventually I began to drive a car to transport my daughter and her friends, but it was a chore, with more stress than enjoyment.

In 1971, during a year off between college and graduate school, I started to swim. I liked to say I swam for mental health, but of course, physical health was a benefit too. I'd swim at YMCA's or health clubs, or the hotel pool if I were on a business trip. I'd swim in the ocean whenever I could. I'd swim three to six times a week at home, and every day on beach vacations. My sense of well-being always benefited from a swim. In the depths of winter, I'd usually put my pool membership on hold and take dance or aerobic classes. A fitness program was built into my life.

My Type A personality propelled me through school and into a career. Along the way, I took occasional detours into the spiritual world. For about four years in the 1970's, when I was 23 years old until I was 27, I practiced transcendental meditation on and off. Once, I had an out-of-body experience, which I found fascinating. Sometimes, I'd meditate on the New York City IRT, on my way to work. When I skipped meditating, I'd have an acute headache. That lead me to conclude I'd developed a dependency on meditation—an addiction to it—so I decided to stop the practice completely.

During my late thirties, I'd studied visualization techniques, attempting to master the skill of focusing on what most mattered to me. A system called DMA posited the concept of "current reality": what's going on in your life at this moment constantly shifts and changes. If you maintain a clear mental picture of your "vision" (what truly matters to you, what you truly want) eventually, current reality and your vision will coalesce to become one and the same. You will have manifested your vision and attained what you truly want. The theory—which, as an artist, I know to be true—is that the creative process is just that: a process. If you know, feel, and see the result you want as if it already existed, you'll find a way to manifest it. Along with this theoretical base came meditation-like visualization exercises, with breath control as a beneficial by-product.

As for prescription drugs, instinct told me not to play around with the chemistry of my body. At 25, I'd been on the pill for a year and hated feeling bloated. When my generation approached menopause, with the exception of two friends and myself, every woman I knew in my age range took hormone replacement therapy drugs as soon as she experienced unpleasant symptoms. When I had hot flashes and trouble sleeping,

I increased the frequency of my swimming to help alleviate those symptoms and discomforts. No hormone replacement therapy for me.

By 2004, the nightly news was punctuated with back-to-back commercials touting the benefits of all varieties of prescription drugs for people my age. Middle-aged baby boomer actors became advertising stars. I was the one who vehemently and smugly criticized people for being so weak as to need all these drugs, and for being so willing to take them. Didn't they understand that stuffing all these chemicals into their bodies would alter natural biological balances? How could immediate discomfort make people so shortsighted that they'd take drugs for everything? Didn't they care about their bodies' integrity over the long run?

With a healthy diet and no need for prescription drugs, I preferred natural remedies to help manage the excess energies of my body and my mind. Swimming, walking, and dancing burned calories and provided time alone for meditation of sorts, time to sift and process the challenges of my career.

These are the reasons my family and friends would probably have considered me "The Healthiest Person We Know."

"Just Shoot Me"

So the two physical drawbacks I'd been noticing—some discomfort in my legs and a different quality of discomfort in my hands—escalated, I became concerned about them.

Sometime in 2002, I called my brother Larry to ask if we had arthritis in the family. He said not really, and suggested I take glucosamine sulfate, allowing six weeks for it to have a positive effect. I started to take it, and continued through 2004. Any positive effects were psychological only. In the fall of 2003, when I had my annual physical, I told my doctor that I sometimes felt my legs were going to fall off at the knees. She assured me they wouldn't.

During the winter of 2004, I experienced something strange when I swam at the YMCA in Boston's Chinatown. More accurately, I wasn't experiencing several sensations that I'd taken for granted during my thirty-three years of swimming. I couldn't get air as I swam. I also couldn't get speed, an endorphin high, or color in my cheeks. When I tried to do the backstroke, my head felt so heavy and dull that I had to flip over and switch to the crawl. I figured the HVAC system in the pool area was to blame for poor air circulation, and that it was in need of repair. It never occurred to me that perhaps the problem was within me, and I was the one in need of repair.

In April of 2004, I was hyperactive, even more than usual. I was in motion—fast motion—most of the time, whether at home or out. No matter how tired I might have felt, settling down at night took hours. It became a family joke, only no one was laughing. In the middle of a mid-April night, I sat up in bed and as I stood, every muscle in both legs, from hips to toes, contracted simultaneously. My legs took off. Careening as mechanically as a robot, at a speed faster than I can imagine even now, I traveled on legs as rigid as steel. Racing toward a wall, I thrust my right hand against a door jamb to avoid slamming into it, got through the doorway, and braced both hands against the edge of the sink to break my speed before I smashed into the mirror. There I stood for several minutes, letting my body calm down. Then, moving very consciously and in slow motion, I was able to get myself back to bed, and back to sleep.

In the shower the next morning, my body was vibrating, somewhat like a concussion that wasn't limited to the head. I questioned whether I was stable enough to drive a car and deliver my daughter to school. Concluding that I was, I decided there was no need to trouble my husband Bill about the rigid leg event.

I made the round-trip drive safely. Returning home and entering our dining room, I sat at the table where Bill was reading the newspaper and drinking juice. I exploded into sobs—something I almost never do. With the sobs shaking all of me, including my voice, I told Bill what I'd experienced the night before.

"If this is a degenerative neurological disease, I don't want the medical costs to bankrupt us for you and Sara," were my words, and I meant it.

"Just shoot me," was my message and I meant that, too.

Later that morning I called my primary care physician, Beverly Woo. Highly regarded by her patients and her peers, Dr. Woo conducts her internal medicine practice with intelligence, insight, and compassion. Diagnostic intuition supplements her knowledge and experience. Although the waiting room may be full, each patient benefits from this doctor's thoughtful attention and her dedication to each one's health and well-being.

When I learned that Dr. Woo was out of town, I relayed my experience of the previous night to the covering physician. He was unimpressed. Middle of the night leg muscle contractions were somewhat common for people who were "on their feet a lot," he told me. When I spoke with my doctor a few days later, she, too, was unconcerned. The strain, pain, and rigidity in my legs lasted three weeks.

On April 29th, 2004, Bill's and my sixteenth wedding anniversary, Sara accompanied us on the one block walk from our home to the Boston Public Garden. In May of 1989, when our daughter was seven months old, we had donated a weeping Japanese cherry tree to this beautiful park. Coincidence combined with luck, and the tree was planted in the exact spot where Bill and I were married. Each year our "family tree" is the first in the park to blossom. By our anniversary, it's in full flower. Visiting the tree and taking a family photo is an annual custom.

On this particular evening, my experience was very different from years past. I was able to walk only in very small steps, with my feet only a few inches apart. My legs still had residual pain and limited range of motion from the severe cramping weeks before. Wearing dressy sandals with low heels made walking even slower and even more difficult. I couldn't keep pace with my family.

After we took our pictures, Bill was impatient with my pace. Frustrated, he got the car. We drove a few blocks up Beacon Hill to a restaurant where we were meeting friends for dinner. For my whole life prior, this would have been a quick and easy walk. Now it was an ordeal, and, although I smiled sweetly and tried to maintain a good attitude, I was disconcerted by an undercurrent of muted pain and emerging worry.

My Knees Break

By the second week in May, I was walking normally and considered the leg-cramping episode a one-time oddity. In May and June, I felt okay.

Then, on July 2nd, exquisite pain in my left knee woke me around 2 a.m. I saw in my bed and I felt in my body a black steel jaw, like earth-moving machinery, clamp shut over my knee.

There was pain the next day and restricted walking, but I moved around and lived normally. On July 4th, we had our usual rooftop party with a few friends joining us for dinner and our prime view of the Boston Pops concert, complete with spectacular fireworks. Our apartment is on the top two floors of our building and during the course of the day and that evening, I probably made twenty trips up and down a long flight of stairs, back and forth to the roof. Pain and stiffness in my right knee and leg surfaced as a constant presence in my awareness.

Once again in the middle of the night, the black steel jaw returned, this time clamped over my right knee. Again the pain was extreme, but not to the same degree as I'd experienced with the left knee. Now I really became unable to walk in any normal way. My steps were tiny and shot with pain. My legs hurt constantly. Within a few days, ascending and descending stairs became impossible. To move between the upper and lower floors of our apartment, I became dependent on the communal elevator. One day I set out on an errand and, after half a block, turned back because the effort of walking was too difficult.

In mid-July I attended a two-day continuing education seminar at the Harvard Graduate School of Design, where I had earned my Master of Architecture degree. Bill was distressed by my lack of locomotion and, although he rarely offers medical advice, he insisted I see my doctor. During the seminar's lunch break, I hailed a taxi from Harvard Square in Cambridge to Brigham and Women's Hospital in Boston. My ability to walk had become so limited that navigating public transportation was out of the question.

Dr. Woo fit me in between scheduled appointments. As I described what I'd been experiencing, she examined my knees.

"There's no redness or swelling, so there's no bacterial infection. That's the worst that could happen."

These types of things happen as people get older, she said. She assured me that the problem would ease up over time. Her sense of relief relieved me.

"At least I don't have cancer of the knees," I laughed.

Through the Summer

As even a short walk had become untenable, staying home took precedence over going out. There was a nauseous, sick feeling present in me. Increasingly, I stayed home, often sitting in an oversized white armchair. Sometimes my legs rested on the matching ottoman; most times, they just hung down to the floor.

"Don't you ever leave the house anymore?" Sara asked one August day. Her tone held disbelief. All her life she'd known me to be active—out and about, on the move, wanting and enjoying action and adventure.

But it was summer, and I'm a swimmer.

During every summer since she was four, Sara and I had taken pleasure in the half-mile walk to a nearby outdoor pool. Our route varied. Usually, we strolled along the Charles River Esplanade, sometimes along picturesque Charles Street, and occasionally along the edge of Storrow Drive, which separates the Charles River from the city.

As a young child, my daughter would sit on the pool deck at the shallow end of my lap lane. While I swam, she orchestrated elaborate scenarios with her Barbie dolls. It was here that she had learned to swim. Now, as a teenager, she enjoyed swimming and sunning poolside with her friends.

In order to swim this summer, I needed to drive to the pool. What a bizarre change this was. We're a one-car family, so either I'd be driving and paying for parking, or Bill would be dropping me off and picking me up. Using the car upset me. Keenly aware of pollution since I was a teenager, keenly aware of global climate change now, I had no desire to add to either of them.

Swimming in nature was a bust, too. With Sara's buddy Becca Goldklang, we drove to upstate New York. Although most of Bill's family converged on the house we rented on Keuka Lake, and although we all maintained good spirits, incessant rain put a damper on outside activities. When I braved the lake's gloomy waters, I found my legs didn't respond to my brain's instructions. Forget about swimming. In the water, even walking became an ordeal.

Since the mid 1990's, I'd been experiencing weakness in my legs, especially on these summer walks. The late summer of 2004 kicked my discomfort to a new level. Pain became a disability.

Life was out of balance, but we didn't yet know how dangerously the scale had tipped.

Around Labor Day, through a full night and into the next day, I experienced heart palpitations that were violent and unrelenting. An emergency room visit crossed my mind. Fortunately, the pounding, rapid heart rate normalized, and the ER visit never happened, but the memory of fear stayed with me.

Into the Fall

Intermittent nausea and nostalgia wrapped around my days. Like a rock climber who's beginning to lose her grip, I flailed around in search of stability. For me, the Gratton family is stability personified. Originally Bill's friends, Duncan and Pat Gratton became my friends, too.

Bill had introduced Duncan to the real state business and the two had collaborated on several projects. Pat, a veteran flight attendant, welcomes every opportunity to meet people and explore the world.

For the past several summers, our families had vacationed together at Squam Lake in New Hampshire. The kids: Sara, and Christina and Johnny Gratton, delighted each other and their parents as they swam, played, and made art projects together. My daughter was growing up fast, as were Christina, thirteen, and Johnny, ten. Wanting to hold on to their playful childhood friendships, and our pleasure in them, I convinced my family and the Grattons to skip town over Columbus Day weekend and head south. Our excuse: Sara's sixteenth birthday. Our destination: Atlantis.

The place was big, busy, and hot. Our families enjoyed the amusement-park amenities and the range of restaurants. The main beach was perpetually closed due to rough tides. In the gentler bay, we bathed. Salt water felt great, but my undependable legs restricted me to bathing rather than swimming.

While the kids eagerly climbed the faux Mayan pyramid, patiently waited their turn to board a boat, then bravely slid down a pitch black tunnel into the shark pool, I demurred. I was scared, scared of the long, steep climb in broiling sun, the steep drop in utter dark, and the face-to-face encounter with sharks. Besides, this thrill was for kids, and I was a grown-up.

On our next-to-last day, all three kids urged me to join them.

"I know," said Christina, "Johnny can go first, then Sara and I will go in the next boat. Then, you can go right behind us. We'll sing all the way, so you'll hear our voices and you won't be afraid of the dark."

They did, and I did. They gave me courage. The climb was hard on my legs and strained my heart. The staff at the top was bossy and loud. No turning back. First Johnny sat in his boat and slid into blackness, then the girls, then I. Sing they did, and their singing kept me feeling connected and safe. The dark descent was thrilling. When my little raft shot out of the vertical tunnel and into the horizontal one, seeing the sharks so close, just on the other side of thick glass, was chilling. Seeing and hearing the children filled me with love.

None of us could have predicted how black a tunnel I'd soon descend in real life, how crucial love and friendship would be to my sense of safety, and how necessary song would become to my soul.

Detective Doctor

I typically saw Beverly Woo once a year unless I had an especially pernicious flu. Occasionally I'd get a prescription for an antibiotic; more often, I'd be told to let the virus run its course.

This year my annual physical was scheduled for October. My knees and legs still weren't normal and their movement remained limited. Kneeling was impossible as it generated hideous pain.

I told Dr. Woo I sometimes worried that my heart would explode. She ordered some blood tests and a week or so later, I received a letter from her. The lab results showed an elevated level of C-Reactive Protein and an elevated sedimentation rate. Since these might indicate inflammation somewhere in my body, she suggested I might want to see a rheumatologist. She recommended Dr. Bonnie Bermas.

When I called Dr. Bermas' office to book an appointment, I was told that her earliest opening was January 4th—three months away. I took it.

But the gnawing, nauseous sensation in my abdomen and the ongoing sense of trouble in my knees and legs told me I couldn't live for three months feeling this way. I left a message for Dr. Woo; I wondered if it would be okay to ask her for a favor. Could she please try to schedule an earlier appointment for me? She was able to do so, and on November 11th I went to see Dr. Bermas.

I knew her schedule was packed and I suspected she was under pressure with many pain-filled people to treat; yet she greeted me calmly and warmly as though she were truly glad to meet me.

In her small office, I told Dr. Bermas my medical history of great good health with lots of physical activity, as well as the recent developments in April and July, just as I've told you. She listened, asked questions, and recorded the information with rapid-fire speed onto her computer. Then she asked to examine me.

Nothing in the exam seemed to indicate a quantifiable diagnosis, except that I couldn't move the lower halves of my legs much. The range of motion was limited, and motion generated an achy, stretchy pain as though an elastic band had gone brittle, become riddled with fissures, and threatened to shear and break.

Dr. Bermas wrote a prescription for the steroid prednisone, with the instruction to take 20 milligrams a day in the hope that this would reduce any inflammation and resolve the problem. She walked with me back to the waiting area and scheduled an appointment for a progress check in one month.

Taking a daily prescription medication was an experience for me. I didn't like the routine or the ritual. Now I sat each morning at my dining room table, measured out the proper number of pills, and swallowed the steroids. Nothing changed in how I felt.

On December 9th, once more I told Dr. Bermas how I was feeling—no change. When she examined my knees and legs, she found no change. She ordered a blood test, asked me to keep taking the Prednisone, and scheduled an appointment for the following month.

In the new year of 2005, I had that January 4th appointment. Neither my body nor my blood showed signs of improvement. Hating the daily drug dose, I asked if I could please reduce it or eliminate it. The doctor agreed.

Following protocol, she ordered another round of blood tests, and I began to whittle down the Prednisone.

The next day, Dr. Bermas telephoned me, a surprise in itself. She asked a question, phrasing it almost as a favor.

"To help alleviate my perplexity, would you be willing to have a CAT scan?"

This was big news. What could it mean? I'd never had scans or anything like them. Maybe it was denial, or maybe it was acceptance, but instead of panic, I felt calm. Or numb. I said okay. Dr. Bermas told me she wanted a scan with some color in my blood so she'd be able to see more clearly what was going on. Her scheduling assistant suggested a CAT scan appointment for the next day. That was too quick a turnaround for me, so she offered a couple of other options.

I went into my husband's office to tell him of Dr. Bermas' request, and asked if he would please come with me when I had the scan. Never one to like hospitals much, but loving me very much, Bill said yes, and we agreed on Saturday as the most convenient date.

The First CAT Scan

On Saturday afternoon, January 8th, Bill and I set out for the hospital. I'd dressed nicely; I wasn't going to present myself in a schlumpy, sloppy way as if I were a sick person in need of pity. I wore a gray sweater set with darker gray trim that my daughter and Becca had helped me select during our summer vacation, and decent pants—not blue jeans.

In the basement—or, one of the basements—of the hospital was a relatively grim and impersonal waiting area. I checked in and received two bottles of a pink drink (I had my choice of flavors; I chose pink). I was instructed to slowly swallow all of the liquid over the course of exactly two hours, at which time I'd be called for the CAT scan.

I chose two seats for Bill and me in a corner, opposite a large wall clock, as far away from other people and as private as possible in a compact space. I decided to mete out the beverage and drink it in ten-minute segments, and visually divvied up the bottles of pink liquid into twelve portions.

As I sipped, and as I became aware of my measured breathing which helped keep me calm, I observed the other patients. A man who appeared older than I, but probably wasn't; skinny, a few sticks of hair on his head, dressed in leftovers. A woman, who appeared younger than I, but probably wasn't, with a serene demeanor, carrying a series of thick folders containing her medical records. I felt compassion for them. I felt sad for them because they were sick, or waiting to find out if they were sick.

Bill sat with me, still; first reading, then doing a crossword puzzle.

In two hours exactly, my drink was drunk and my name was called. I instinctively spoke up for myself. In what was to become part of my consciousness, behavior, responsibility, and ritual, I reminded the receptionist that my doctor had ordered dye for my blood.

"Contrast," she corrected me. "Yes, you'll have that."

In the CAT scan room, the technician asked me to remove my shoes and surprised me by telling me to remain dressed. Again, to her, I mentioned the dye.

"We'll do one scan without the dye, then I'll give you intravenous contrast and we'll do the second scan."

A CAT scan doesn't take very long. My throat, chest, and upper stomach were the areas of interest. The first scan was done.

Then the technician had a lot of trouble getting the IV needle into a vein. It took a few tries and she got frustrated. I stayed calm but felt this didn't bode well.

The second scan, with contrast, was done. I sat up, put on my shoes, and went out to join my husband.

On this dark, winter weekend afternoon, as Bill and I slid from the CAT scan area into a dark, grim corridor hundreds of feet long, we saw only one person in the far distance. Approaching him, we recognized him. What are the odds of that? A physician, our acquaintance had a medical emergency that day. He'd come to the hospital to care for a patient.

In the elevator ride up out of subterranea, the doctor asked us what brought us to the hospital.

"I had a CAT scan," I said.

He said nothing.

Endoscopies

The weekend passed. Late Tuesday afternoon, January 11th, Beverly Woo called. She'd looked at the CAT scan results with Bonnie Bermas, and had invited a third doctor to help interpret what they were seeing. She said she'd like me to have an endoscopy. She'd already spoken to a colleague of hers, and asked me to call his office the next morning to schedule an appointment for the test. I agreed, we signed off, and I relayed the conversation to Bill.

At 6 p.m., the phone rang.

"Hello," said a beautiful male voice with the perfect British accent. "Is Karen Lee Sobol there?"

This was surprising if not shocking. A specialist I'd never met was calling me at home, at night. Even more surprising, if not alarming, he was offering me an endoscopy appointment with him at 9:15 the next morning.

I was surprised but not alarmed. I felt honored to be receiving such personal, prompt, and caring attention. Surely this was all a very good sign. The test could be done soon and I could be done with doctors.

Check-in time for me was 7:00 a.m. at the doctor's office. Check-in time for Sara was 8:00 a.m. at school. Since our destinations were in opposite directions, a friend agreed to drive our daughter to school so Bill could drive me to the appointment, then home. Anesthesia would be involved.

Our destination was a satellite branch of Brigham and Women's Hospital. Set in a parking lot shaped like a squared-off doughnut, the boxy facility was spacious and impersonal. After checking in, I sat with Bill for a few minutes. As an architect, I appreciate big open spaces, but this waiting room had too much open space. I felt like a small fish in a very big tank. As clouds of gray snow plastered themselves onto wide plate-glass windows, I felt socked in.

When my name was called, Bill and I walked to a small room with a desk and a couple of chairs. Then the routine began. All of it was new and surprising to us: releases to sign, explanations of the procedure, a couple of anatomical drawings showing how the endoscopy tube enters the mouth, slides down the esophagus, etc. The technician's manner was so matter-of-fact. If she saw and experienced all this as simple and routine, why wouldn't I? I'm sure I asked a few questions, but she moved me along fast. Bill was directed back to the waiting room. I followed the nurse, almost at a trot, as she led me to a big, ward-like room, and assigned me a bed.

Why did I need a bed? It was early morning, and I'd just gotten out of my own bed.

A different nurse came to me, along with instructions to take off my shoes, and a plastic bag to hold my other belongings. She acted like my new best friend, and I latched onto her as though she were. Pretty quickly, though, she left, replaced by another nurse, also acting like my new best friend. The human connection, a personal relationship, was very important to me—an anchor in this bland environment with sick people scattered around in other beds. I asked if I could sit up; I wasn't tired and I wasn't sick. Also, for quite some time, lying flat had created an uncomfortable sensation in my head, similar to the discomfort I'd been experiencing for about a year in the pool when I tried to do the backstroke. The head of the bed was cranked up for me and, for about an hour and a half, I observed the rhythm of activities around the nurses' station and watched the hands of the wall clock progress. Occasionally someone came to check on me, but mostly I was alone.

Eventually it got to be nine o'clock. Yet another nurse came, untethered my bed, and transformed it into a sled which she easily glided through the ward and into a treatment room.

In person, the doctor was as energetic and gentlemanly as his voice on the phone had been the night before. As the sled-bed nurse began to administer anesthesia, I felt myself in a floating kind of state, aware of the doctor, the nurse, and my somewhat passive part in this scene. I felt sensations of the endoscopy tube's travels in me, dulled by anesthesia. No tissue sample was taken for a biopsy. It was all very quick.

Once the endoscopy tube was out of me, the doctor stood to my right and said, "It's normal."

Hooray! I knew it! I was fine, this was over, and it was time to go home.

The nurse had a different view. She wheeled my sled-bed back into its original parking space in the ward, although now I was in "recovery" rather than "prep." She informed me I had to wait for the anesthesia to wear off.

I told her the good news, "It's normal," and asked if I might speak with the doctor again. She went to check and returned to say he'd started another procedure. If I were willing to wait, he'd be able to see me eventually.

Earlier during the "prep" phase, I'd noticed a small refrigerator with very small cans of cranberry juice, apple juice and ginger ale. Offered a drink as part of "recovery," I happily accepted a ginger ale.

After a while, I was allowed to put on my shoes, be discharged, and rejoin Bill. He'd been sitting, waiting, stalwart, patient for over two hours.

Although I was very happy to report the doctor's findings, I wanted confirmation and verification. Perhaps in that floating anesthesia state I'd misheard? So Bill and I sat, maybe for another half hour, until the doctor joined us.

"It's normal," he repeated. "You can go home."

Out into the snow and home we went, with huge relief. I still felt physically awful, but apparently, I was all right. I called Dr. Woo with the good news.

But a couple of days later, she called me. She'd like me to have a second endoscopy, with a biopsy. She could schedule it for exactly a week after the first one.

January 19th was already a landmark medical date. On that day, my friend Valerie Amelbert was scheduled to have elective brain surgery.

Recently, out of nowhere, one of her brothers had suffered a ruptured brain aneurism. Deeming it hereditary, his doctor had suggested all the siblings be examined for the same problem. Valerie's examination revealed an aneurism. Not wanting to risk the disabilities that her brother now endured, she bravely chose surgery. When she'd called to tell me, her matter-of-fact attitude and her courage struck me as almost unnatural. How could anyone possibly sound so calm, so rational, and as trusting of her doctor as she faced a medical procedure that could permanently handicap or kill her? I didn't get it, but of course I expressed support.

I'd already been mentally and spiritually focusing on Valerie's good health and success. Now, learning that I'd be undergoing a diagnostic medical procedure while she was undergoing surgery gave me a very bad feeling.

This time, my endoscopy appointment was at the real hospital. The waiting room was so small and so crowded I couldn't bear to be in it. Instead, I paced in the second floor corridor, a walkway open to the hospital's atrium lobby space below. As I studied the framed prints on the wall, my mind interpreted their psychedelic colors and mandala-like patterns as portents of my good health.

When my name was called, again there were releases to sign and explanations to hear.

This time I was shown directly to the procedure room, which looked to me like an operating room. Two male nurses were in attendance; vital signs were checked. Two doctors I'd never met would be performing the endoscopy and the biopsy. Although I was assured I'd remain conscious, an oxygen supply was placed in both my nostrils—quite a pleasant sensation—anesthesia was administered, and I was out.

On Saturday, January 22nd, dark and biting cold as it was, I walked over to Massachusetts General Hospital to visit Valerie.

Sitting by the bed was her sister Leslie, and the family resemblance was lovely. On the right, near her hairline, Valerie's head bore a long, rough-looking vertical scar with big, rough-looking stitches. The brain aneurism had been successfully released; the pressure imbalance had been corrected.

When I asked how Valerie was feeling, she said she had a headache. We laughed.

Given the circumstances, it was a short visit. Valerie's son Danny walked me to the elevator.

He confided some of his current struggles and concerns to me. Worried about his "Mommy," and under pressure at work, he was tired and skipping meals. I told him to take good care of himself because being healthy is the most important thing. We parted sweetly.

Now, finally—with that sickish sense in my stomach, and the growing awareness that I was somehow probably very sick in my body—I was beginning to understand what my father had meant all those times he'd told me, "Karen Lee, when you have your health, you have everything."

Telephone Trauma

A series of phone conversations with Dr. Woo punctuated the last week and a half of January.

She and Dr. Bermas, along with a consulting doctor, were looking at the CAT scan and, presumably, the biopsy results. A series of possible ailments and diseases were mentioned. Worst case: an inflamed esophagus. Could be a lymphoma. There seemed to be a thickening at the top of the stomach. Did Bill and I want to come talk about this in person? Maybe that would be better.

Since it seemed that my doctor's and my communication was good, and open, there didn't seem to be a need to talk in person, so I passed on that suggestion. Besides, I didn't have much energy to troop around in the cold.

On February 1st, Dr. Woo called to say she'd set up an appointment for me with another physician. Young, knowledgeable, skilled at reading and interpreting CAT scans, this physician joined Dr. Woo and Dr. Bermas as part of the team reviewing my diagnostic test results.

The appointment was set for 8:45 a.m. on Thursday, February 3rd at 44 Binney Street, Boston. I was given a phone number.

For each appointment in January, Bill had been my companion; of course, he agreed to join me for this one. Not wanting to inconvenience or impose upon him, at about 4:30 the preceding afternoon I decided to call the doctor's office and find out exactly where 44 Binney Street was.

I dialed.

The phone rang and was answered: "Dana-Farber Cancer Institute."

Imagine my shock?

I called Dr. Woo.

Irate, furious, I asked, "Why am I going to Dana-Farber?"

In hindsight, it occurs to me that my daughter may have heard me ask that question.

Habit, Home, and Heart

Perhaps this is an appropriate place to mention a habit, a room in my home, and an interior dialogue between my body and me that were all in play by this time and that had continuing roles and importance through the next year and beyond.

The habit I have is to take notes of telephone conversations. I have what could be considered a complete diary—on 8½ x 11 inch papers—for all the telephone calls, research, and the hospital visits before, during, and after the Twelve Weeks. The start date is when I first asked to see a specialist about the pain in my knees. The notes fill a few file folders and a couple of loose-leaf binders. Most are stuffed into a small green paper shopping bag with yellow rope handles. As one phase of my medical odyssey ended and a new phase began, I'd retire one set of notes and launch another. I'd absorbed whatever had already happened and acted upon it. Information became part of the process, and contributed to progress. Who needed all that paper and past history around, when almost every day there was more information to learn and analyze, and new, dire medical challenges to face?

The room is my dining room. It sits on the southwest corner of a big building, with views of Boston's Back Bay to the south, and the Charles River to the west. The light is ever changing. On bright days, sunlight floods the room, and we track the subtle shifts of the sunset through the seasons. Loving light, I love being in this room.

Beginning on dark afternoons late in January of 2005, I sat at our dining room table talking with Dr. Woo and taking notes on the information and diagnostic speculations I was hearing. From that spot, I made the phone call to hear, "Dana-Farber Cancer Institute," followed immediately by the furious phone call to ask, "Why am I going to Dana-Farber?"

As for the dialogue between my body and me, this began either just before or just after the CAT scan. It began as a sort of prayer, with a lot of scare. The very small elevator that leads up to our apartment has a stainless steel reflective ceiling. Often in the past, during an elevator ride, I'd crane my neck, look up, make eye contact with my eyes' reflection, and try to ascertain whether or not I was a good person. As my mother would have said, quoting Shakespeare, "The eyes are the window to the soul." Now as I looked up and met my own gaze, I tried to "see" if I had cancer.

Sitting in the dining room, thinking about the possible problems the CAT scan and the endoscopies were indicating, I felt disbelief about my heart and me.

About those October blood test results, and the high C-Reactive Protein levels. At the time, this was a new term to me. Now, it was everywhere: the "Science" section of *The New York Times*, the nightly news, everywhere. CRP as it is called, was being connected with all varieties of serious diseases. It has an important predictive value for cardiac disease. Maybe a dying heart caused my thudding blood. Maybe that late summer sensation—my rapid, pounding heart, feeling ready to explode—signaled some terminal heart condition.

Even though my father, my mother, my uncles and—as I later learned, some of my cousins—had histories of heart disease, my heart and I had always been a great team. Intrinsically, I'd always known my heart was healthy, and the genetics of coronaries and hypertension had skipped over me. Hadn't we been swimming together, my heart and me, for thirty-four years? How could it be that my heart was sick? That we—it and I—might die soon because of it?

By mid-afternoon I'd find myself exhausted and on the verge of sleep. I would need a cup of strong coffee, the fourth or sometimes fifth of the day, to jump-start my heart.

What had been intermittent, visceral nausea became almost constant as each dark day brought no relief to my legs, and many dark days brought bad news through the telephone.

Although these early conversations with my body were telling of unhappy, unwelcome circumstances and omens; the ability to think about, visualize, and talk to my organs, blood, and bones would evolve into a powerful tool and resource for healing and for cure.

"Hi. You Have Cancer."

On Thursday, February 3rd in the big, open waiting area of Dana-Farber's Gosman Adult Clinic, I was furious. Livid. Why was I here? I didn't want to be. I didn't belong here. During a very long wait to see the doctor, my rage stayed at white light pitch.

The first hard part was just going through the doors into the building. Bill and I parked in the garage attached to the main clinic—we got a great space, by the way—entered an elevator, descended a couple of levels, and were deposited into the cancer center.

Checking in felt horrible. Why did they ask me my date of birth? Why did they give me a hospital bracelet? Why did they draw blood?

I chose seats for Bill and me that were as isolated as possible, but over the course of our hour and a half wait, the placed filled with patients and their companions—husbands, wives, kids, and friends. No secluded place remained where I could hide, or, better yet, escape. My anxiety became a physical vibration, and it wasn't good.

Why did a secretary take me into a tiny room and ask me to fill out a questionnaire about the history of lymphoma in my family? Bright yellow papers, a couple of pages, stapled together.

"I don't have lymphoma," I snapped. I was mad. I ripped the papers in half and pitched them into the trashcan. I rejoined Bill in the waiting area, to wait some more.

One saving grace for my psyche, which helped me not go nuts: on the waiting room's walls were several beautiful, framed silkscreen prints. Fixing my attention on Andy Warhol's day-glow colored chrysanthemums and Alex Katz' one-dimensional trees helped me control my temper.

Bill read the newspaper and appeared composed. He was the stable foil to my mental, verbal, and physical bouncing around. Eventually, my name was called. Read from a chart, actually. I wondered, "Why is there a chart with my name on it?" Bill and I stood, and joined the clinical assistant. I don't remember having my vital signs taken, but knowing the protocol as I now do, there's no doubt that they were.

Then back to the waiting room, to wait some more.

Eventually, Bill and I were shown into a small room crammed with four chairs, a built-in desk and computer, and a compact examination table. A blonde woman entered and introduced herself. A nurse, named Linda.

She asked me terse questions and seemed to expect brief answers, but I became loquacious. In fact, I talked almost hysterically, and at length. I spoke passionately about my history of good health, except in regard to when my legs cramped and my knees broke. Like a trial lawyer before a judge, I argued in favor of my health, hoping to bring in a verdict of "Not Sickly."

The nurse sat, immobile, eyes fixed on mine, saying little, writing nothing. My mind tried to make her warm and caring, but that's not what she was projecting, nor what I was feeling. No matter what I said, or how much I protested about my good health, she remained unresponsive. It wasn't a conversation. It was a monologue. It lasted a tiresomely long time.

Four days later, my view of Linda changed, and my respect for her grew. A couple of weeks later, when I retrieved copies of my medical records, I was surprised to see that she had recorded, after our meeting, and almost verbatim, everything I'd said. She also had some nice, if patronizing, observations about my demeanor and behavior. I had initially thought of her as a highly skilled recording device; a robot. Two months later, she became a valued, though discreet, guide.

Finally, a doctor joined us: a hematological oncologist, or blood cancer specialist. I was ready; I had been ready. In my lap sat my list of questions, the key one being: "Might this develop into cancer?" with many related concerns. In my hand was my pen. In the room were Bill and I, Linda, and now the doctor.

"Hello, I'm the oncologist. You have cancer," was pretty much the way the first twenty seconds went. Or so it felt to me.

The three others were seated on one side of the room. I—me, the one with cancer—I sat across from them, isolated. I saw and felt that the spatial divide signified the health divide: I was going to die of cancer, and they were going to live.

The doctor's opening line or two wiped out most of my carefully composed, neatly written queries. Why bother asking?

But since I react to panic situations by going dead calm, I made a conscious effort to maintain my composure and tried to conduct this meeting as though I were an equal participant. Holding onto my pages of notes and my pen, asking my questions and recording the doctor's responses, helped me stay reasonably grounded and somewhat sane, and lent me some sense of control. Honestly, though—I had cancer. The others were all in control, not I. I spoke calmly. I attempted to sustain conversation. I wanted to be an equal. I wasn't.

The doctor had a couple of questions for me.

"Do you have blurry vision?"

Absurd! Ridiculous! My eyesight was 20/20. Practically barking "No," I rejected the idea of impaired vision as random and not relevant to me.

"Do you have night sweats?"

"What are night sweats?" I asked. I got no answer.

The doctor told us I had lymphoma, of which there are thirty-five types, some Hodgkin's, some non-Hodgkin's. Mine was non-Hodgkin's. It developed very slowly. Years—even decades—could go by without it becoming a concern. People live with this a very long time with no problems, no effects, and no need for medical intervention. So I was told.

"Think of it as diabetes," the doctor advised, almost dismissively.

Is he nuts? "CANCER IS NOT DIABETES!" my mind screamed.

Later, when Bill and I talked it over, he reminded me of the "Think of it as diabetes" approach. Being from a medical family, I made it clear that I rejected that premise instantly and completely. I never wanted to hear that statement again.

Based on the blood test results, the CAT scan, the endoscopies, and the biopsy result, the doctor said he was "ninety-eight percent sure this is marginal zone lymphoma." To confirm the diagnosis, he'd like to do a bone marrow biopsy. This could be scheduled either four days from now, or a month later. Bill's and my eyes met, and I felt certain that, as I said "Monday," our minds were united.

An appointment was booked for Monday morning. We left.

Now I did want to see Dr. Woo. When Bill and I arrived at her office, she made time to talk with us. I said I had cancer. I asked about treatments. Didn't they carry toxicities that could set the stage for other cancers?

Yes, she affirmed.

At about one o'clock, Bill and I pulled up in front of our building.

"Are you going to be all right?" he asked.

"Yes."

After we kissed goodbye in the car, Bill went on to work, then to his company's annual seminar and dinner. Luckily I had a lunch plan with Bill's sister Susan, and it was time to meet her. Usually she and I saw each other at family gatherings, so I'd been looking forward to time just with her. And now, I was grateful not to have to be alone with my thoughts. On the subjects of my health and the morning's news and events, I said nothing. After lunch, Susan came home with me, and visited with Sara when she arrived home from school.

In the evening, with my husband out and my daughter doing her homework, I sat alone in our living room, in a shocked trance.

Thinking that Sara was out of earshot, I called my friend Sherri Mahne, and told her I had cancer. In hindsight, I believe my daughter overheard my end of the conversation, and learned the terrifying news second-hand, the same day Bill and I did.

The next day, Sara traveled with a group of teachers and students to Washington, D.C. to participate in the Model United Nations. Sixteen years old, she was a sophomore in high school.

Bill and I were home alone. Bill couldn't possibly have been kinder, more tender, or more loving—even though I had cancer. We cried. We hugged. We made our love for each other known.

"Just shoot me" never crossed my mind.

Potluck

Despite our equilibrium-shattering news, on Saturday, February 5th, Bill and I stayed with our social plan to attend a potluck dinner for the parents of our daughter's high school class.

The hosting family included one of Boston's preeminent chefs, whose recipes Bill admired and cooked. At home that day, our kitchen percolated with the luscious aromas of the chef's lobster stew—Bill's contribution to the potluck menu—as well as a personal gift and tribute to our host.

That evening, with two giant pots securely packed in the car, Bill and I aimed for the suburbs. Just inside our host's back door was a good-sized mudroom where guests hung their coats before entering the house proper.

Bearing his pots, Bill preceded me. From the kitchen and living room, a multitude of voices floated into the mudroom, engulfing me and pinning me where I stood. I felt isolated, not only physically, but also existentially. Immobilized, I tried to figure out how I could possibly join the party and attempt to behave normally.

After several minutes, I numbly entered the house. Forty or fifty couples, the proud parents of the class of 2007, stood chatting about their kids. Side-by-side with the chef, Bill dished out the lobster stew, which our host as well as the other parents relished.

At the upper level of the spacious family room that doubled as a banquet hall, I exchanged greetings with a couple I knew. He's a doctor, she's a nurse. Recently medicine had become my world. Although I found myself smiling, I was unable to sustain a conversation of more than a few sentences before needing to move on. "How are you?" that universal, blasé greeting, the question everyone asks, but no one really cares about; it was too painful to bear.

Standing alone, now inundated by the buzz and hum of human voices speaking unidentifiable words, I heard the sounds of life, of the living. I felt as if I'd already crossed over; participating, speaking, were no longer options for me. Soon sound would fade and disappear, too. I'd never before appreciated it so. With all my being, I absorbed as much sound as I could.

The chatter, the laughter, the rhythms, and the buzz—it was all so rich. How I would miss hearing, when I was dead.

What potluck.

On Sunday, February 6th 2005, my fifty-seventh birthday, Bill and I watched the New England Patriots win the Super Bowl. Numb inside and out, I couldn't feel the joy in their victory.

The First Bone Marrow Biopsy—Cancer Cures Denial

On Monday, February 7th, 2005, Bill and I returned to Dana-Farber for my bone marrow biopsy. We were at Dana-Farber for the second time in our lives, and the second time in four days. I know my anxieties couldn't have been more screamingly intense, yet a paradoxical, parallel, anchoring calm, almost an auto-pilot "I'm in control" mechanism, was operating in me too.

As we experienced the usual long wait, there were a lot of sick people in varying conditions of pain, along with the dishevelment that comes with disease. There were plenty of husbands, wives, and adult children there to shepherd the cancer patients.

Although this date was chosen based on the doctor's schedule, I never saw him. It was the nurse, Linda, who would offer me anesthetic medication and perform the first of three bone marrow biopsies I would undergo over the course of the next sixteen months.

"Sign this release." She handed me some hospital forms.

I signed.

"Take this." She gave me a tiny Ativan tablet, in a white paper cup. "Swallow this."

I took it. I swallowed.

"Squeeze this syringe of morphine slowly into your mouth."

I squeezed.

"Slower."

Mentally, I was trying to act collaboratively, as if Linda and I were colleagues, members of the same team. We sat together, close together, due to the smallness of the room, for five minutes after the last drop of morphine had been squeezed. Then she led me to an examination room.

It was the largest room I'd seen in the clinic so far. No windows; opposite the door was a wall of built-in cabinets with a work shelf. In the center of the room, parallel to the entrance and the work area, the examination table took center stage.

Linda introduced me to the man who would assist her. She asked me to remove my clothes from the waist down, then she and the man left to allow me privacy. After I'd undressed as told, I sat on the table facing the door. When the nurse and the assistant re-entered, two young women entered with them.

"These women are medical students from Europe. They're with us for the day. I wonder if you'd mind if they observed the procedure?"

I agreed.

At Linda's instruction, I lay on the exam table, on my stomach. I turned my face to my right, away from the nurse, the assistant, the work shelf, and the tools. I was looking at the two observers.

The breath and mind control powers of meditation, which became a key player through this process of diagnosis and treatment, cure and beyond, came into play at this instant.

My ability to breathe calmly, and very slowly, automatically kicked in.

Linda said, "I know this is humiliating."

I responded with "It's okay. I know it's important."

One of the young women said something like, "This is the kind of thing my mother would take pictures of for the family album, for all of us to see." I detected a hint of a laugh in her tone.

Although my body lay motionless and my breathing approached a meditative state, inside my thoughts burned with fury and insult. How stupid! How dare she? I wouldn't let this horribly inappropriate (and to me, in that spot at that moment for that reason, utterly insulting and truly humiliating) comment go. Thoughts traveled through my mind about calling Linda tomorrow to ask her to reprimand this woman. She was there with my consent as my guest, to observe and to learn; not to make insensitive, hurtful small talk.

Thoughts about how I'd handle this drifted. Linda was about to start drilling into my left pelvic bone. She must have told me a few things about the procedure. She and her assistant worked together at my left side, the two women observing to my right. My breathing became deeper, calmer, and slower as the work to extract marrow from deep inside my body began.

One of my character traits that I have always found annoying and not necessarily effective, is that faced with a crisis, I become dead calm. Panic never happens.

Now, as if guided by an invisible hand, the slow, deep breathing I'd learned from meditation years ago automatically kicked in. In some deep and unconscious way, breath control now assisted me to remain calm, relaxed, aware, and still as Linda's metal drill screwed its way to the core of my bone.

The morphine was working, so for the most part, I heard the drilling rather than felt it. I experienced a cacophony of loud grinding, and felt an incessant dull sensation. I held my body completely still, and breathed to get my brain through this.

There was a fair amount of blood. When she was done, Linda placed a patch over the wound and gave me instructions on caring for it over the next few days. She suggested I lie still for a while, to rest and regain my bearings.

Eventually I sat up, facing the two students.

"So you know, there's nothing funny about cancer. Nobody wants it in the family album."

I surprised myself. I said it, and it was done. The women left immediately. Now I see that that moment was the beginning of a new honesty for me. It was also the beginning of my standing up for myself, and fighting for myself, in a very new way.

As I would say to Bill a few weeks later, "Cancer cures denial."

Linda offered me ginger ale, which I gratefully accepted. I thanked her and her assistant for their work and their care, as well as for the ginger ale.

By apologizing for the inappropriateness of the medical student's remark, Linda let me know she was on my side.

She told me I was the best patient she'd ever had for a bone marrow biopsy.

"Really?" I didn't think I was so special.

"People writhe, people scream."

It didn't seem hard to me. My calm, my breathing, my "I know it has to be done" point of view would stand me in very good stead in the coming months.

Linda told me the lab would need a few days to analyze the bone marrow sample.

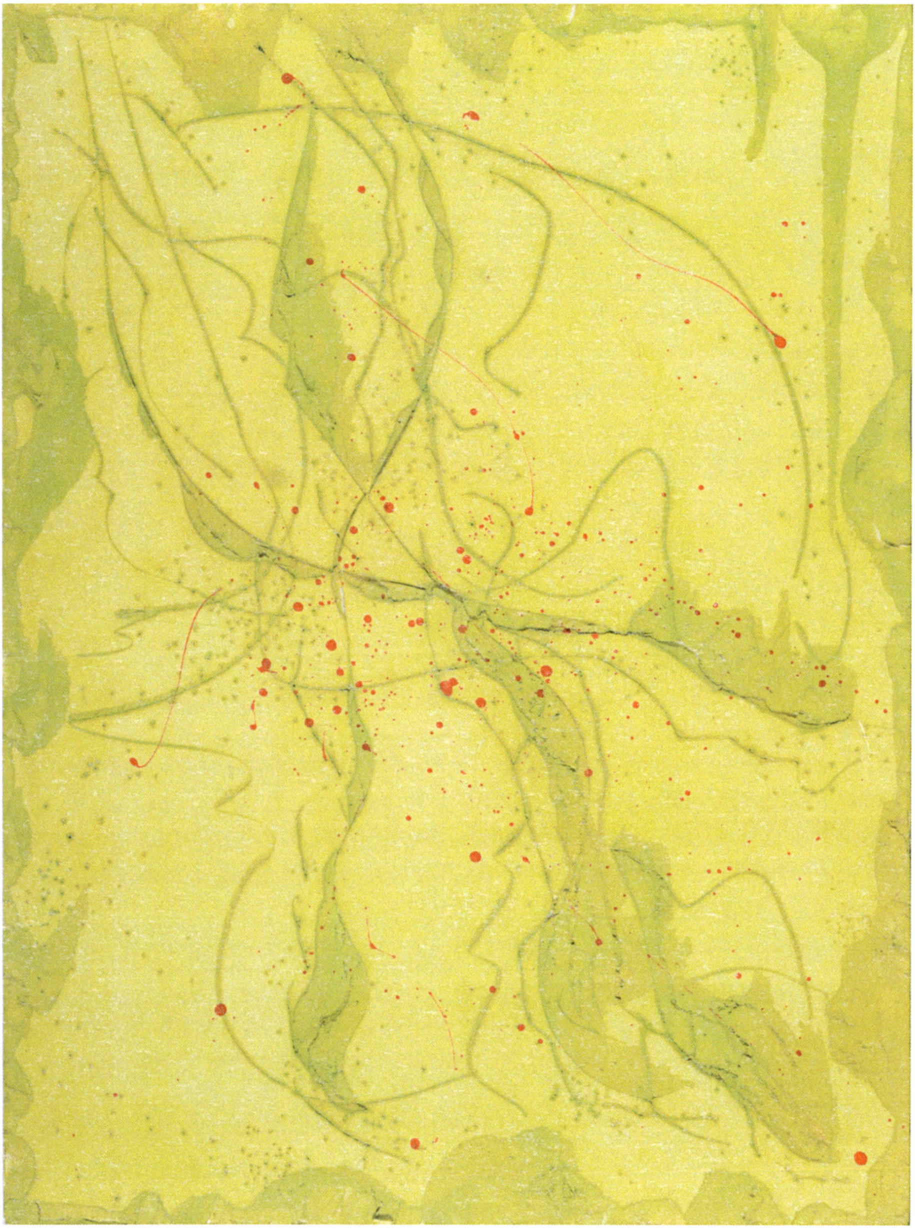

"Call the doctor on Friday," she advised.

Once at home, I fell into bed. A narcotic sleep lasted three hours, and I missed a funeral I'd planned to attend.

A day or two later, during a phone conversation with my mother, she asked, "Karen Lee, did you have a good birthday?"

"Sara was in Washington," was my response.

I deflected the question. I never answered it. How could I?

Apparently, cancer doesn't totally cure denial. At least not all at once.

Waldenstrom's Macroglobulinemia

The next three days had a blurry numbness to them. Awareness. Adjustment. Acknowledgement. "Cancer." "Cancer." "Cancer."

Friday, February 11th was another dark day, especially by late afternoon when I sat at Bill's desk and telephoned the oncologist.

The bone marrow biopsy results were in, and they did indeed provide more information about the lymphoma.

"You have Waldenstrom's Macroglobulinemia," the doctor said. "Let me spell that for you."

He did.

As I listened, I wrote. I underlined the different parts of Macroglobulinemia and made a diagram of their meanings.

"Waldenstrom is the name of the doctor who discovered the disease. Macro refers to very large cells, globulin means antibody or protein. Emia means 'in the blood.'"

Once again the doctor forcefully, yet in an ironically off-hand manner, assured me that there was nothing to worry about. Although incurable, this disease was extremely slow to progress. "Watch and wait," was its motto. The diabetes analogy was offered again, I suppose to reassure me?

He went on to say that, now that "we" knew the exact lymphoma I had, "we" could ask for more specific tests. "We" scheduled an appointment for me to return to the clinic in a month, on Monday March 7th.

Feeling sick in my stomach and dark in my heart, I walked the few steps from the desk to a bookshelf. I pulled down *Gray's Anatomy*, plopped down on the sofa, and flicked on a reading lamp. It was time to learn something about lymphoma.

I'd never given much thought to the lymphatic system; why would I? My mother's medical school text had full color renderings; this layman's version had delicate black and white drawings. I was surprised and dismayed to learn that the lymph system is everywhere. It's composed of glands, the small vessels that link them, and the spleen. It's almost as extensive as the circulatory system.

It's part of the immune system, and its job is to help protect the body from infection and foreign substances.

If my lymphatic system had cancer, my body must be riddled with it. I sank into despair.

During the next three weeks, I was heavy in body, heart, and mind. In public, I kept my face set, unsmiling, unresponsive to my neighbors. I had cancer. I was going to die. I had the right to be unbending. I carried a death sentence.

I asked Bill not to mention my diagnosis to anyone in our family. I didn't want Internet information or advice from his relatives, and I felt the news of my having cancer would kill my parents. So, we kept it very quiet.

From childhoods of poverty during the Great Depression, both my parents forged impressive careers. After serving as an officer in the army during World War II, my father Noah became a successful businessman. After attending college and medical school—both on full scholarships—during the war, my mother Myra became a solo-practitioner. She chose obstetrics and gynecology as her specialty, because delivering babies was a happy component of medical practice.

Noah, now ninety, had survived a series of near-death experiences ranging from two massive heart attacks to a ruptured gall bladder. Myra, eighty-two, suffered from hypertension and a variety of other ailments. Neither of them needed more worry or stress.

In these early days, I told only a tiny number of very close friends that I had cancer. The people I did tell were Mary Ting, Pat Gratton, Prudence King, and Sherri Mahne.

A graduate school classmate, Mary Ting had befriended both Bill and me. Quite by chance, I'd introduced Mary to her husband Todd Springer, and I like to take credit for their beautiful children. Mary and Todd are both architects, and theirs is a talented family. In New York or Boston we'd visit museums and meet at their home or ours for holidays celebrations.

My New York City architecture career and Bill's Boston real estate career converged to bring Dan Miller and Prudence King into my life. In 1987, when Bill and I were dating, he and Dan collaborated on deals and, by chance or by design, Dan's long-time partner Prudence became my client on a campus planning project for the University of Massachusetts in Boston. Together we attended plays and enjoyed Passover Seders.

Pat Gratton, the seasoned flight attendant, had observed for some time that I wasn't behaving in my normal ways. The past summer she'd been surprised to see how sedentary I'd become. During our trip to Atlantis in October, she'd watched with concern as I walked at less than a snail's pace, and gingerly stepped into the sea. Even so, the news of my cancer hit Pat hard.

When Thomas Mahne joined my daughter's third grade class, his mother Sherri and I soon became friends. A smart businesswoman with a kind and generous heart, Sherri helped me navigate the politics of the playground and the challenges of parenting.

As the severity of my disease began to reveal itself and I adjusted to this new reality, I would gradually take a few more people into my confidence. Beginning in March, with great heartache, I began to tell people whom I thought were friends about my cancer. Some embraced my family and me. Without becoming intrusive, they made it clear they were there to help us. They responded with kindness, sensed my need for privacy, and reached out to me from time to time with a supportive note or a humorous one.

Some pledged to help us out no matter what, but their pledges and what I'd thought was their friendship quickly evaporated. Others took the news in silence and never spoke to me again. Not a call, not a note. Although this still astonishes me, I can understand it.

Just the idea of cancer is terrifying. Perhaps these people were afraid they'd catch cancer? Perhaps it was just too creepy to stay in my world? Perhaps they hoped that discarding my family and me would keep them safe from my sickness.

I learned lasting lessons about who was on my side and who wasn't.

Once we had a name for the lymphoma, Bill and Sherri were on the Internet immediately.

"It's very rare. It's more common in men than in women. It's more common in people over 65." These were Bill's findings, and I seemed to be somewhat of an anomaly in both the sex and age categories.

"Karen Lee, people live with Waldenstrom's for decades," Sherri comforted me in her assertive way. "You'll die of something else."

Reassuring to both of them, but not so reassuring to me, the one with the cancer.

Internally, I was doing a lot of adjusting, and hating it. Over the past few weeks, I'd become aware that I was really sick; I just hadn't known I was sick because of cancer. This single fact was more than enough information for me to grasp and attempt to metabolize. More information, the Internet, weren't for me. Not yet.

During this period, Bill ran interference for me. Internally, I wasn't in denial, but externally I behaved as if I were. Bill did the worldly work. He found and bookmarked thirteen Internet sites on Waldenstrom's Macroglobulinemia for me. He later told me that upon learning the name of the lymphoma, his first telephone call had been to our neighbor Fred Rosen. In addition to being one of the most sophisticated people we knew, Fred was a pediatrician, a brilliant researcher, and one of the world's top experts on blood. He reassured Bill that people do in fact live with this cancer for decades with no need for treatment.

Seeking a specialist in this disease, Bill also called a business colleague and close friend, Donny Levine. Donny gave Bill the phone number of a relative in California, a cancer researcher, and said, "Call him now." Multitasking at his office, Bill was on the Internet and on the phone with the California relative. The relative's recommendation came through the phone line with absolute certainty: "Dr. Steven Treon, Dana-Farber, Boston."

Bill had simultaneously found Dr. Treon on the Internet.

The Good Girl

Since I was a girl, I was always the good one. The good student, the hard worker, the one who—for the most part—followed the rules and succeeded within the parameters other people established. I'm not proud of this, but charm and good looks sometimes came into play and helped me achieve whatever my goal happened to be at the time.

Now I was flailing, without a guide. I saw and felt myself to be utterly alone, with nothing to hold onto and no one able to know my terror or enter my ring of isolation.

Intuition told me the sets of other people's rules that I might typically employ—to get good grades, win a design contract, or build a relationship—couldn't help me. Charm versus cancer? Forget about it. My decades of good girl skills weren't a resource now. I couldn't enlist them, and I certainly couldn't rely on them to get me out of cancer.

So faced with the news, and the knowledge, that I had cancer, how exactly did I choose to handle that news and that knowledge in February and the first half of March, 2005?

I decided to make it go away. But how?

There must be some tricks, rules, or lifestyle changes that could chase away the cancer. And I was willing to try those tricks, follow those rules; willing to overhaul my habits to make myself well. I'd do anything to end the cancer and avoid medical treatment. I figured I could do it by being a good girl in new ways.

Diet as a cure came to mind. I heard about the author Andrew Weil, MD. Thinking that two books would cure my cancer faster than one, I bought a copy of both *Eating Well for Optimal Health* and *8 Weeks to Optimal Health*. Surely, eating a lot more salmon would eradicate the cancer and I'd be healthy again.

But there were a couple of problems. First, as I've said, I already ate well, and I loved salmon. For most of my life, my food choices read like the American Medical Association's wish list for a healthy diet, for the most part. Second, although from time to time I enjoy creating tasty, pretty meals, I hate following recipes. After perusing Dr. Weil's books and getting the gist of them, I realized that I lacked the energy and discipline to center my life on a new menu-planning program. So much for that cure.

Non-Western medicine came to mind, specifically Chinese herbs. I called a few people whom I felt might be able to put me in touch with a Chinese herbalist. I was surprised to discover that the thought of using non-Western medicine, remedies, or techniques for health had never occurred to most of the people I called. Only one of my friends was receptive to my request, and able to provide me with a contact, Dr. George Wong, in New York. But, she advised me, he was traveling, and unreachable.

When he returned to his New York office in early March, I spoke with Dr. Wong. I told him what I knew: lymphoma, non-Hodgkin's, non-threatening, and I wanted it to go away. I described the nature of Waldenstrom's Macroglobulinemia as best I could at that time. Patiently, he listened.

His first reply was disappointing: his herbs couldn't cure lymphoma. His next remark was reassuring: if he could have just three months, his herbs could definitely strengthen my immune system, making my body better able to withstand the eventual assault of chemotherapy, should it become necessary.

Even though this wasn't the response I'd wanted to hear, I felt a connection and a trust with Dr. Wong. He listened to me, and responded with respect. He was eager to see me soon, which I greatly appreciated. We made a date to meet at his office on March 17th.

"Did I have lab reports?" Dr. Wong wanted to know. It would be most helpful for him to see my blood test results.

Although it hadn't occurred to me to look at the lab reports myself, and I had no desire to see my sickness documented in black and white, of course I agreed to get copies for Dr. Wong.

With my state of being in these early weeks consisting of terror, shock, and misery, I equated my reading the Internet information Bill had bookmarked with my going public about my cancer, and for a couple of weeks, I just couldn't do it.

While I appreciated my husband's thoughtfulness, I've never been much of a researcher or a fan of the Internet. But I was beginning to realize: if I did some research on this lymphoma and could understand it, perhaps I could find a way to outsmart it.

Home alone one morning, I sat at Bill's desk, turned on his computer, and went to the bookmarked sites. Here's what I saw: a history of the disease, statistics about how rare it is, a definition about tumor cells overproducing the antibody IgM, reassurances, á la Sherri's, of patients' active lifestyles, support group information, and an organization called the International Waldenstrom's Macroglobulinemia Foundation (IWMF).

My reaction was rejection. I hated all of it. I flew through it fast, feeling that even seeing information was an act of acceptance that would make my sickness worse. Nonetheless, I copied down the telephone number of the IWMF. I dialed. When a recorded message came on, I steeled my nerves, and left my name and number.

When I received a return phone call, I hastily explained my situation. The woman I spoke with was matter-of-fact. She suggested a support group and provided the phone number of the group leader for my region. She had some pamphlets she could mail to me. "Would that be helpful?" she asked.

The pamphlets arrived in a couple of days and sat unread for weeks. As for support groups: for me, this was a private journey.

"Who Cares?"

Weighted down, bearing heavily the knowledge that I had cancer, Bill and I trudged through the days and through our home. Quietly, Sara did, too.

Often, one of us would begin a sentence or initiate a question, typically about something mundane, aimed to elicit a response or an action from the other. In the old days, the routine response or the automatic action would have been quick in coming.

These days, the lackluster truth came instead.

Within the new frame of reference in which we were now immersed, "Who cares?" became our motto concerning the everyday matters of life and home.

With cancer, when you view a life as though it's in a funnel—spiraling downward, options narrowing, the only exit is death—who cares about anything else?

Free Fall

I have always had a passion for painting and making sculpture. In my twenties and thirties, it translated into my career as an architect. In my fifties, it became my calling as an artist.

During the first year of college, in class I was the dutiful student; in my dormitory room I was the free-spirited artist. On my bedroom floor, I'd place a canvas and paint.

By sophomore year, I felt disillusioned with academia and increasingly drawn to painting. Looking around Harvard, I realized that there was one place on campus where students were able to work with their hands and make things—new things—like drawings and sculptures. Rather than taking a semester off to reconsider my options, I took a flying leap into the Visual and Environmental Studies major. If I liked it, I told myself, I'd stay in school. If I didn't, I'd be out of there.

As it turned out, working in the Carpenter Center's studios delighted me. Architectural history fascinated me. Rather than pursue the path of the artist, I chose the more conventional career path of architecture. Why not apply my creative energies to practical projects, places where people could live, work, and feel good?

During my architecture career, I often had drawing, painting, or sculpture projects going on at home. The design sketches for one of my most beautiful projects were done in watercolors. But my career demanded so much time and energy that my art was relegated to a minor role.

In 2001, when my daughter entered middle school, I signed up for evening classes at Boston's School of the Museum of Fine Arts. With energy and enthusiasm, I threw myself into the challenge and fun of making art.

During the next four years, I experimented with painting, sculpture, and collage. The school's print shop became my second home. When my work was exhibited in the school's galleries or sold in the annual sale, I felt honored.

The winter semester of 2005 found me taking a Wednesday evening painting and collage course, as well as a Saturday morning lithography course. Along with my enthusiasm came two new companions. First, in January, the nausea of fear warning me that something was terribly wrong, and then, in February, the nausea of terror, reminding me I had cancer.

As if I needed reminding.

Rarely pre-planned or cerebral, my work springs from emotion and intuition. My working method is physical. I use my whole body as I draw,

paint, print, and sculpt. It's an interactive process. My mind knew I had cancer, and my body felt it.

As I worked, a new color palette appeared. For some paintings, hot pink served as background; against it, I spattered drops of red enamel or splashed jagged branches of black ink. Visceral images pulsed like my over-worked heart. Other canvases had backgrounds of shimmering whites, also clawed by red and black.

In the print shop, hot pink and acid green clashed on my plates and on my paper. Dots and slashes of color played across their surfaces.

My energy for life was at an all-time low, but my energy for art was flying.

In class, my tendency was to keep to myself and stay focused on my work. I enjoyed the company of classmates and occasionally became friendly with some, but it's fair to say my demeanor was more private than social.

One Saturday morning, as the class gathered around a large table in anticipation of a demonstration by our teacher, the woman next to me became chatty. About my age, she chose me to receive the burdens of her life.

She'd had cancer. She'd had treatment. She was currently okay. Her husband, an alcoholic, had lymphoma. He, too, had had treatment. From time to time, his lymphoma reared its ugly head. She had no idea why he was still alive, she said.

My outward response was a sickly smile. My inward response was a gripping distaste. Why did she and her husband both have cancer? Why was his cancer a lymphoma, as was mine? Why did I have to know any of this? And, what was I supposed to do with it?

I had an urge to bolt. Get out of there. Go home and sulk.

But I stayed. Through that semester, although my physical strength was diminished, the force of my art remained intact. My body of work had power. It pulsed with life, and with blood.

Courtesy Call

Arthritis wasn't my problem. Nonetheless, I made an appointment to return to Dr. Bonnie Bermas. I wanted to thank her for her attention, her care and her respect.

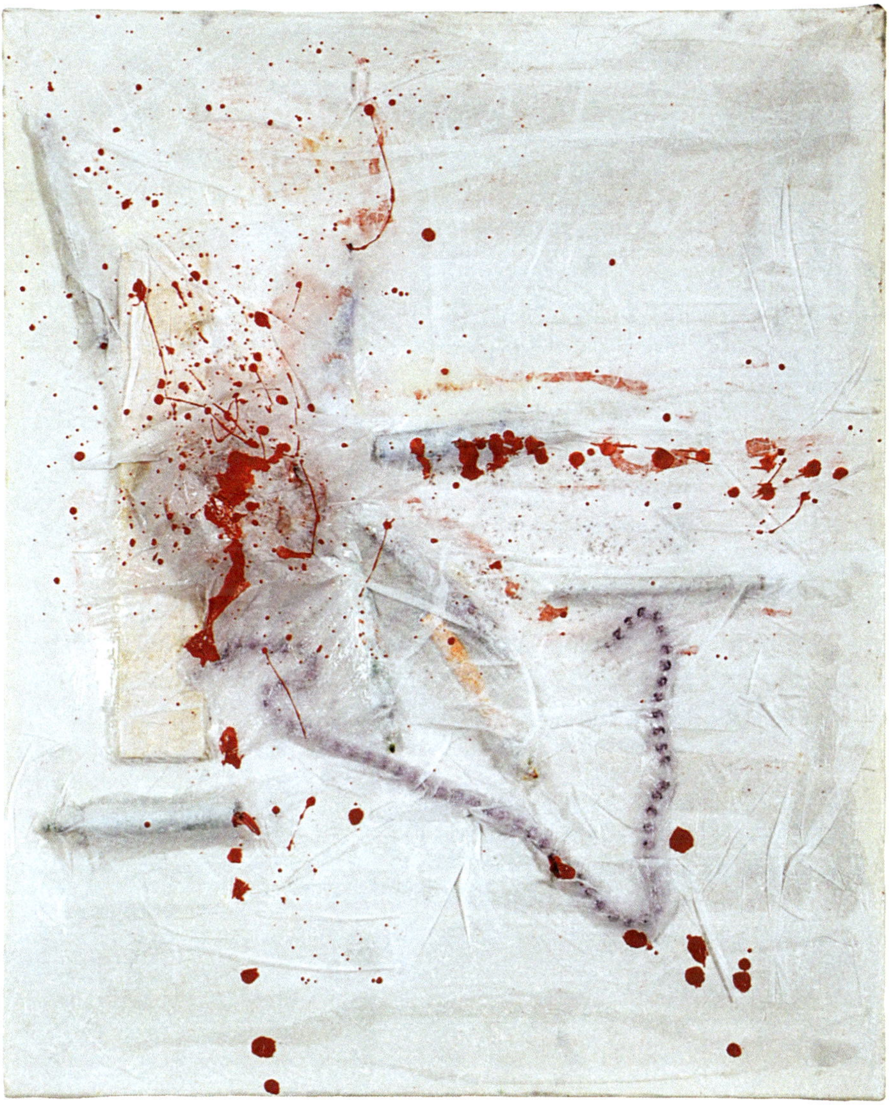

When I arrived at the hospital on February 17th I found the rheumatology wing clogged with people in wheelchairs or on walkers, with bloated legs, barely able to move. Their suffering and pain filled the air. I felt sad and compassionate for them, and sorry that they were so sick. My empathy for them overrode my concern for myself.

Dr. Bermas welcomed me, and seemed surprised to see me. In her small office, an unexpected, and ultimately inspiring, conversation occurred.

She wasn't happy. She said that, although she knew she'd done the right thing for me from a medical standpoint—following the clues, requesting diagnostic scans and tests, and ultimately assisting in finding and defining my lymphoma—she wasn't at all sure that this was the right course of action from an emotional standpoint.

By telling me a story, she explained the dilemma she was feeling. A few years ago, a spot of cancer had been found on one of her father's lungs. Surgery removed the spot and one hundred percent of the disease. He was healthy, and he was cancer-free. He chose, however, to define himself as a "cancer survivor," and that became his identity.

Dr. Bermas' line of reasoning was that, had the tiny spot gone unnoticed, it might have never developed into a threat, and her father could have enjoyed a normal life, identified by health rather than by cancer.

Now, here I sat, diagnosed with a latent lymphoma that would lie dormant and not be a danger to me at all, presumably for many, many years, if ever. Dr. Bermas genuinely liked me, and would have preferred that I not suffer with this knowledge.

I found myself consoling her. Having the diagnosis was okay, I told her. At least we might now have some understanding about why I'd been feeling so bad for so long.

We parted warmly.

Although I didn't register the importance of it at the time, the doctor's story was the first to convey to me the message that a person can have cancer and still have a choice.

The Gates

Even though the focus of my life and my emotions was mostly self-centered, I happened to leaf through *The New York Times*. My perch was the over-sized white upholstered chair in our dining room; the newspaper's perch was the matching, over-sized ottoman.

The legendary artist couple Christo and Jeanne-Claude had created their expansive environmental, experiential sculpture and performance piece in Central Park. Conceived decades earlier, *The Gates* was finally built. A temporary installation, for just two weeks it would be available for all to enjoy.

Photographs showed bright orange fabric suspended from bright orange metal. What a contrast to the brown bark along the paths and within the swards! Volunteers who'd assembled it, visitors who strolled through it, and art critics who reviewed it spoke in one voice: "Phenomenal!"

I told Bill, "We really can't miss this."

As he always does, Bill made it happen.

There wasn't a hotel room to be had in New York City on Saturday night, February 19th, so Bill conceived an alternative. We would travel to New York by train on Sunday, and return to Boston Tuesday.

Sara's childhood friend Lindsay Rabkin joined us. Because Monday was President's Day, the girls had a couple of days off from school.

In anticipation of this colorful event, I painted my fingernails bright orange.

Eager for a break from our all-too-frequent hospital visits and resulting bad tidings, we happily boarded Amtrak's Acela Express. Although Bill's and Sara's long legs competed for stretch space, the train ride was a pleasure.

From New York's Penn Station, we hailed a taxi, dropped our bags at our hotel, and headed directly to Central Park.

As great good luck would have it, Mary Ting and Todd Springer's youngest son, Sean Springer, had the privilege of volunteering for Christo and Jeanne-Claude. For eight weeks, Sean had worked with hundreds of other volunteers to erect *The Gates*. This day, we'd made a plan to meet Mary and her family, and our nephew Lane. The idea was to explore the project together, then have lunch.

At our rendezvous point, the park entrance just south of the Metropolitan Museum of Art, Mary awaited us, beaming.

Brilliant winter sun. Enough wind to get *The Gates* flapping and laughing. Thousands of people engaged and enthralled.

"Come, come," Mary motioned us to enter and follow.

She led us to Sean, a talented sculptor. And what a vision he was! Dressed in a tan jumpsuit with orange trim, sporting orange Oakley sunglasses, Sean seemed to be cut from the same cloth as the largest public sculpture in history. Were his clothes and sunglasses a standard-issue uniform? No, these were Sean's personal additions.

Delighted, we surrounded him. From his jumpsuit pocket, he discreetly removed small swatches of *The Gates*' vivid orange nylon. Equally discreetly, he distributed swatches to us. Each day during the two weeks that *The Gates* would stand, each volunteer was allotted some swatches, souvenirs for visitors. Sean was kind to be sure we received some.

In the sparkling sunlight and chilly winds, we wandered, utterly enchanted. Luminous orange fabric fluttered below glowing orange lintels framed by gleaming orange posts. Banners bellowed with the wind; metal glistened in the sunlight. Individually, each gate looked like a musical note; together, they were a visual symphony. Blasting winds smacked and snapped the banners, and we heard *The Gates* make music of its own. It was a sound and light show that needed only nature to present it. Eventually we left the park and enjoyed lunch. Transported out of myself by the magic of *The Gates* and love for family and friends, I felt very happy. Mentally and sensually, I was exhilarated. Physically, there was no accompanying adrenalin rush. It would be a long time before I figured out that my thick, sick blood simply couldn't move fast enough to deliver that rush.

Late that evening, we found ourselves seated at the Friday's bar on Third Avenue in the fifties. At that hour, it was the only place still open for a basic meal. Sara and Lindsay sat between Bill and me.

All day and into the night I'd been distracted by people I love and the magic of our trip. Now, without warning, the grim reality of cancer dug its nails into me. Suddenly I found myself off my stool, head buried in the shoulder of Bill's jacket, sobbing. I was so scared. I didn't want to die. I didn't want the girls to know I had cancer, and be scared, too.

That night it snowed. In the morning, a white blanket lay upon Manhattan. To Central Park and *The Gates* we went.

This day the magic was different. Absence of sunlight, presence of snow, much colder air. Being Monday, many fewer people floated through the fantasy that was real. A few tall inches of pure white snow rested on the lintels of *The Gates*. Thick lines of snow delineated the trees, lawns, pathways—all white, absorbing sound, establishing quiet.

Again, we found Sean. We enjoyed a hot chocolate at the boathouse near the frozen lake. Again, the experience was unique. This was a one-of-a-kind, once-in-a-lifetime phenomenon. Experiencing it once was remarkable. Experiencing it twice was extraordinary.

What a tribute to the creative spirit, and the collective soul. Twenty-five years from concept to creation. Christo and Jeanne-Claude never gave up, never lost sight of their vision to build *The Gates* during all that time. For those two weeks in February, millions of people received their gift and experienced an uplifting joy.

There's a role model for us all.

For me, it was a welcome respite from the immersion in diagnosis and disease, and a reminder that commitment and hope have power.

The Hardest Part

It's fair to say I was more afraid for Sara than I was for myself. Stunned with the news that I had cancer, fear of telling my daughter paralyzed my emotions at least as much as the diagnosis did. How terrifying for a young girl to learn that her mother has a murderous incurable disease? How painful. How unfair. How terribly scary.

I postponed. I perseverated. I vented and rehearsed the wording and the sequence of what I'd say to her. How to present it so it had a degree of comfort and hope?

To one acquaintance who's a therapist specializing in adolescents, I said I planned to assure Sara that I'd be okay.

"That may not be true," he replied.

Instantly, I dismissed his negativity. Grudgingly, I acknowledged that it might be unwise to make my daughter a promise I might not be able to keep.

Trolling for help, I called Dana-Farber, expressed my dilemma, and was offered the name of a staff psychiatrist. When I called, the receptionist advised that the doctor was extremely busy. Most likely she wouldn't be available for me.

I blurted out the headlines of my dilemma.

A diagnosis of incurable cancer.

A teenaged daughter.

A small, close-knit family.

I needed help; I needed guidance.

I gave the receptionist my phone number.

To my surprise, within the hour, the psychiatrist returned my call. First, she listened. Then, she advised.

"Tell her you have cancer. Tell her you have good care. With teenagers, it's best to be brief: ask her if she has any questions. Tell her tonight."

Thanking her for her time and hanging up the phone, my mind told me "She's nuts." The curt bluntness of the message she proposed shocked me. It felt brutal to me. More important, and worse, hearing it would feel brutal to my daughter, or so I thought.

I delayed longer and postponed the conversation. In that purgatory of grappling with the diagnosis myself, the challenge of telling Sara became hell.

Back at home after *The Gates*, with a carefully orchestrated statement, I finally delivered the message to my daughter. Rather than say "lymphoma" or "blood cancer," I used a more neutral term: blood disorder. My fear of her fear was my editorial agent.

First, I thanked my daughter for being so supportive since that first week in January, with that first CAT scan. Of course, I'd told her as each new diagnostic procedure was scheduled.

"They'll know how to help you," she'd said.

Now I began by saying she was right. Because of a couple more tests, the doctors figured out that I had a blood disorder. White cells were manufacturing something abnormal.

"This thing is indolent," I said. "It's lazy and very slow to develop. I've had it for quite a while. It's not caused by anything I did or anyone else did. It's not contagious, and it's not hereditary. There's no need to treat it now.

"The good part is the doctors can monitor it every few months. Someday, if it needs to be treated, it can be—so you were right about their knowing how to help me.

"The doctors assure me about you, that you're very healthy. I'm fine, and I'll be fine. If you have questions, thoughts, or worries, just ask. Daddy knows, too, so you can ask him, too."

After she listened, my daughter asked me four succinct questions.

"Why Dana-Farber?"

"What's it called?"

"Why not treat it now?"

"Why did you tell your friends?"

Always the closest of confidants, she and I, Sara felt hurt that I didn't confide in her first. I answered each question as best I could. As I've said, in hindsight I believe she'd overheard my end of the conversation on the evening of February 3rd, when I told Sherri I'd just received a diagnosis of cancer. Surely she'd heard pieces of my many phone calls with Dr. Woo. Of course she knew about the CAT scan, as well as the endoscopies. Clearly something was wrong, and my daughter knew it.

Sometimes I wonder if the Dana-Farber psychiatrist was right, and immediate, honest communication really is the best and least painful choice.

The Leash and the Time Bomb

On Monday, March 7th, exactly four weeks after our first entry into Dana-Farber Cancer Institute, Bill and I were back. Checking in was again a horrible, infuriating drill for me. Being told to go around the corner to have blood drawn, then waiting another hour and a half past our designated appointment time, again generated extreme anxiety and anger in me.

This is when I first began to notice that in a cancer hospital you can't make assumptions about who's a patient and who's not. Wanting to isolate and distance myself from phlebotomy—the small room with four stations where patients' blood is drawn—hating everything about this, I decided to wait outside in the hall. When I saw another woman standing there, I assumed she, too, was waiting her turn. I stood next to her, but not too close, figuring I was in line.

After a while, a woman came out of the phlebotomy room and joined her companion, the one standing next to me. They left together.

I learned to read the signs. If a couple is seated together, or a family is seated together, don't judge or be guided by appearance or age. Don't make assumptions about who's sick and who isn't. The one wearing the hospital bracelet: that's the patient.

This day I had with me three pages of questions to ask the oncologist.

Eventually, someone called my name. Was the wait finally over? Was it time to see the doctor? No, it was time to check my vital signs—weight and blood pressure, and hear a question I despised: "Are you having any pain today?"

Then back to the waiting room.

Finally my name was called a second time, and Bill and I were shown to a room that seemed even tinier than the one we'd been in a month before.

Linda soon joined us. Looking at the results of my bone marrow biopsy on the computer screen, the nurse remarked with muted surprise that the tumor cells were a "minute population." When I tried to ask a few questions, it was clear that she wouldn't be answering them. I stopped talking. What was the point?

When the doctor arrived, I was welcoming and looking forward to a dialogue to ease my worries. Now we could settle in and focus on a discussion that would answer my questions and alleviate the horror of all this. Or, so I hoped.

That day the doctor was hurried, distracted, and not interested in my questions. He dismissed them, brushed them off; he brushed me off. He wasn't interested in me as a person, or so it seemed.

When his cell phone rang two or three times, he took the calls. When I asked questions, they weren't taken seriously, nor were they answered.

He asked me the same questions he'd posed four weeks earlier. Any blurry vision? Any night sweats?

Having thought about these questions over the past month I attempted to ask for help in figuring out the answer to the night sweats question. Four points were on my list:

I've never been 57 before.

I've never had my knees break before.

I've never had menopause before.

I've never had cancer before.

How to distinguish hot flashes from night sweats? I asked for help here, and got none. I'd been waking up in the middle of the night with a lake of water between my breasts. I'd sop it up with my nightgown. Although I never made the connection then, I believe it's fair to say those were night sweats.

The doctor had a message to deliver: from now on I'd need an appointment, and a blood test, every three months. He told us that the results of today's blood tests should be back by week's end, and suggested I call him on Friday.

With our daughter's spring break approaching, Bill asked the doctor whether it would be all right for us to take a vacation. He assured us that would be fine.

Although she sat immobile, I noticed that Linda seemed to be sending me signals with her eyes, as if she wanted to convey some kind of silent message. As the doctor stood to exit, and Bill and I felt we were being pushed out the door, I persistently stated my two key questions of the day:

"Am I on a leash?"

"No, not at all," was the doctor's dismissive, almost mocking answer.

"Is this a time bomb?"

Again, "No."

As Bill and I stood to take the two steps to the door, Linda extended her hand to me. Her business card lay on her open palm.

"Call me anytime," she said.

I took the card.

The Choke Chain and the Ticking Time Bomb

Between Monday and Friday, I didn't think about the blood test results, nor did I feel any particular anxieties about them. Mostly, my feelings were neutral. On Friday—another cold, dark gray, airless day—I sat at Bill's desk and dialed the oncologist's number.

Late in the afternoon, he returned my call.

Once the bone marrow biopsy revealed Waldenstrom's Macroglobulinemia, the doctor knew which elements of the blood to analyze, that is, what questions to ask, to determine the degree of disease. For example, questions about the sedimentation rate and cardiac reactive protein were now superseded by analysis of the blood's viscosity and protein level.

The answer was mainly bad.

The doctor said the blood analysis showed a viscosity of 3.2; normal blood viscosity is 1.6. Based on a single sample, he said the amount of protein was more or less stable.

"Sometime in the next few months, we'd like to start treatment before the solubility reaches 4.0, when typical symptoms like blurry vision occur."

Stunning news! Not so very long ago (four weeks to the day) the message was that I'd be fine for decades, and that I should regard this cancer as nothing more than a latent imbalance. Right now, it revealed itself to be threatening my life.

I asked what "treatment" meant.

The non-negotiable answer was fludarabine, rituximab and hydrocortisone.

I asked about the drugs.

"Why do I need a steroid?"

Apparently, it was to counteract the impact of the other drugs. This wasn't making sense to me.

How much of the drugs will be prescribed, and what would they accomplish? What was the treatment schedule? My questions seemed more than reasonable, at least to me.

Fludarabine, I was told, is an "old" chemotherapy drug. I guess this was designed to comfort me? Rituximab isn't chemotherapy, but a synthetic antibody that binds to the tumor cells. Hydrocortisone would protect me from the other two.

"Why?" I asked.

"We can talk about it when the time comes," was the non-response.

The prescription: four to six rounds of treatment. Each round consisted of receiving drugs five days in a row, once each month. I'd also be on a diet of antibiotics.

Ideally, the drugs would help reduce the life-threatening blood viscosity, caused by the tumors cells overproducing IgM cells. With this treatment, the lymphoma usually goes into remission. It could stay quiescent for a year, maybe two.

"Then what?" I asked.

"We repeat the treatment cycle. Another patient, an eighty-six year old woman, is currently in remission that began eighteen months ago."

Rather than give me encouragement, this made me angry. I was, after all, only fifty-seven.

The oncologist assured me there wouldn't be many side effects.

"You won't lose your hair," she said.

Hair? Hair! I was dying! Why would I possibly care about my hair?

"We're picking this up at the tail end of 'watch and wait,'" I heard the doctor say. "You've had this a long time."

As I listened, I felt in my gut and I knew in my spirit, the treatment she described would kill me. I knew my body wouldn't be able to live through these drugs, or this schedule. I knew I had to trust my instincts.

About the treatment cycle, which would seem to define my life and my family's, I asked: "Why would I want that situation?"

Many questions came to mind as I listened and jotted down notes.

"We'll talk about that when it's time to start treatment," was the answer.

"You have no choice, and there's nothing to discuss," was the message.

During one brief phone conversation, the assurance that having this cancer was a non-event crashed and burned. The leash I'd asked about became a choke chain, and the time bomb was ticking.

On that day, when I heard the edict that, in a few months, I'd have to begin "treatment," I knew four things instinctively and for sure. First, the course of treatment being dictated would kill me. Second, as a thinking person, I did not exist for the diagnosing oncologist. Third, I needed to be respected and listened to, and treated as an intelligent person by my doctor. Fourth, I needed a different doctor.

My intuition, instincts, and awareness became a conscious presence. I heard them mentally and felt them viscerally, the "gut feeling." The clarity and simplicity of the message couldn't be denied or ignored, so I listened, accepted, and trusted it.

Trust in myself powered my drive to survive.

As soon as Bill came home, I told him the news. I was a wreck. He was stalwart. We were both extremely shaken.

I've no doubt Sara picked up on all of this immediately. Even so, feeling and dealing with my own emotions and thoughts, and wanting dearly to protect her from being scared about my being so sick, I waited several days before directly telling my daughter this new, even worse news.

In our living room, on our sofa, I told her that, as a result of recent blood tests, the doctor said I'd be needing treatment in the next few months.

"Why not now?" she asked.

She's so smart, so loving.

"Why wait? Why let it become worse, more dangerous?" was the meaning behind her words.

These were my sentiments, verbatim.

As her crew coach wrote later that spring on my daughter's report card, "She always asks the one question that everyone in the boat needs to have answered."

Now my emotions plummeted. Real cancer. Really bad cancer. Really bad cancer in a really bad stage.

I'd be dead really soon.

During one conversation, Bill said something about fear, as if his understanding of that emotion matched mine.

"It's not fear. It's terror," I snapped.

Bill would be a widower, out having a new life, while I was out being dead.

So many of us have engaged in the hypothetical speculation: "If I had a dread disease, if I knew I were going to die soon, if I had only a month or a year to live, what would I choose to do with my life? How would I use the time I had left?"

For me, now, this was no longer theory, and no longer speculation. I felt like I'd felt that first time in the consultation room at Dana-Farber, with Bill, Linda, and the oncologist. There are two kinds of people in the world: the ones who have cancer, and the ones who don't.

There, in my bedroom, I felt isolated, and I felt doomed.

Visit with Fred

Still running interference for me, shielding me, protecting me, and now shifting it all into a higher gear, Bill again called our neighbor Fred Rosen to tell him the news.

A contender for the Nobel Prize, Fred was a pioneer in identifying and creating treatments for a host of pediatric autoimmune diseases. Blood was his specialty. Cultured and sophisticated, he spoke eight languages and loved the opera.

When Fred invited Bill and me to talk with him, we eagerly accepted. As usual, I had with me a notebook, a list of questions, and notes about my blood test results.

Fred gave me his full attention as I brought him up to date: the severity of my lymphoma was on the verge of becoming life threatening, and I'd been told treatment would be needed soon.

Fred asked about the viscosity and IgM levels revealed in my most recent blood tests. He knew the numbers were too high. He taught Bill and me that our immune system produces five antibodies. "They come in five flavors," he said. "IgA, IgD, IgE, IgG, and IgM."

Each has a unique function in protecting and defending us from disease. As we listened, Bill and I got a crash course in this segment of the immune system.

IgA protects the sinuses and gastrointestinal system from bacterial infection. IgD sits on the immune cell and acts like a magnet, attracting any type of infectious agent to itself before it reaches the immune cell. IgE can sense allergens and parasites, and plays a role in responding to allergies. IgG provides long-term immune protection.

IgM registers the first alarm when the body needs to mount an immune response. When we need protection against infection, IgM jumps into action like the Marines. Because it's a large cell, IgM is referred to as a macroglobulin: a big blood cell.

In Waldenstrom's Macroglobulinemia, tumor cells cause overproduction of IgM cells, which in turn thicken and clog the blood.

Fred asked what drug the doctor would be giving me.

"Fludarabine."

"He's bringing out the heavy artillery." Only a spontaneously raised eyebrow indicated his feeling about this course of therapy. "Seven years," he said.

I drew a blank.

"You have seven years once the fludarabine starts."

Well this was precise. Dying seven years from now was better than dying right now. Maybe Sara would marry young, and I'd still be alive to attend her wedding after all.

Incurable

Instinct told me I needed to find some treatment options and a different oncologist. Fred's information reinforced and confirmed both the instinct and the need. After the visit with Fred, I began to feel a sense of struggle; I wanted to wriggle myself up and out of cancer's prison. Rather than accept and surrender to other people's definition of my lymphoma as incurable and likely terminal, I wanted to be well and live.

Reaching out for help, I called two friends, both doctors.

"Who do you know who can help me get well?" I asked them.

Both suggested well-known, well-respected hematological oncologists. The names on their lists overlapped, and as they related the specialists' credentials, it sounded like my doctor friends, knowing what they did about Waldenstrom's Macroglobulinemia, were concerned about my being nicely ushered into death as this incurable disease progressed. Given their training and experience, their conclusion was logical to them. It was, however, unacceptable to me.

From her medical school days, one friend had a clear memory of this lymphoma. A textbook had used an image of railroad boxcars to represent the big IgM molecules, and their ability to jam end to end, clogging blood vessels. The crack-up sounded grim and irrevocable.

I noticed a bizarre disconnect. I wanted to get better, which I'd expressed clearly. I felt misunderstood, belittled, and betrayed. It felt as if my friends had already accepted the irreversible progression of the disease, and my non-negotiable death. Not what I wanted.

My hope, even though it was at this point vague, was taking root, in opposition to the lack of options and lack of hope other people had for me. My optimism to live faced their seeming certainty that I wouldn't.

To paraphrase a line from one of the musical numbers in "Chicago," I saw myself alive, and they saw me dead.

Red Tape

As for making a shift from passive to active, out of necessity it was time and I was ready. I took the name and phone number Bill offered, and called the office of Dr. Steven Treon at Dana-Farber.

The recorded message scared me. Following the basic greeting came a series of menu choices that went something like this:

"If you are a patient participating in the Bexxer clinical trial, please dial 3."

"If you are a patient participating in the alemtuzumab clinical trial, please dial 4."

Terrified, I hung up.

After calling a couple of times and hanging up fast, I redialed, held on, and spoke with an office assistant.

With conscious control of my words and my voice, I stated my diagnosis and the current state of the disease as I understood it. I requested an appointment to see Dr. Treon.

Well there was something I hadn't understood. I was told that in order to schedule such an appointment, a doctor's referral was necessary. I found it surprising that my own request wasn't enough—after all, why would anyone frivolously ask to see an oncologist—but I kept with the program and called Dr. Woo.

When I mentioned Dr. Treon to Dr. Woo and spoke of him as a known expert in the study and treatment of Waldenstrom's Macroglobulinemia, she agreed to try to reach him and interview him on my behalf.

A week or so later, on a Sunday, she called. She'd contacted two specialists she knew; both were available to see me. She'd also spoken with Dr. Treon, and they'd enjoyed a cordial conversation. She felt comfortable with him as a researcher. As for his clinical abilities, well, that was less clear.

Here was the very good news: with Dr. Woo's referral, it would now be okay for me to call Dr. Treon's office and try to schedule an appointment.

Once again, I dialed Dr. Treon's number at Dana-Farber. This time, I responded to the recorded message: I was in the category of "new patient," and left my name and phone number.

When the office assistant returned my call, her manner was businesslike. Yes, with the referral from my doctor, she could book an appointment for me. The next available clinic date to see Dr. Treon was April 1st. As the schedule that day was very full, and Dr. Treon liked to take his time meeting new patients, she suggested I consider waiting a few more days. Liking her logic, I booked an appointment for April 6th.

With that date set, a quiet, non-verbal instinctive process began in me. Although I was far from ready to begin seriously addressing my disease and its current severity, certain preparatory steps came to mind. It was time to begin marshalling any resources I had, including human ones. Recalling Linda's barely perceptible nod of the head and the message her eyes had conveyed when she'd extended her open palm with her business card, I had it in my mind for a few days to give her a call.

When I telephoned, she answered at once.

She wanted to know how I was doing. This in itself was interesting; she seemed to care. Maybe she wasn't as detached as her demeanor in the clinic seemed to indicate. I told her of my upcoming appointment with Dr. Treon. I asked her if there were any other questions I should be asking, anything else I should know.

"You've asked more questions than any patient I've ever met. Usually, when people are told they need cancer treatment, they ask only two questions: Where do I go, and what time?"

Her tone conveyed respect. I asked for her advice and I remember her parting words: "Ask Dr. Treon what he has coming down the pike."

I heard these words as the ultimate encouragement—and that about said it all.

Shifting Gears

Booking an appointment to meet Dr. Steven Treon pinned me firmly to Western medicine, but I remained determined to investigate traditional non-Western medicine, too. The time had come to meet Dr. George Wong.

On March 17th with enthusiasm and hope, I left home around seven o'clock in the morning, and walked the few blocks from my home to Boston's Back Bay Station. I'd borrowed my daughter's favorite book bag and filled it with snacks, pens, paper, and my 1984 Panasonic Walkman.

In the 1980's, on my walks from my loft to my office, I'd listened to Michael Jackson's "Thriller," Blondie, and whatever else was popular at the time with this Walkman in my hand. To my daughter, it's a clunky antique. By this time Bill had planned a trip to Mexico for us during Sara's spring break. Whenever I traveled, I loved to try to learn or brush up on the language of the country I was headed for, so I thought I'd use the train ride to listen to Spanish language tapes.

During my career as an architect, designing support buildings for New York's commuter railroad systems became one of my specialties. I have a deep appreciation and respect for this mode of transportation, and I always look forward to a train ride.

This particular day, as I boarded Amtrak's Acela Express, I noticed the "Quiet Car": no cell phones, radios, or loud talking, and very few passengers. Perfect for my mood. From Boston to New York, attractive towns and picturesque views of the Atlantic Ocean border the railroad tracks.

Outside, all was beautiful. Inside, I suffered.

I arrived in New York City a couple of hours before my appointment with George Wong, PhD. Even bearing the miserable burden of cancer, I felt free and happy to be in a city I love. With my thoughts sometimes blurry, I'm not sure how I got from Penn Station to Madison Avenue and Fortieth Street. Because my ability to walk wasn't normal, this was a considerable distance for me. What I am sure of, though, is this: summer skirts, tiered, brightly colored, splashed across Express' windows. First on 34th Street, then in other store locations, the skirts seemed ideal for my daughter. Perhaps I'd buy her one or two here, today. If not, I'd surely buy her one or two in Boston.

Once on Madison Avenue, I abruptly found myself drenched in music and noise—high school kids, marching bands, bus motors, teachers regulating and shepherding the kids. The Saint Patrick's Day parade was soon to begin!

Being surrounded by young people, jammed onto narrow sidewalks between busses and buildings, helped me feel happy. I loved the energy, and I loved being alive to feel it. I flowed along with this river of life, engulfed by many different high school groups. As I advanced north, I did my own march to their cacophonous warm-up medley. I delighted in the uniforms, the rainbows of colors, and the sheen of golden fringes. The day was gray with a hint of drizzle, but the experience was vibrant and colorful.

Shoulder to shoulder with so much life—peppy kids, energetic teachers and bandleaders—and so much vibration—voices yelling, singing, and laughing, tubas panting and puffing, drums banging—I experienced a sense of vibration within myself. Body and brain were unified in an experience that was sensual rather than mental. The feeling was freeing and exhilarating.

At 57th Street, I turned east and stopped in the Belmora luncheonette. Needing comfort food, I ordered eggplant parmesan. I appreciated the food, as well as the life and health of the pizzeria's staff and patrons.

Then it was time to focus and get myself to the appointment with Dr. Wong.

The Strang Cancer Prevention Center seemed to be an odd name, but an optimistic one. As I was buzzed in, the voice on the speaker directed me to the executive office. When I arrived I was greeted, and invited to hang my coat and have a seat while I waited for Dr. Wong.

I should tell you I was dressed like a "schlub": comfortable travel clothes, with no style and not much shape. I was feeling victimized. Me—in a cancer center.

While I waited for Dr. Wong, I observed a woman named Helen Marx. She stood in her assistant's cubicle, pacing, clearing up some personal business related to her husband's death. Probably a couple of years younger than I, she was stylishly dressed, with a great pair of flat shoes. Although our clothing was the same in content—unadorned V-neck tops, simple slacks, not much jewelry—she looked classy, a woman who felt good about herself, and I looked bland, a woman trying to go unnoticed. Possibly that had as much to do with body language and self-image as anything else. Though short, Helen stood tall. Though tall, I sat slumped.

Dr. Wong arrived, greeted me, and led me down a couple of hallways to his one-room office. He sat behind his big dark wood desk; I sat in front.

Although small, the room felt grand. There were bookshelves, plants, some statuary. Mainly and marvelously, there was Dr. George Wong.

First, he listened. I told him the background, about my legs and knees, and my inability to walk normally or get air when I swam.

We talked about cancer. Breast cancer research is his specialty. He said it's insidious. Push it out the front door and it comes in the back door. I asked if he felt birth control pills contributed to breast cancer. He had no doubt that they do.

We were together about an hour and a half. During this time, I learned more from Dr. Wong about my disease, and why I felt the way I did, than I had from anyone else. As I rested my elbow on his desk, with the lightest touch possible, Dr. Wong felt my pulse. The disease created anemia—that's why I lacked energy. It was difficult for my disease-thickened blood to deliver sufficient oxygen to my body—that's why I experienced a lack of air. Dr. Wong counseled that he needed three months for his herbs to make me stronger and build up my immune system to better withstand chemotherapy. But the herbs alone couldn't combat the disease. Chemotherapy was imperative.

Using elegant calligraphy, Dr. Wong wrote a prescription for an herbal drink. That same afternoon, he planned to take the prescription to a sterile factory in Chinatown. The chemists would make up a two-month supply of herbs, then ship them to me. Dr. Wong advised me to heat and drink the contents of one pouch each morning and each evening.

Feeling grateful and also feeling better because I had learned and understood more about my body's response to the disease, I said a warm and appreciative good-bye to Dr. Wong and headed back to the executive office area to retrieve my coat.

For some reason I didn't understand at the time, Helen Marx greeted me and invited me into her office. It was a small space, with a feeling of intensity and a life fully lived.

She sat behind her desk; I slumped in the guest chair opposite her. She told me some stories. She used to volunteer at Strang. A couple of years ago, her husband had been diagnosed with stage four renal carcinoma: kidney cancer in its most advanced state.

Told he had six to eight weeks to live, Helen's husband chose surgery, which removed most of the tumor. After that, he opted for palliative care only, to keep him as comfortable as possible.

For the next four months, he and his family enjoyed a good quality of life. Then, the situation declined. It was eight months from diagnosis to death.

Helen's second story involved a friend, a thirty-two-year-old man who had been diagnosed with a form of leukemia, and was told he had only a few months left of life. He and his family decided that rather than accept the treatment—and prognosis—offered at the diagnosing hospital, they would "shop around." At a different hospital, they found a very aggressive treatment, and the young man chose that. He was now doing very well.

Helen looked at me fully, and leaned into me with her mind and with her heart.

"You're going to be fine," she said. "I know it."

I didn't believe her.

She offered me her business card, asked me to stay in touch, and told me to feel free to call her anytime. We said goodbye, and I took a taxi to Penn Station.

During the train ride to Boston, something shifted within me. "My first shot is my best shot," I thought. When I arrived home, I said to Bill, "Up until now, we've been chained to the front of a runaway locomotive. That's over. From now on, you and I run this project."

Lab Rat

The more I thought about my situation, the bolder and braver I became.

Incurable disease, advanced state, lethal treatments, a life punctuated and defined by more lethal treatments, death.

Versus:

Excellent health, except for the cancer. So why not seek out and go for the most aggressive experimental treatment I could get?

The term *lab rat* came to mind. Why not? Why shouldn't I choose to be a human lab rat? The best case: I'd get better. The worst case: The experimental treatment would kill me, and the knowledge gained by my death would help other people get better. Win-win.

My first shot is my best shot—the thought that had come to me on the train ride home after I'd met Dr. Wong and Helen Marx—became a foundation of my thinking as I formulated a strategy for getting better.

My body would never be healthier, stronger, or better able to withstand and recover from treatment than it was right now.

For about six weeks, I had been a cancer victim. But even within that cage, that emotional cell on death row, I found myself in profound touch with my intuition. It was guiding me to think for myself rather than accept what other people thought about my cancer and my prospects for life.

From St. Patrick's Day on, I became a person first, albeit one who had to face—and face down—cancer.

Trust

One morning I went back to the Internet to look up Dr. Steven P. Treon. I'd quickly read through his credentials, which included his role as one of the planet's experts on this disease, and noticed that he'd published some articles related to his work. I'd dialed his office number, and asked the office assistant if she'd please mail me his articles.

"There are quite a few," she'd replied. "May I fax you the list of their titles?"

Later that day, my fax machine delivered at least twenty pages, each filled with single-spaced listings of Dr. Treon's published articles and papers. I glanced over a few pages worth of titles, understood pretty much nothing, and deciding to trust that this body of work didn't need my attention, I set the package aside.

Trust also took root in other parts of my life.

Two things I'd always been afraid of were flying and driving.

But, hey: now that I had cancer—death inside me—flying, or rather, fear of crashing, wasn't scary at all. Rather than a white-knuckle anxiety attack, flying brought relaxation.

As for driving, having lived in cities my whole adult life, I never needed or wanted a car. Only when I was in my 50's did I drive on a regular basis to get my daughter to and from school. As a driver I was timorous, angry, and lacking in both confidence and skill.

With cancer, my awareness increased, as did my driving skills. I still don't much like driving, but I became an excellent driver.

I surprise myself.

Transformation on the Beach

With Sara's school break nearing, we prepared for our trip to Mexico. We stayed in the province of Quintana Roo, which I find one of the coolest place names on earth.

When our plane landed and we disembarked, heat and palm trees greeted us. Cancun's airport was a festival. The path leading out to ground transportation was wide, busy, and noisy. Lining the route, people loudly urged us to sign up for sightseeing trips and tour packages. Many held colorful signs showing Mayan pyramids, pristine beaches, and tropical fish. Usually all this welcoming activity would delight and relax me, putting me in an open state of mind. This day, however, the opposite reaction occurred. The music, invitations, and gay colors felt intrusive and offensive. Instead of opening up, I shut down.

Bill had arranged transportation for the ride south from the airport to our hotel. When we located the correct information booth, I slowly became aware of a bizarre bodily experience.

The conversation about our transportation took on a confrontational tone. The agent seemed not to understand our reservation. I felt he was sidestepping Bill's request for the pre-arranged car service and insisting we sign up for a complicated tour package in which we had no interest.

Although Bill was calmly pursuing a path of reason, I found myself becoming very mad. I intervened. I repeatedly asked the agent the same couple of questions, and became increasingly aggravated when I perceived his answers to be repetitive and rote rather than responsive.

At this moment, an odd awareness arose in me, almost an out of body experience. Although my behavior had familiar feelings—I was hyper, upset, and agitated—I noticed that there were none of the familiar corresponding physical sensations. Rather than feeling my heart racing and my body keyed up to match my mood, I felt absolutely nothing. There was no adrenaline rush. Only dullness was in my torso. It was as if I were disembodied, disconnected from, and disengaged within myself. It was as if I existed as two separate entities: one an actively unhappy, upset mind, the other an utterly lethargic body.

Eventually, a ride was negotiated and we arrived at the hotel. About forty-five minutes drive south of Cancun is an old-style hotel complex called

Maroma. Gardens with colorful tropical birds and an undisturbed beach predate the mid-1990's mega-resort construction known as the Mayan Riviera. It's glorious. As Bill, Sara and I unpacked and settled in, we appreciated the beauty of the place as well as the change from cold weather to hot, and the change of context. Bill and I welcomed the break from school for our daughter, and appreciated the break from home and hospital visits for ourselves.

By this time, I'd already developed the beginning of a routine. My decades-long habit of drinking coffee first thing each morning had changed about a week earlier, as soon as I'd received the first shipment of Dr. Wong's herb pouches. A new tradition continued on our terrace near the sea. Each morning, along with coffee, came a pot of hot water. I immersed a plastic herb-filled pouch into it and, after a few minutes, snipped open the pouch and drank the warm, dark herb mixture. Each evening, I repeated the ritual.

Whenever I mentioned my herb drink friends would grimace.

"Does it taste bad?" they wanted to know.

Taste? How it tasted never occurred to me. I believed in its healthful contents, and that was all that mattered.

At the edge of the sea, always a place of happiness, renewal, and inspiration for me, a new ritual began to form. Barefoot and alone, I found myself for the first time since being diagnosed with cancer acknowledging to myself that I had cancer; I was able to accept it as a fact.

Motivated by wanting to be alive and healthy, I found myself using a mantra-like technique from my DMA days.

I stated to myself (at first silently, and after a few days, aloud) my current reality: "I have Waldenstrom's Macroglobulinemia."

I asked myself (at first silently, and after a few days, vocally), "What do I want?"

I answered: "I want to be totally healthy and cancer-free."

I formally stated my choice: "I formally choose to be totally healthy and cancer-free."

Up until now, even though I understood I had cancer, I was too scared to really, fully accept it. Now, at this time, in this place, being able to say it made it somehow less personal and more objective. It was oddly freeing. As I focused on being rid of cancer, I felt energized and encouraged.

With the pounding surf providing background rhythm and plenty of sound, I found that I could speak in full voice, in full view of other people, yet have my words audible only to me.

Magic in the Mangroves

Although the hotel beach and grounds were keeping our family very happy, it seemed we should take a day trip and do some exploring on the Yucatan Peninsula. Visiting ancient Mayan sites was an obvious choice. We talked it over, and Bill asked Sara where she might like to go.

"Sian Kian looks interesting," she said.

Sian Kian is Mayan for "where the sea meets the sky." A much shorter, much cooler drive than the road to Chichin Itza, the narrow dirt road to Sian Kian had only one car on it—ours—and led us through a primordial jungle to a nature preserve and national park. We were the only visitors there.

With a Mayan guide, Bill, Sara, and I boarded a small motorboat, then set out across a circular bay of very wide diameter. At its opposite side, we entered a narrow waterway, one canal in an elaborate system that the Mayans had built. After visiting a tiny, ancient building, our guide provided each of us with an orange life vest and a black rubber inner tube. As we entered the water and settled into our tubes, our guide waved us off, promised to meet us downstream, gunned the engine, and left us in his wake.

We floated. We drifted. We laughed as our respective tubes slowly spun, in random circles, powered by eddies in the canal. For the first time in months, we were silly and relaxed together.

With our seats in the inner tubes' centers—that is, in the water—and our bodies draped over the tubes' sides, we could use our hands and our legs to guide ourselves (to some degree), and to move downstream faster. For a while, we all did.

Needing to rest, I stopped kicking. Then it occurred to me that I didn't have to rush. As my husband and my daughter kicked along and progressed together, I chose to drift. I relaxed and made a conscious decision to really look and see the mangrove trees clinging to the canal's shore; to notice leaves floating up to me, to hear the water, the wind, the birdsongs, to feel the life and the health surrounding and embracing me. In everything, I saw promise of my cancer-free good health restored. I felt it as a fact. It was calming and encouraging.

Eventually my tube and I floated up to our guide and the boat long after Bill and Sara arrived. They laughed and joked, thinking I was lost and gone.

Little did they know, I was anything but.

Litterbug

As I walked with purpose along the beach, consciously acknowledging I had Waldenstrom's Macroglobulinemia, and consciously choosing to be completely healthy and cancer-free, I began to notice signs that supported my hope.

On one of my meditative walks between our room and the restaurant, with the sounds of the surf complementing the sounds of my mantras, I spotted a small piece of paper on the sand. When I was in grade school, every year the city sponsored a clean-up campaign whose slogan was "Don't be a litterbug." When I lived and worked as an architect in New York City, long before recycling was common, I'd save my cans and bottles. Every couple of weeks, on Saturday mornings, I'd pay for a taxi and schlep my trash uptown to Manhattan's only recycling center. Since 1989, stewardship of our natural environment has been a passion and an avocation. So picking up a scrap of paper on a pristine beach was for me, a reflex action.

It was a boarding pass. The name: SOBOLEVO/S. What are the odds of SOBOL showing up on a random boarding pass on a beach in a foreign country, let alone being spotted and picked up by me? To me, this was hope personified. I analyzed the letters, the numbers, and I saw in each confirmation that I would live, healthy and whole.

On the hotel's exquisitely landscaped grounds, an occasional stray leaf appeared in my path. I collected and kept a few tough, rounded yellow leaves that were rutted by bumpy red sores of disease. I equated the leaves' sores to my diseased blood, focusing totally on the healthy leaf body vanquishing the bloody disease. Although all the leaves' colors have faded to pale brown, they still rest on my desk.

To this bright place where colorful peacocks strutted among flowers so bright they were almost gaudy, Sara and I introduced our own color. As for the tiered drawstring skirts floating in Express' display windows that dreary St. Patrick's day in New York City, I'd found them in Boston and bought two. One was hot pink, the other acid green. Lucky to wear the same size, my daughter and I wore the skirts interchangeably. They floated with us to the beach or to dinner. Versatile, the skirts got us through vacation and through the summer.

In January, they'd become my uniform.

The Cure Concept

When I developed a stomach problem severe enough to require a doctor's help, lucky for me the hotel had a doctor on call. Arriving with his black satchel and his teenaged son, he was the consummate gentleman.

"I will cure you," he said. "I know for sure I will cure you."

I appreciated his certainty more than he could have imagined.

Aware that my body's chemistry wasn't normal, and worried—even paranoid—about possible adverse effects of the antibiotic the local doctor had asked me to take, I telephoned the oncologist back in Boston. When he told me to take the antibiotic by all means, somehow I understood that this issue was the least of my worries.

As for the local doctor, with the medicine he gave me right away—right there on the veranda—and the antibiotics he left with me to take over the next few days, cure me he did. My stomach returned to normal. Better still, my mind experienced another shift. The concept of cure was introduced. Why not use this medical event as a stepping-stone and a model to cure the cancer?

I incorporated this experience into my mantras-on-the-beach. They went something like this: "I had a violent stomach sickness. The doctor here assured me he would cure it. It is completely cured. I have Waldenstrom's Macroglobulinemia. What do I want? I want to be totally healthy and cured of cancer. I formally choose to be totally healthy and cured of cancer."

Although I hadn't yet met him, I began to weave Dr. Treon into my vision.

The mantras became part of the architecture of my consciousness. Over the next many months, they evolved to address my progressing cancer and the choices I had to make. Eventually, they evolved into long and detailed prayers.

My mind and demeanor were calmer and more composed for our departure from Mexico than they'd been at our arrival. Back at the airport with a little time to spare, Sara and I decided to check out the gift shop. A colorful bazaar offering local crafts, it presented thousands of items from jewelry to sculpture.

While my daughter examined silver beads, I was drawn to painted wooden animals. I chose two, and spent only a few pesos.

A mostly yellow fish and an angry-looking red bird with green feet, these small figures landed on the windowsill in my bedroom. For me they became icons of health and hope. As I awoke, I saw in the yellow fish life and longevity. I saw it conquering the angry, red bird of disease, whose green legs and claws represented restored good health.

With less than a week between our return to Boston and my appointment with Dr. Treon, I was ready to be ready.

Back to Biology

Home again in late March, my attention focused on the upcoming appointment with Dr. Treon. With Sara at school and Bill at work, I retrieved the IWMF's bulky packet and settled down at our dining room table to read.

The long side of the rectangular table parallels south-facing windows. I sat with my back to the windows, feeling the warmth of the sun. Opposite the table, there is a buffet-type chest with a built-in mirror. During the next several days, as I sat and read and thought, as I took notes and made sketches for many hours every day, never once did I allow myself to look in the mirror. I felt as if seeing my reflection would confirm how sick I was. I couldn't face seeing my own face.

After taking the IWMF's newsletters and booklets out of their envelope—a major threshold in itself—I began to read. The contents and presentation were excellent, but I found myself asking questions. I needed more general information about the blood and lymph systems, as well as more detailed information about the immune system and the body's ability to respond to cancer.

Almost automatically, I went for Sara's high school biology book, which is, in fact, a college textbook. *Biology: Concepts and Connections* became an invaluable resource. As I read about the lymph system, questions came up about bone marrow. As I read about bone marrow, questions about the skeleton arose. For hours at a time, I flipped back and forth from the index, fitting together an intricate collage of the body's structures and functions. As the lenses of this kaleidoscope shifted into sharper focus, a clearer understanding of both my body and my disease emerged.

As I jotted down notes and drew diagrams, I framed questions. Ironically, the cancer began to seem less personal.

Learning about the disease and human biology comprised the first piece of my self-education. Learning about treatment options comprised the second.

If the first piece was fascinating, the second was sobering.

Established chemotherapy and radiation treatments had varying degrees of success; in this case, they were defined as *remission*: how long the disease remained repressed before it again became life threatening and required more treatment. The traditional treatments carried high degrees of toxicity and tended to destroy stem cells, thus slamming the door on future procedures that might utilize and rely on stem cells.

Experimental treatments had their own sets of risks. Long-term toxicities were yet unknown; success rates were not yet quantified.

What I knew for sure was that I wanted to destroy as little of my body and its resources as possible, and that I wanted to leave the opportunities for a range of future treatments as open as possible. The less damage done by drugs or procedures, the better the prospects were for my health and longevity.

I also knew I wanted this cancer to be assaulted as ferociously as possible in the first round of treatment. I felt brave, and bold, and healthy,

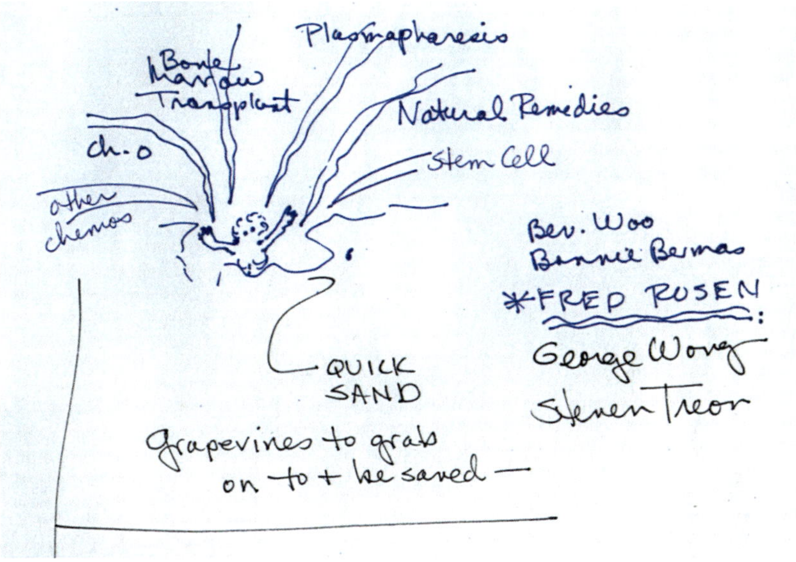

and strong—ready, willing, and eager to welcome very aggressive treatment. I wanted the cancer attacked, annihilated, and gone.

This thinking became the cornerstone of my attitude, my philosophy, and my goal as I prepared to meet Dr. Treon.

With my research completed for the time being, and my questions and goals formulated, I found myself with four pages of handwritten questions. I obsessively re-wrote them a couple of times, so they were neat and orderly. I wanted to be sure to cover them all when I met the new doctor.

During a phone conversation with Sherri, I relayed to her some of what I'd learned about established treatment options, and my hope and excitement about the upcoming appointment with Dr. Treon.

"Karen Lee," she said, "when you're drowning in quicksand, reach for a different branch."

A Different Branch

As if by magic, a different branch presented itself.

Not long after we knew I had cancer, the telephone rang unexpectedly. Elizabeth Ting was calling.

Mrs. Ting or Ma, as we call her, is Mary Ting's mother. From her first words it was clear that Mary had told her mother all we knew at the time about my diagnosis: some type of non-Hodgkin's lymphoma, very slow to develop, no need to give it much thought.

Always an ally and a friend, always active in supporting my good health, Mrs. Ting told me she'd spoken with her son Peter about my situation. Peter is a doctor, and it seemed cool that Mrs. Ting had consulted with him before she called me.

"This lymphoma is easy to cure," she said.

Great news! But how could they—she and Peter—be so sure? Of the thirty-five types of lymphomas, a few were considered curable; Waldenstrom's Macroglobulinemia wasn't one of them.

"Peter says you will have to have chemotherapy," Mrs. Ting continued.

Rotten news—how could Peter be so certain?

The day before my first appointment with Dr. Treon, calling me both to say hello and to offer her unique brand of help, Mrs. Ting made a suggestion that would radically change my relationship to my cancer. When she'd told her weekly prayer group about my situation, her friend Margaret had an idea; she knew of an audiotape that might be helpful. Her conversation with Peter was medical; her conversation with Margaret was spiritual.

I appreciated the sentiment, but for a variety of reasons, ranging from my limited ability to walk to a bookstore to information overload, I felt overwhelmed. Thanking Mrs. Ting, I told her I couldn't deal with finding the tape right now.

No problem. My 86-year old friend assured me she would find it for me.

"Only Connect"

My research done, my four pages of questions with a few sketches neatly rewritten and reorganized, I felt only calm optimism as my April 6th appointment with Dr. Treon approached. I was looking for, and expecting, a happy ending.

At home that morning, as I anticipated the day and asked myself "What do I want?" a realization came. If only I could reach this doctor—if only I could connect with him—I felt I could convey, and he would comprehend, my aspiration to be well. My objective focused on just this:

making a human connection, person to person. We could become a team. We could both be on the same side.

I dressed very nicely, choosing the pink sweater with the pink fur-like trim that I'd worn the Sunday we'd first seen *The Gates* in New York City, just five weeks before. I wanted to present myself as a person with dignity. I wanted the doctor to meet me as someone with roots and meaning outside the cancer center, a person who was part of a family, a community, and the world.

"Only connect" is the introductory phrase to E.M. Forster's novel, *Howards End*. I'd chosen the quote for my artist's statement that begins my professional resume. That day, it was my spiritual mantra.

When Bill and I arrived at the cancer clinic, I still felt out of place; I still felt I didn't really belong there.

After locating my chart, the receptionist told me to have a seat.

"What about blood tests?" I asked.

I experienced an odd mix of feelings:

Defiance: "I know more than you do. I'm an insider. I know the drill."

Superiority: "I know what you should be doing, and you're not doing your job."

Conflict: "I don't want any part of this anyway."

In the most gracious way, she re-checked my chart.

"There's no order for blood tests. Dr. Treon usually does that after he sees the patient."

Well this was certainly new, and interesting. A few hours later, I'd begin to understand the reasons and the wisdom behind this sequence.

Once again, our wait was very long. Periodically, and impatiently, I'd ask how soon we'd be seeing the doctor. The response was always the same: the clinic was very busy. No time estimate was offered. Bill read newspapers as I tried to maintain my composure and suppress my discomfort at being there at all.

As was my wont, I chose seats as far away from other people as possible. My isolation was, as usual, short-lived, because patients and their companions arrived, checked-in, and filled up seats in a steady flow. I stood. I paced. I studied the prints on the walls.

We waited. We waited an hour and a half. When my name was finally called, Bill and I stood as one person and walked to the end of the waiting room where the nurse's aid stood.

"You can wait here," she told Bill. "I'll be checking her vital signs, and then she (meaning me) will be coming back out here."

Eventually, Bill and I were taken in to an examination room. Unlike the miniscule, windowless rooms of our two previous visits, this room was spacious, with daylight flowing in from high windows. On a wall near the door, a mirror hung. As we waited—still—for the doctor, I looked at myself in the mirror for a moment. I had the self-assurance to do that.

We sat, Bill on the far side of the room, I next to the desk with the computer. I took out my notes and a pen. I focused. I wanted to be sure to ask all my questions and cover all my bases, at least all I was aware of at the time.

When Dr. Treon entered, Bill and I rose to greet him.

As I introduced myself, I said, "I'm here to be your cure."

"We don't use that word with this disease," was his deferential response.

As we sat and settled in, the doctor spoke with commitment and excitement about his work to unravel the tangled roots of Waldenstrom's Macroglobulinemia. Just recently, his research team had discovered something called mast cells. With enthusiasm, the doctor said he believed these would provide a vital link to understanding the source of this lymphoma, and to developing better methods to treat it.

And he and his team had just received a donation that established his lab as the Bing Center for Waldenstrom's Macroglobulinemia.

Now that Bill and I were up to date on current events in the research world, it was time to focus on my particular case in the clinical world.

What followed was a conversation that lasted an hour and a half. Dr. Treon was patient, kind, truly a citizen of the world, and very, very smart. He told us that he has personal familiarity with cancer. His father had had three types of cancer, and his mother two. Both were currently healthy and doing well. The three of us exchanged information about our backgrounds. Of Greek origin, Dr. Treon was fluent in five languages. In addition to his MD degree, he had a master's degree in biology, and a PhD.

As the time unfolded, my questions were asked. Dr. Treon took his time as he answered them in great depth. When his beeper sounded a couple of times during the consultation, he checked it and, in the most respectful way, excused himself from the room. Each time he returned, he gave us his complete attention.

As I outlined the history of how I'd been feeling, and what my body had been experiencing, for the past year—because it was one year before, the previous April—that the middle-of-the-night, full leg spasms took me over, Dr. Treon's attention was compassionate. To re-enact how my legs had taken off without me I stood, and, with rigid legs, sped across the room, robot-like. The doctor watched, astonished.

Based on my research of the International Waldenstrom's Macroglobulinemia Foundation pamphlets, I expressed my desire for radical, aggressive treatment.

"I'd like to have a stem cell transplant."

Dr. Treon's polite, but clear response was, "We won't be doing that."

I felt his response was rooted in concern for a patient's well-being in the context of this particular disease, rather than in a lack of open-mindedness.

When Dr. Treon had reached for my chart, I noticed how thin it was in contrast to another, which was almost two inches thick. I vowed my chart would stay very, very thin.

Looking over the results of the bone marrow biopsy, Dr. Treon remarked on the light involvement of tumor cells. It was about 10%, and he was used to seeing about 30%.

"You may not really be a Waldy," he said.

"If I'm not, will you still be my doctor?"

"Yes. Would you mind," he asked, "if we did another bone marrow biopsy?"

How could I say no? He scheduled it for April 20th.

Another request: Dr. Treon would like the results from another CAT scan. Would I mind? Would it be okay with me to have the scan done at Dana-Farber this time? He scheduled that for April 15th.

Looking over the lab reports from recent blood tests, Dr. Treon noted the degree of anemia.

"Would you mind eating more meat?"

In the course of responding to my questions and educating us about the disease and his research, Dr. Treon made a clear diagnostic statement.

"Where I part company with my colleagues is this: when I see a problem in the eyes, I start treatment."

I respected the individual philosophical position he expressed but, at the time, to me, it was theoretical, not personal.

As part of this induction exam, Dr. Treon wanted me to have an ophthalmology exam at the Schepens Retina Associates Foundation. A handsome young man joined us, and Dr. Treon introduced him with sincere praise and respect as Zachary Hunter, a young member of the doctor's research team.

Could Zachary please call over to Schepens and ask how soon they could see me? At the end of our appointment, Dr. Treon told us the ophthalmologists had time available to see me right then. But that was really too much for me all in one day, so he scheduled an appointment for the following day.

Attentive to the bureaucracy of specialty medical care, I asked Dr. Treon about a referral for the eye exam.

"It's part of the study," he replied.

I was in it now. I felt embraced, welcomed, cared for as a lab rat.

After we talked for a long time, and I learned a great deal, Dr. Treon asked if he could examine me. With the lightest and most experienced touch, he checked my throat and stomach areas. Dr. Treon checked off many boxes on the phlebotomy sheet then handed it to me. Zachary would escort me to the phlebotomy room, and my blood would be drawn on my way out of the clinic.

As I was preparing to say goodbye, I asked the doctor one last question.

"Sometimes I feel like my heart is going to explode."

His response: "Fair question. Stay hydrated. Water won't do it. Drink Gatorade."

On our way to the car after the blood was drawn, I said to Bill with reverence, "This doctor understands cancer at the molecular level."

Soon, we would too.

Schepens: The First Visit

The next day I was back at Dana-Farber (by myself this time) at the information desk near the front door.

Zachary Hunter had offered to meet me there, to escort me over to Schepens.

No light in the sky, that spring day.

We threaded our way on empty sidewalks bordered by residential-style lawns. Just a block or so away from, and more or less parallel to Longwood Avenue, the address of Children's Hospital, Harvard Dental School, Harvard Medical School, and a dense pack of related medical facilities, I found myself on a bucolic stroll.

In my warm and inviting way, at this moment partially fueled by nervousness, I asked Zachary about his background (math) and how he came to be here.

"Dr. Treon found me and asked me to come."

Behind the chitchat, I felt wary as a cat. I had no expectations or anticipations about this eye appointment, but I was on edge.

In the eye doctors' office, Zachary and I received a warm welcome from Gilbert Feke, PhD, the foundation's senior scientist. When Zachary headed out to Dana-Farber, I headed in to have my eyes dilated.

Back in the waiting room for what seemed like a very long time, I soon lost the ability to focus on a magazine, so I alternately sat and paced. Looking out over treetops, I watched them lose clarity.

Then came a series of eye exams, each performed by a specialist. Ultra high-tech computerized photography, aimed at exploring the microcosms in my eyes. Blackened rooms, the only searingly brilliant light aimed into and through my eyes. Me: still, seated in one room after another, the focus of everyone else's attention.

What were they looking for? I asked. Distended veins and signs of hemorrhaging—indications that the blood had become so thick, and the tumor-generated IgM cells so profuse, that blood could not move or flow.

The final exam focused on the retinas. I was placed in a very high chair in a pitch-dark room. It felt like a pod on a spaceship. With the help of a searingly bright pinpoint light, the doctor looked for hemorrhages.

It was like being on the set of a sci-fi movie.

The question: was I the star of the movie or the captive, abducted alien?

"The eyes are the window to the soul," one of my mother's favorite Shakespeare quotes, came to mind again. In this case, the eyes, whose network of veins is so easy to see and examine for health or for disease, also proved to be the window through which the doctors glimpsed the progression of the cancer.

On this date in April 2005, everything looked all right to the ophthalmology team. That was good news. With normal optical blood vessels, there was no alarm that I needed cancer treatment soon.

Seeing as though through fog, I descended in the elevator and slowly picked my way to Longwood Avenue. Feeling slightly unsure of myself and the unsteady way I was experiencing a familiar world, I flagged a taxi and sat very still.

Now I did have that blurry vision the diagnosing oncologist had asked about. Exhausted, I took my aching head and went to bed.

The Second CAT Scan

On April 15th, tax day was the last thing on my mind. It was the date of my second CAT scan, and I went alone this time. For some reason I felt safer at Dana-Farber than I had at the big hospital. Perhaps I felt I was under Dr. Treon's gentle, protective wing.

On the lower level of Dana-Farber's clinic building, the waiting room felt spacious and peaceful. Carpet and upholstery were sophisticated and calming; very good art dotted the walls.

Not many people in the waiting room. Really only one group plus me. During the two hours that I sat silently, measuring out small portions of the special CAT beverage and sipping slowly, I appreciated that Dana-Farber's drinks tasted much better than those at the hospital. I also benefited from the warmth and camaraderie of the other waiting group.

There were three women, two middle-aged, one young and in her 30's, and two older men. The two men sat very close to each other, solving crossword puzzles. They were such a team, talking over the clues, how many letters a word had, which letters were already in place. Experiencing their friendship vicariously made me feel happy, especially because I figured one of them was the cancer patient, here for a scan, distracted from his worries by his buddy.

Wrong. It turned out that the young woman was the cancer patient there for a scan. The older people were there to keep her company and support her.

Like I say, never assume who has cancer and who doesn't. When it comes to cancer, assumptions and stereotypes don't matter. Not looks, not age, not color, not attitude. The one with the hospital bracelet—that's the patient.

After two hours of sipping the drinks and visiting the bathroom, the CAT scan took only a few minutes. This time the IV needle went easily into a vein on the nurse's first try.

The Second Bone Marrow Biopsy

With a tiny number of exceptions, every time I went to Dana-Farber, Bill went with me. Depending on the service or procedure, Bill would stay either with me or in the waiting room. For a bone marrow biopsy, to me and to him, there was no question that the waiting room was the better place for him to be.

Compared to the bone marrow biopsy experience I'd had on February 7th, this second experience on April 20th was lighter, brighter, and even though it hurt more, it felt better.

In a smaller but sunlit room, it was only Dr. Treon, a nurse assistant, and me. For quite a while, the three of us stood—Dr. Treon and I on one side of the examination table, the nurse on the other.

There were papers to consider, and releases to sign.

"Would you mind," Dr. Treon asked, "if we take a couple of extra samples of your bone marrow, for research purposes? The research may not directly benefit you."

Of course, I said yes. This doctor had already done so much to help me by sharing his energies and enthusiasm, his commitment to his research and his patients, and teaching Bill and me so much in our first meeting alone. Being respectful of us, he earned our respect in turn.

I signed all the papers I was shown.

For a few moments when Dr. Treon stepped out of the room, the nurse and I chatted—about him! She was Spanish-born and felt warmth, respect, and comradeship for the doctor. She admired his linguistic skills. She admired him.

Then Dr. Treon returned.

Showing that I knew the drill—actually, that's a pretty funny phrase to use here, since a drill is used to penetrate the pelvic bone and suction

out the bone marrow—and still standing eye level with the doctor, I said, "I'm ready for the morphine."

"Morphine? Why would we use morphine?" he asked.

I explained my previous drug dose, for the first bone marrow biopsy.

Dr. Treon's method was different. A local anesthetic only, injected at the biopsy site. He saw no need for anything more.

Now it was time for me to be on the exam table, with the doctor on my left and the nurse on my right.

Once the anesthetic took affect, Dr. Treon began the procedure, that is, he began to drill into my pelvic bone. I think four separate bone marrow samples were extracted, one to be analyzed as part of my diagnosis, the others to be used for research.

This time I was less aware of the sensations and vibrations of the drilling, but quite aware of the sensation of suction deep inside bone, and body essence spiraling up and out of my body. Deep, calm breathing, and the doctor's talking me through each step, eased the process.

Even with power tools, drilling through bone requires a lot of physical strength. Being right-handed, Dr. Treon always drills on the patient's left side.

"On days when I do a few biopsies, I take Advil at night," he told us.

When Bill took me home, I rested, but there was no morphine to sleep off.

Now there was a fresh set of test results for Dr. Treon's information and evaluation: an exhaustively documented, comprehensive examination of the circulatory system as seen through the eyes, a second CAT scan, and a second bone marrow biopsy.

All the test results were in agreement. There was definitely lymphoma. The bone marrow biopsy confirmed its name: Waldenstrom's Macroglobulinemia. I was officially a "Waldy," and I was grateful to be Dr. Treon's patient. The quicksand's downward spiraling vortex seemed to lose some speed. I felt I could tread water, so to speak, rather than continue to sink.

But that wasn't necessarily true for my family.

"Save the World"

For the person who has it, cancer is terrifying. For his or her family and caretakers, it's brutal. Throughout our family's ordeal, Bill kept mostly quiet. He was the "strong, silent type" personified. Sara too remained stoic, observing everything, saying nothing about my sickness (at least not to me) and keeping her own counsel.

From January through March, as I kept my bad news private, I assumed that my daughter's life at school would remain "business as usual." That was a mistake.

On a winter evening, as she sat with a copy of *Macbeth* on her lap and a pencil in her hand, my daughter looked up and said, "Mama, I can't write my paper."

As if on automatic pilot, I became the cheerleader, saying encouraging slogans like, "Of course you can," and "Make an outline."

I reacted as though this was were just a momentary snag for my motivated, studious child. In my desire to protect and shield her from my fright and uncertainties about having cancer, I utterly denied that she might have them, too. How I wish I'd sat with her, hugged her, and opened a conversation with something like, "I love you. This is scary, isn't it?" And then just listened.

During a routine phone conversation, my daughter's English teacher told me Sara had written an essay for a different assignment. Since it mentioned me, the teacher felt she shouldn't discuss it with me.

My heart sank. I imagined my daughter was criticizing me. Was I a terrible mother? Was I failing my child? Did she hate me?

Weeks later I found the essay lying on our hall floor. Its title: "Save the World." In it, my daughter poignantly described the shock, pain, and terror of my cancer diagnosis. She said we just found out "we" will soon be needing chemotherapy. It was more important for her, she said, to help the sick and feed the hungry than to stay in school. She wanted to use her energy and her time to save the world and help people in trouble, and she wanted to do it now.

My daughter was screaming for help, and a young teacher decided she was better able to manage the crisis than we parents were!

My daughter's words showed me the time for secrecy was over.

When I met with the school director, she taught me that when a young person is faced with a terrible situation and has to be strong at home, she might not be able to maintain her strength at school. She suggested I alert the high school principal about our family's challenges.

To the principal, I wrote a letter. Here are some excerpts:

"When 2005 began, our family had no hint of what was about to unfold. Starting on January 4th, diagnostic tests occurred weekly and bad news came a few days after each test. During February and into March, we were first told that the lymphoma was indolent, then we were told that it was advanced. Our family was stunned. Sara understood a great deal about this disease, thanks to her biology course last year. She remained strong, supportive, and encouraging, and showed great strength at home.

"Sara, Bill, and I are very optimistic about my eventual return to good health. Nonetheless, we live with the presence of cancer every day. There's no doubt that my daughter's emotions and her ability to concentrate on schoolwork are profoundly affected."

With more support from her classmates, Bill, and me, through fear and uncertainty, my daughter navigated through the school year with as much courage as she could muster, and with grace.

No Doubt

As for that "different branch," a small package from Mrs. Ting arrived in the mail. It contained a cassette: *Secrets of Your Own Healing Power*, by Wayne Dyer, PhD.

I was touched, and appreciative. Rather than listening to the tape right away, I procrastinated. Or, perhaps I waited until the time was right.

In any case, the tape was with me for a couple of weeks before I located my 1984 Panasonic Walkman.

On a sunny Sunday afternoon, while Bill watched TV in the living room and Sara immersed herself in homework, I settled down in the big, white upholstered chair in the dining room, donned my headphones, and started the tape.

At first it seemed interesting. After twenty minutes or so, it seemed fascinating. Halfway through, I needed a pad of paper and a pen. What I was hearing had become not only informative, but also inspiring. Animating dire medical stories with compassion and humor, Dr. Dyer presented a belief system based on an individual's commitment to good health against all odds. Citing case studies of people in medical crises, and referring to healers in societies more closely linked to nature than our own, he told stories of people who were able to regain good health. He also told of people who were able to avoid sickness in their lives and remain well. At the core of each situation lay a belief in good health, with absolutely no doubt about it.

After meeting Dr. Wong and Helen Marx, my attitude had shifted from cancer victim to project manager. Following the transformation on the beach, my view of my situation was frank, and my outlook for my future was positive. Before I met Dr. Treon, gloom, doom, and negative thoughts about my life dissolved. As I listened to Dr. Dyer explain his philosophy, another transition occurred. From then on, doubt had no place in my heart or my thoughts. I believed only in healing and health.

Although I listened to the tape only once, I referred to my notes a couple of times. The stories, the facts, the hypotheses Dr. Dyer conveyed wove a network of physical health generated and sustained by the mind and the spirit. His outlook and his message penetrated my soul, and I believed them.

Suggesting that meditation could provide a foundation for both physical and mental well-being, Dr. Dyer mentioned a tape of his called *Meditations for Manifesting*. I made a mental note to find it.

Rhododendrons

Although I knew that there was a few month window until I'd need treatment, I decided it was time to tell my brother Larry. He lives on the other side of the continent with his wife Lorraine and two teenaged daughters, Florence and Jenna. In 1980, when my brother married, he and his bride left the east coast for good. Two years later, my parents followed them west, and left New Jersey for good.

The phone call was very, very hard. As I told Larry my story, I felt myself dissolving. Fortunately, we had a happy topic to discuss. Jenna's Bat Mitzvah was scheduled for May 7th. It was important to my brother, and to me, that I be there.

As Dr. Treon had suggested, I began drinking a sports drink called Propel. I asked Larry to please pick up a case of it for me.

Nice as it would have been for all of us to attend my niece's bat mitzvah, as the school year was coming to a close, my husband and my daughter stayed home and I traveled west alone.

High above the continent during the evening flight west, for the first time I listened to Wayne Dyer's second tape, *Meditations for Manifesting*.

Dr. Dyer's resonant voice spoke of the strength of our minds to bring into our lives that which we truly want. He presented an ancient meditation technique, and then demonstrated it. It involves using one's voice, repeating the sound "Ah" for twenty minutes each morning, and the sound "Om" for twenty minutes each evening. The morning meditation sets up optimism; the evening meditation is one of gratitude. In the dark, in the sky, in an aisle seat, I listened. Muffled by the airplane's repetitive hum, my voice timidly practiced vocalizing along with the voice on the tape.

When I arrived, the case of Propel I'd requested awaited me in Larry's garage. My time was split between staying in my brother's home and in a nearby hotel.

My mother Myra was eager to take me for a ride around the neighborhood. The rhododendrons were in bloom, and she wanted to show me some of her favorites. In New Jersey, rhododendron bushes with purple flowers had sheltered the front of our house.

Now, my mother drove me up and down the hills pointing out rhododendrons so big they resembled trees. And the colors of their flowers! Whites, pinks, reds, and of course, purples. What a delight! She called them rhodies, a term that was new to me.

For some reason I'll never know, my mother's narrative about the rhododendrons was interspersed with stories of friends and relatives, with a common thread. That thread was lymphoma. My Aunt Shirley, my cousin Frank—relatives by marriage, not by blood—the neighbor in the house ahead of us, the friend in the house to the left. All had lymphoma of one type or another. She told me about their histories, and their deaths. Despite her factual recount, sad sentiments lay beneath her words.

It was absolutely weird. Weighed down by my own lymphoma, and feeling awkward about keeping my sickness secret from my parents, hearing about all these lymphoma situations was bizarre. I stayed silent.

It was very sweet of my mother to share the natural beauty, and her enthusiasm for it with me. Perhaps it was prescient on her part to also discuss lymphoma.

During those few days in the west, the new form of meditation I first tried during the flight became a key element every morning and every evening. In my brother's home, I meditated in the guest room, in the bed that had been mine in New Jersey. Often my eyes drifted open, and in the waving evergreen branches, cloaked in fog outside the window, I saw hope dancing.

At the hotel, I'd meditate on my balcony overlooking a broad, wide river, beautiful in the fog. With a cup of coffee in my hands, wrapped in a thick wool sweater, I sat in the chilly mist, unaware of the cold or of time. With morning "Ah's" and evening "Om's," my voice spontaneously developed rhythm, melody, and tone. Their underlying foundation was my intention to be healthy and cancer-free. My energy focused on being well and on my love for all my family.

During Jenna's bat mitzvah ceremony, it was an honor and a pleasure to be seated on the bima, in a semi-circle with my family.

After the service, my mother sat in a chair in the front row of the now-empty synagogue. Dressed elegantly as always, she'd worn high heels. Her legs hurt so badly that she couldn't stand. Because my own legs and knees had been suffering so much pain for the past thirteen months, I'd brought along an extra pair of shoes so I'd have the option to change out of my low-heeled boots. When I offered my mother my boots she initially waved me away, but within a few minutes, she accepted my offer. Sitting next to her, I helped pull the boots onto her feet. It was an unusual and tender experience for the two of us. Although she complained that the boots were heavy, wearing them helped her get through the evening's celebration with more comfort and less pain. I felt grateful and happy to be able to help her, she who had helped me so much.

That evening, during a festive dinner and reception, my father Noah took great care to deliver food from the buffet tables to my mother and me. It was though his legs were instinctively doing the work that ours could not.

Duplicity? Hypocrisy? You might ask. Was it dishonest to keep my disease private? I think not. In the three months since receiving the cancer diagnosis, adapting, adjusting, accepting a new reality was all very much a process, and a difficult one. Shifting from terror and despair to optimism and hope, living mindfully in the present, catering to the needs of my sick body—these were the currents of life for me. Privacy and quiet time allowed me to keep more energy for maintaining emotional stability. Now feeling stronger within myself, the sense of separateness and isolation diminished. In a sense, I lived in parallel mental worlds; for me at that time, the conscious choice was both practical and appropriate. I'd call it instinctive self-preservation.

Big Blood Disease

In mid-May, I returned to New York City for my second appointment with Dr. George Wong. I'd arranged to meet Mary Ting for friendship and lunch before going to Strang to see Dr. Wong. Mary and I were both looking forward to a couple of hours together.

Again, I took an early morning train from Boston's Back Bay Station.

A block or so into my walk I realized I hadn't meditated and definitely wanted to. Meditate on the train? Repeating "Ah" aloud for twenty minutes? Not likely. So I started right then, as I walked, chanting Wayne Dyer's morning "Ah" meditation. It was exciting to chant in motion, more or less in tempo with my stride.

Again, I'd packed food; in fact, it was the same menu I'd taken to New York in March. Instead of water, I carried three plastic bottles of Propel. Thanks to Dr. Treon's tip about keeping myself hydrated, I drank plenty of it every day. Again I was dressed in comfortable pants, a simple cotton V-neck top, and walking shoes. Even though my knees and legs had intermittent weakness and pain with limited stamina, I still hoped to be able to walk around New York.

Although my menu and my wardrobe were more or less the same as on my March trip, what was radically different this day was my outlook. I was only and always positive about my health now. I enjoyed the train ride completely; private time, the scenery, and a stroll or two to the café car for coffee.

Mary and I met at Fifth Avenue and 42nd Street, in front of the main entrance of the New York Public Library. Hugging each other, and so glad to be together, we decided to have lunch and then take a stroll through Central Park.

It was my first return to the park since February, and *The Gates*. In place of bright orange banners, bright green leaves waved above us.

In the delicious mid-day sun, we talked, and wandered, and aimed ourselves toward the east side of the park and Strang. Mary likes to walk quickly; I couldn't.

"I need to sit down," I said as we approached Fifth Avenue.

"Okay, I know a good place. It's on Lex," Mary said, as she kept moving.

Lowering myself onto the nearest bench, I said, "I mean now."

Mary stopped, turned back to me, and said, "Oh."

Weak legs, a heavy body, and lack of energy necessitated my stopping immediately.

So, we sat, we chatted, and I tried to regain some strength.

As my appointment time with Dr. Wong approached, my friend and I said good-bye, and I took a taxi to East 72nd Street and Second Avenue.

I arrived early and enjoyed a cup of coffee and a cookie at a nearby bistro. It was fun to sit on a bench outside the bistro, soaking up the sights and sounds of the people around me. In March I'd felt only despair; in May I felt delight and appreciation for life.

At Strang, I was again buzzed in and went to the executive office where Helen Marx greeted me like an old friend.

In George Wong's wing, I waited quite a while outside his office. Nearby sat a man and woman with a sick child, about four years old. I felt so sad for them, and so sorry that they had to be here. With no chair available for me, I walked purposefully and rhythmically around a small area that formed a knuckle between two hallways. Silently, I chanted about being healthy and being cured.

I was neither anxious, impatient, nor angry about having to wait. I could hear muted conversation coming from Dr. Wong's office, and knew he was helping a patient.

When Dr. Wong's door eventually opened, a slender woman exited. Dr. Wong greeted me, invited me in, and apologized for keeping me waiting. He asked "How are my herbs doing? How do you feel?"

I told him I appreciated his herbs and felt they were helping. Although I didn't tell this to Dr. Wong, I believe that the ritual of drinking the herbal potion from its pouch each morning and each evening, and saying a silent prayer for health each time, contributed mightily to my feeling better in attitude and in body. The sickly, nauseous presence of fear was gone.

I told Dr. Wong some of what I'd learned about categories of drugs used for treatment of Waldenstrom's Macroglobulinemia. I told him about Dr. Treon, and that Dr. Treon and I shared an understanding and a comfort level about my participating in one of his clinical trials, should my lymphoma ever advance to a state that required treatment.

Dr. Wong asked a few questions, and then wrote a new herbal potion formula for me in his beautiful calligraphy. As in March, Dr. Wong would take the prescription to the pharmacy factory in Chinatown, and my herbs would arrive at my home in a couple of days. This time, Dr. Wong mentioned an ingredient or two that he was specifying to help build up my immune system. Information I didn't need to know. I said good-bye to him, and to Helen Marx, then headed back to Penn Station.

Walking from Boston's Back Bay Station home in the early evening, with a much lighter sky than I'd had in March, I chanted aloud Wayne Dyer's evening "Om" meditation, to a much lighter step.

The new shipment of herbal drink was thicker and oilier than the first. My ritual of two pouches a day, accompanied by silent thanks and prayers, continued through the summer, until mid-August. Then another system of rituals and drugs began to take root.

From time to time, Dr. Wong and I talked on the phone. He was back and forth to China, working side-by-side with colleagues and their research teams. Since he'd met me, he'd been searching through Chinese medical texts for information on Waldenstrom's Macroglobulinemia. During one of our conversations, he was excited about a discovery he'd made.

"I found your disease. In China it's called Big Blood Disease."

My Favorite Equation Ever

During the summer of 2005, my family and I knew that cancer had become an impending life threat for me. Once again, with perfect timing, the IWMF was there to help. This time the help arrived in the newsletter. Along with breaking news on research and patient support groups, there was a book review. The book: *The Anatomy of Hope*. The author: Dr. Jerome Groopman, a Boston-based hematologist and oncologist. Leukemia, lymphoma, breast cancer, and AIDS are his realms.

Here's a quote from the IWMF's article: "Speaking of the 'biology of hope,' Dr. Groopman writes, "Belief and expectation—the key elements of hope—can block pain by releasing the brain's endorphins and enkephalins, mimicking the effects of morphine. In some cases, hope can have important effects on fundamental physiological processes like respiration, circulation, and motor function." In this doctor's experience, "people with hope fared better, felt better, and lived longer."

From Dr. Groopman's statement, I created this equation:

Hope=Belief+Expectation

Through the pain of disease and the assault of treatment, this formula kept my mind focused on health. I completely believed and totally expected that I would become well.

College Reunion

June 2005 brought my 35th college reunion. It was a multi-day affair, with a wide range of events and meals. Even with cancer, events go on. As I registered and walked into the first event, a picnic-like social and supper, I felt good, I felt happy, and I felt open rather than self-conscious or shy. I made new friends with more frequency than I welcomed old ones. It was here on an open lawn, watching and listening to the Harvard marching band, that a new, deeper connection and much more openness to music first came to me. It was a beautiful development of my experience on St Patrick's Day. I realized that my twice-daily meditations using rhythmic breathing and my voice were building in me a new resonance to harmony and vibration. A marvelous side effect was more receptivity to music, and less inhibition in enjoying it.

I felt no desire or need to announce my state of sickness, to discuss it, or to confide in anyone. As I observed my classmates, a few hundred of whom showed up, I felt self-contained in my awareness of being sick. When Bill joined me later in the evening, I welcomed his presence and felt guarded by his strength.

Up to this point, only two classmates, both women, knew I had cancer.

Friday afternoon, relaxing with one of them and another woman with whom I'd become close in New York after college, I told of the lymphoma. The friend who was learning of this at that moment didn't react or respond. To this day, I have yet to hear from her, not even the question, "Are you dead or alive?"

Family Reunion

When I was a kid, our family's social life consisted mainly—well, entirely—of get-togethers with other Sobol families. My father was one of twelve: nine boys and three girls, brought very close by shared experiences and the drive to survive through poverty, the depression, World War II, and the post-war boom that brought comfort and security to the new middle class. Growing up first in Syracuse, New York then in Newark, New Jersey, as adults, all twelve settled within a few-mile radius of Newark. Eleven married and had their own kids. Several re-married and had more kids. My brother and I have fifty-three first cousins. We definitely had the critical mass for plenty of social life within our family circle.

Over time, about half of the family stayed in New Jersey, or at least in the northeast. The rest extended our boundaries—Israel to the east, the Pacific coast states to the west.

For the July 4th holiday in 2005, my brother organized and hosted a Sobol family reunion on the west coast. Bill, Sara, and I attended, along with about fifty relatives. For my husband and my daughter, being surrounded by so many Sobols, many of whom they were meeting for the first time, resembled a Berlitz total immersion course in a new language. For me, it was old home week. The jokes and the memories were familiar and comforting. The joy of seeing my daughter laugh and cavort with cousins of various ages provided a new dimension of happiness. My cousin Richard's daughter, Shoshanna, a few years younger than mine, formed an instant attachment to Sara. When Shoshanna installed herself in our hotel rooms, my daughter enjoyed the feeling of having a little sister, and our suite became action-central for the weekend.

Always aware that I had cancer in me, and choosing to keep my disease private, I maintained a balancing act between my external behaviors and my internal realities. With various family members in ever-shifting groups, I sat at the pool's edge, enjoyed casual chats, group dinners, and a baseball game followed by holiday fireworks. I learned of career successes or failures, heard heartening stories about my cousins' kids, and some heart-breaking stories, too. But I was never quite there one hundred percent.

Outwardly engaged yet inwardly reserved, I maintained a now-customary mental vigilance. I lived, as it were, in two worlds. Always aware of my cancer, many realms of reality co-existed within my mind. Respect for my body's limited abilities dwelled side-by-side with the desire to participate in life and become cancer-free. Although Dr. Wong's herbal drinks were no longer a daily presence, Propel most certainly was. Back again on the hotel terrace that fronts the wild river, I meditated twice a day as I had here in May. In every bird, duck, treetop, and river current, I saw always and only life—and the assurance that I would live free of cancer.

My time with my parents was much too short. Private time was nonexistent. Within two weeks, they would know I had cancer and become my wellspring of guidance, encouragement, and support.

Eager to be home for the July 4th Boston Pops concert and the fireworks celebration, Bill, Sara and I boarded an early morning flight.

Publicly, July 4th was a big date. Privately, July 6th loomed high on my radar screen. My second appointment with Dr. Treon was only hours away.

July, Again

Like the summer before, in order to swim at one of the neighborhood pools, I needed to drive. Unlike the summer before, my family and I now understood why. On the medical front, we treaded water. While I meditated every morning and evening, and drank Propel all day long, my thoughts and feelings about having Waldenstrom's Macroglobulinemia were mostly neutral.

For my spiritual well-being, my morning and evening meditations focused on being cancer-free. For my physical well-being, Dr. Wong's herbal drinks had fortified me for four months, but he and I tacitly agreed no more were called for. Dr. Treon's Propel continued to hydrate me. The upcoming clinic appointment seemed routine rather than alarming, because I felt safe in the care of my doctor. Learning more and researching more, I prepared new lists of questions to ask him.

Can Waldenstrom's Macroglobulinemia metastasize? Can it cause other cancers? Is the immune system's function compromised? Is it okay to eat shellfish and sushi? What precautions can I take to protect myself?

At Dana-Farber, our wait time was shorter than it had been on previous visits, and our conversation with Dr. Treon was briefer than the one in April. Focused on my well-being and meticulous in tracking the progress of my cancer, Dr. Treon wanted to see detailed information about the health of my blood. He also wanted an update on blood circulation in my eyes. Calling Schepens, he scheduled an appointment for me within the hour. Then he checked boxes on the blood work form and sent me to phlebotomy.

Once I was under Dr. Treon's protective wing, phlebotomy became less hateful to me. At this blood-drawing session, the phlebotomist was a young, handsome, big-bodied African American man. He was very gentle, and very kind.

Emotionally able to engage in a little conversation, I said something about how rough it was to be dealing with cancer, meaning both for him and for me.

"Everyone here has experience with cancer," he said. "That's why we work here."

He meant personal experience, and told me his aunt had died of breast cancer. He and she had been very close. His sense of loss and pain was still vivid.

Back to Schepens

The second round of eye examinations at Schepens was as detailed as the first had been, but there were three notable differences.

First, while I'd found the April examination fascinating, the July examination seemed tedious. Second, on April 7th, all of the specialists were ready and waiting for me. On July 7th, the retinologist was nowhere to be found, which necessitated another appointment on another day specifically so that I could see him, and he could see my retinas. Third, when the exam results were analyzed and reviewed, the findings were ominous.

As the optical veins were examined, they appeared distended and bulging. As the retinas were showcased through that brilliant point of light, hemorrhages were seen.

In the blackened room that reminded me of a spaceship, the retinologist announced, "There are hemorrhages in your eyes. There could be hemorrhages in other organs too, like your kidneys. Or your brain."

That put a perspective on it.

"Looks like you'll be getting treatment soon," he said.

I didn't like this prediction.

Within a few days, Dr. Treon and I spoke. He reported that the serum viscosity had risen to 3.7, and the IgM had gone up a notch, to 4400.

Did he think I could go away for a summer vacation, say, in a few weeks, I asked.

"Yes, you can go. But go now. I'll need you soon."

That put urgency to it. He'd received the ophthalmology data from Schepens, and what he saw was a call for action.

Circling Our Wagons

As for the motto of Waldenstrom's Macroglobulinemia—"Watch and wait"—we were watching, and the waiting period was expiring. The ticking time bomb was about to detonate. Hemorrhaging retinas and sausage-shaped optical veins left no doubt about it.

As for the choke chain, I'm happy to tell you it had dissolved and disappeared months ago. Because I felt so safe in my doctor's care, and because my mind nourished my body with the vision of being cancer-free, the strangling terror and the pervasive nausea of the previous summer and winter had ceased to be and were no longer players in this game of chance.

The next phase of the game—the life or death battle to combat the cancer—would surely still involve a significant component of chance. Facing a new type of free-fall, I felt optimistic.

We didn't yet have a specific timetable, or a specific treatment, but there was no doubt that the start date would be soon and the treatment would be powerful.

There was also no doubt that it was time to tell my parents, Bill's parents, and Bill's three sisters. No way would I begin any form of chemotherapy without my family's being aware of it. Dying from treatment was surely a possibility. Having my family learn I was sick, after I was dead—no, not an option.

Twelve hours after I'd spoken with Dr. Treon, Bill had reached all of our parents and all of his sisters. To each he'd relayed the news of my lymphoma, its current degree of danger, and the necessity for impending, as yet unspecified treatment. In return, he'd received empathy and support which he relayed to our daughter and to me.

I felt, as usual, shielded by Bill, and relieved that our larger family circle was now aware of our immediate family's crisis.

Contrary to my fears, my parents didn't drop dead upon hearing their daughter had cancer. Quite the opposite. My father and my mother, each in his or her unique way, became unwavering sources of encouragement and courage for me in every realm of this journey with neither a road map nor a known destination. My mother's medical empathy included emotional and psychological support, as well as insights into the doctor-patient relationship. My father's own experiences of being on that knife's edge between living and death—and his intuitive sense for remaining in life now—revealed him to be a gifted healer. While my mother's words and ideas grounded me, my father's linked me with less tangible, but equally sustaining, realms of energy and thought. Together, they were the perfect complement and a foundation of strength for me.

Within two days of learning that Dr. Treon—or more accurately, the advanced state of my cancer—now set our family's schedule, Bill found and rented a house on Squam Lake. Within two days of that, we packed our family, including Lindsay and our big blue raft, into the car and aimed north.

On and off, over the past few summers, we'd enjoyed relaxing in this peaceful place. Often, Lindsay and various members of my husband's side of the family came to vacation with us. Usually, the Grattons joined us and expanded the fun.

In past years, everyone had a few months' advance notice for the open house and a reunion. This time, with just a few days' notice, the Grattons and several member of Bill's family spontaneously dropped what they were doing, packed bathing suits and sweatshirts, and came to us in New Hampshire.

On a wooded hill that slopes to the lake were two buildings: one a modest ranch-style house, the other a rustic cabin. Bill, Sara, Lindsay, and I moved into the house. Relatives and Grattons rotated through the cabin.

Support Systems

There are four parts to the story during these two weeks—the physical, the spiritual, the personal contact with people I love and who love me, and telephone contact with people offering information and advice. Underlying it all, and making it all possible, was Bill.

First: the physical. Last summer at Keuka Lake, the inability to manage my legs or to trust them to keep me safe had caused me to flee the water. The risk seemed too sharp, and fear won out. This summer at Squam Lake, my legs were still primarily dead weights, but it was my head's dull heaviness that generated fear and drove me ashore. Like an over-ripe watermelon, my head was unable to float. Quite the opposite: my head seemed to feel a fatal attraction to the bottom of the lake. For me, being in the water wasn't an option.

Being on the shaded porch or on the dock above the water were safe options, and in both places my mental focus and sense of calm expanded. Feeling the sun's heat, hearing the birds chatter mingled with my daughter's laughter, was a sensory balm.

Second: the spiritual. Meditation, twice daily, anchored my thoughts. Seated on a corner of the dock, with every breath I focused on restored, cancer-free health. In every bird's flight, in every cloud, on every wave of the water, I saw only hope and health. Every sign was a symbol, and every symbol affirmed life—my life.

Hummingbirds drinking nectar from feeders on the porch, each leaf stretching into the sky's blueness, all showed me a way back into living in good health.

Like Libra's celestial scales, my mind balanced the optimism I've just described, alongside the reality of advancing cancer and impending medical intervention. Easy to be calm while noticing nature, my mind maintained calmness when engaging with issues around my disease. I credit will power, nurtured and sustained by meditation, for this evenness of temperament.

Third: personal contact. From upstate New York Bill's father, Papa, and his wife Diane joined us. From Michigan, Bill's sister Betsy and her husband Jim arrived. During the first week, Bill's family embraced us. During the second week, the Grattons did.

Sara's support system came, too. Sara's friend Lindsay arrived with us, Ann Iannuzzi drove her daughter Liz to the lake, and Cilla Lavin brought her daughter Becca Goldklang.

Able to stay for only two days, Betsy and Jim came with a mission. Suffering from a variety of debilitating diseases, with passion and strength Betsy conveyed that you never quit, you never give up. "Hang in there" is one of her favorite expressions. "I'm hangin' in there" is what she says of herself.

Jim, too, had wisdom to impart. As he told me to expect really hard times during treatment, and guided me to stay strong, his words opened a lens. Through it I became connected to Betsy and Jim as if they were my earthly guides into a realm not yet known to me. The golden light of the setting sun forged the three of us into an unbreakable triangle, the two experienced ones embracing and stabilizing the novice with clarity, encouragement, faith, and love.

When it was time for family members to leave us and return westward, the Grattons cuddled into the cabin. Having even more kids around lifted my mood. Renting a motorboat and piloting it too, Duncan helped relieve Bill of the duties of father and host. As always, Pat was a strong, loving, and supportive friend to my husband, my daughter, and me.

When I needed privacy, friends and family intuitively honored it. When I meditated, the dock was mine. My need for some solitude was balanced by times of hilarious group activity, often in and around the lake. Though troubled by my trouble, Papa and Diane brought laughter, energy, and fun into the mix. Danny, their puppy, thrilled the kids.

One bright afternoon, Sara dipped her long blond hair into the water in front of her. When she swung her head up and back, a shower of rainbows delighted us all. For the encore, Lindsay snapped a picture. A few weeks later, when Bill and I went to the infusion room, that photo came with us. Every day I was there, as I mentally prepared myself to receive my drug, that photo of the joy-filled girl with the rainbow hair filled me with love and kept me mindful of why I wanted to live.

Fourth: the people whose voices brought information and advice through the telephone.

For the first few days, the cabin was empty. When I needed privacy to call my mother or a friend, my doctor or a medical center, the cabin served me well. It was the perfect retreat for complete privacy. With the lake's glimmering surface beyond the screened porch, I sat at a small table and talked on an old-fashioned telephone. Pen in hand, jotting notes, I asked many questions. In turn, I received much information and encouragement.

Ann Iannuzzi had a past career as a blood technologist. She knew the subtleties of Waldenstrom's Macroglobulinemia well, and helped supplement the information Dr. Treon and my own research provided. Her input helped deflate some of my fears.

Maggie Trichon, the owner of a modeling agency in Boston for whom I worked from time to time, is my contemporary. For the past year or so she'd been in a war against brain cancer. I never expected she'd become a medical mentor.

Having heard my story and learned of my impending treatment, she relayed to me the handbook of bringing your own supplies to the hospital. She became my guide into the cancer ward.

"Pack a bag," she said. "Bring your books, your music, and your own food. They'll offer you a sandwich, but I like to bring my own peanut butter and jelly sandwich, and I eat it whenever I want."

Into this rustic space came my mother's voice. She assured me I'd be fine.

"Karen Lee, you're gonna be foyne," in the best Bronx accent.

For the seventh time, Lance Armstrong had just won first place in the Tour de France.

"Karen Lee, I want you to race in the Tour de France. If Lance Armstrong can do it, I know you can, too."

What faith! Absurd perhaps, but just thinking of the possibility, and my mother's over-the-top encouragement, painted a picture of future success.

As we talked of approaching treatment, my mother offered me two pieces of advice.

"Trust your doctor," and "Pretend it isn't happening to you. Pretend it's happening to somebody else."

The first seemed clear, although my doctor and I were about to enter an entirely new realm of trust. The second seemed odd, if not impossible.

From a different phone in a different location, a conversation with Dr. Treon marked the end of "watch and wait" and the start of medical action.

I had questions for him, and we'd been missing each other's calls for a couple of days. He'd left word with Bill that he'd be calling me at 6 o'clock Friday evening.

With the cabin occupied, and his cell phone service at the house sketchy at best, Bill had found a clearing in the woods next to the road where cell phone reception was reasonably good. He referred to it both affectionately and sarcastically as his "office." On this evening, he drove me to his office, and walked a few yards down the road as I dialed the doctor.

Expecting that this was my call, to ask my questions, I was unprepared for Dr. Treon's opening line.

"Let's cut to the chase," he said.

The ophthalmologists' examination results left no doubt that the cancer had reached a dangerous stage. Dr. Treon wanted me to schedule plasmaphereisis as soon as possible. I had a vague idea that plasmapheresis—whatever that meant—reduced IgM levels in the blood of Waldenstrom's patients. As I watched Bill pace in the distance, I had no choice but to agree.

When Bill came back to me and I told him the news, it would be hard to say which one of us was more in shock.

Monday morning, Papa and Diane vacated the cabin so I could use the phone in privacy. Calling Dr. Treon's assistant, I was given the number for the Blood Donor Center at Brigham and Women's Hospital. Calling the Blood Donor Center, I was given an appointment for the next day. Realizing I had no idea what plasmapheresis entailed, and sensing it would help to have some picture of what to expect, I made a list of questions and re-dialed.

The receptionist was patient and thorough as she explained the procedure. She told me that, for three hours I'd be seated, unable to move, with an intravenous needle in each arm. Both IV lines would connect to a type of giant centrifuge. From my left arm, my blood would leave my body and enter the centrifuge.

My blood plasma, dangerously thickened by cancer-produced IgM, would be removed, discarded, and replaced with sterile, healthy plasma contributed by five separate donors. The healthy plasma would be mixed with my red blood cells, and would re-enter my body through the IV apparatus in my right arm.

Much more information than I'd expected, but still preferable to the surprise of hearing it all for the first time as the IV needles were being inserted into my veins.

And so the details of the initial act of treatment came to me through the phone line in the cabin.

Reprieve

Definitely not your normal vacation. At least, I hope not, for anyone. On Tuesday, July 26th, Bill had a meeting in Boston and I had my first appointment for plasmapheresis. We drove to the city Monday night and slept at home. In the morning, Bill delivered me to the hospital. Then Pat Gratton came to stay with me.

A young intern conducted the intake interview. Knowing my diagnosis, his anxiety about my prospects was obvious. I countered with my optimism. It was clear he didn't believe in my point of view, but I did.

The experience of plasmapheresis was far weirder than the explanation, which was plenty weird. The gigantic recliner-style chair was uncomfortable. I was told not to move—at all—for the next three hours. The position of the IV needles, one at the inside vein of each elbow, hurt.

The centrifuge was big, loud and scary. Seeing my red blood fly through clear plastic tubing, seeing my gunky, cancer-laden plasma collect in disposable plastic baggies, seeing liter after liter of clear, healthy, replacement plasma fed into the machine, feeling a new blood mix re-enter my body—bizarre, all of it.

Pat stood by, reading broccoli recipes aloud. Many months later, I realized that may have been a tactic she employed not to entertain me, but to calm herself as she watched what I was experiencing.

When I felt myself growing faint, loudly I called out to the nurse. No time to ask Pat for help. I knew I needed to take action to help myself before I became unable to. Instantly the nurse crossed the room and saw the problem. Letting me pass out wasn't an option. Blood pressure dropping, pillows used for propping, the procedure halted for a few minutes, the crisis was averted.

In a chair across the room, also undergoing plasmapheresis, was a large woman about my age, also with Waldenstrom's Macroglobulinemia. She'd had this procedure many times. She was talkative. In silence, I listened and observed. She seemed relaxed, at ease with it.

I found that odd, but enviable in a way.

When Bill arrived, Pat left.

The procedure finished, my exit by wheelchair was mandatory. In the hospital lobby, the realization that other people's blood plasma was now running in my body gave me an alien feeling. Very hungry, I asked Bill for a hamburger. In the two-hour drive back to Squam Lake, for the final days of vacation, I never uttered a word.

A new reality pushed itself through me—literally—with every pump of my heart.

When Dr. Treon told me that the plasmapheresis had reduced the IgM from 4920 to 2350, Bill and I were overjoyed, as was my mother. This was terrific, I thought. I was getting better.

But plasmapheresis is a temporary reprieve. The IgM kept climbing back to dangerously high levels.

In the first week of July, blood tests and eye exams showed the cancer's virulence and violence were escalating, and its aggressive advance was becoming dangerous. In the last week of July, and almost weekly through August and into September, a series of five plasmaphereses pumped overly-thickened blood out of my veins and pushed thinner, healthier plasma in. But the Waldenstrom's Macroglobulinemia tumor cells produced new IgM as fast as we could pump out the old.

Family Ties

Early in September, Bill's sister Mary and her husband Toep came to stay with us. They delivered an unexpected revelation.

A bit of background:

Several years earlier, Toep had fought a long battle with a rare blood disease: Thrombotic Thrombocytopenic Purpura, or TTP, for short. Mary was at his side, from hospital to hospital, from California to Texas. Miraculously, the disease was defeated and he became well.

As we stood chatting in the kitchen, the couple offered a nutrition tip. For their transcontinental flight, Mary and Toep had brought their own food. Their selection was liquid: a vitamin beverage called Ensure. Although TTP was in his past, Toep had to be continually vigilant to maintain sufficient vitamin intake and obtain adequate rest. Since I was already thinking about fortifying my body to help withstand the onslaught of my upcoming treatment, and Dr. Wong's herbal prescriptions were completed, it seemed that high doses of vitamins would promote that goal. I decided to try drinking Ensure.

Then the couple began to speak of the experience of TTP. Through a year of intensive treatments administered by doctors and nurses, Toep had teetered on the edge of death. I pictured myself about to enter the same world, and attempt to balance on the same precipice.

As they spoke, I realized in a fresh way that Toep had been subjected to, and had survived, two sets of torturous conditions: the disease, and the treatments. By recovering and living, he had literally beaten the odds.

Although I don't recall the exact wording of my question to him, its essence was "How did you do it?"

"I trusted everyone who took care of me. And I always knew I'd be okay," he replied.

The certainty and simplicity of his two beliefs penetrated my consciousness. They reinforced my mother's advice, and helped strengthen my own views. They became, for me, core convictions.

If the Sobol family reunion on the west coast was all about reconnecting, reminiscing, and renewing long-established bonds, Bill's family reunions on the east coast were all about forging new bonds of understanding, encouragement, and love in waters that—for me—were previously uncharted.

Now that our immediate families knew about my cancer and its advanced state, my husband's family came to me to offer their strengths forged by enduring sickness, caretaking and the commitment to remain alive.

It was as if an invisible but unbreakable life force emanated from them to me, holding me safe, binding me to life.

The Intangibles

Late one summer afternoon, on the brink of needing treatment, I sat at my desk and called Ann Iannuzzi. When her husband Ralph answered the phone, I half expected him to say hello, take a message for his wife, and sign off. That had been my experience with many of the dads of Sara's friends.

But Ralph Iannuzzi is an exceptional dad, and soon proved to be an exceptional friend. An MD whose specialty is otorhinolaryngology, he's an ear, nose and throat guy. For him, performing surgery to remove cancer is routine.

In social settings, Ralph—or Dr. Iannuzzi, as my daughter respectfully calls him—is outgoing, a man truly interested in people and excited by life. Now, in this unexpected moment, within the privacy of a one-on-one random phone call, he instantly focused the human side of his medical career on me.

We spoke of attitude. I told him that I was totally optimistic and that my husband, my daughter, our family, and a handful of friends, were wholeheartedly helping and supporting me. His response surprised me.

In his experiences with cancer patients, Ralph told me that the patient's attitude, along with his or her family's and/or friends' love and support, makes a pivotal difference in the treatment's success, and in the patient's quality and duration of life. His own life force flowed through the line as he spoke.

He cited one example from his practice. A youngish woman, a bad prognosis. However, with her family around her, their unfailing support provided an emotional incubator that nurtured her through chemotherapy and beyond. Defying the odds, she was alive and doing well several years after the prognosis would have had her dead.

Listening to Ralph's tone as well as his information flooded me with comfort, hope, even more optimism, and even more appreciation for my family and my friends. Hearing Ralph's encouragement, factual and spiritual at the same time, gave credence to my personal, positive view.

That his message—"Yes, be optimistic. It matters; it makes a difference,"—was grounded in decades of medical practice was wonderfully validating.

Many times during the next year this conversation, and more importantly, this human connection—doctor to patient, friend to friend—came to mind. Many times I relayed the message to others. Many times, I thanked Ralph.

I remember him smiling and saying, "It's the Intangibles."

Back to School

As our family perched at the edge of the precipice named 'cancer treatment,' we were about to enter scary, uncharted medical and emotional territory. We didn't yet know its specific ingredients. Once it began, who knew if I'd be functional in any normal, predictable, or reliable way? Would I be, as I'd posited to Bill back in March, "married to the toilet," retching from the ravages of drugs, infecting fear into the air?

On the verge of free-fall, Bill and I would do all we could in our private realm to take care of our daughter. We had to be sure to weave a safety net for her in her public realm as well.

With summer ending, our family's thoughts turned to school—Sara's high school and my home school, to review the science underlying my disease and treatment options.

Before Labor Day and the start of Sara's junior year, Bill and I made an appointment to meet with the new head of the high school to be sure our daughter would have emotional support if she needed it. One sunny late-August morning, off to school we went.

Bill and I welcomed the principal to the school, he welcomed us to his office, and we began. I told the story of my cancer, of the devastating effects the diagnosis had had on my daughter last spring, of the egregious lack of communication from the school to Bill and me. I told of my choice to enter a clinical trial. With no immune system, I'd be attending no school events. With respect, I made it clear that Bill and I needed to know that faculty and staff would be alerted to our circumstances, attentive to any warning signs in our daughter's academic, social, or emotional behavior, and in immediate communication with us should she show any signs of distress.

The principal's compassionate response was double-barreled. First, he told us that, when his four children were teenagers, he had lost his wife, and the kids had lost their mother, to breast cancer. He knew the ravages of a family's struggle with cancer intimately.

Next, he suggested I talk directly with Sara's teachers. So very private not so very long ago, I now understand that this was the perfect strategy.

Last spring, managing my own feelings and needs as best I could kept me private, introverted, and guarded. Now as a mother, I knew I had to set aside my emotional conflicts in the best interests of my child.

Considering the Options

If the dull thud of thick blood in my head and the sporadic, but encroaching numbness in my hands and feet weren't enough to convince me it was time to attack the cancer with treatment, my doctor's clear, steady guidance certainly was.

Naively I asked whether ongoing plasmapheresis could, in itself, constitute adequate treatment. Bizarre an experience as it was, at least it didn't involve assaulting my body with drugs. "No," was Dr. Treon's one word answer.

For eight months, we'd been talking and learning about the biology of disease and the science of medicine, but the topic was no longer theoretical or distant. Now there was a big difference. The biology was my body, the disease was my cancer, and the medicine, whichever we chose, would soon be running through my blood and bones.

On Thursday, September 8th, Bill and I met with Dr. Treon at the clinic. This time, the meeting had a goal. Dr. Treon would present and explain specific treatment options and we'd have to begin to make a choice.

Since my St. Patrick's Day shift in attitude about me and my relationship with cancer, I'd remained unfailingly committed to three principles. First was the belief that "My first shot is my best shot," and that I'd never be stronger or better able to withstand treatment than I was before I received any. I felt my body could handle so-called "aggressive" treatment. Second, treatment that caused minimal peripheral damage and left maximum options for future treatments, if they were needed, was critically important. Third, I remained unflinchingly determined to take part in a clinical trial. These principles carried me into this next phase, the phase to learn about, and choose, a course of treatment.

A squelching calm sat on whatever fear or panic I had, its weight augmented by my thick, dull blood. My brain heard information and data, but my emotions didn't react much.

"My issue," my doctor stated, "is how to navigate you therapeutically."

Ideally, clinical trials without chemotherapy would attack and reduce overabundant IgM and the tumor cells creating them; the trials would "do no harm" (not permanently damage stem cells and bone marrow, which would limit future treatment options) should future treatment be needed.

As we three sat close together in a small consultation room, Dr. Treon, whose medicine, science, and humanity I trusted completely, spoke in a matter-of-fact way. He gave Bill and me detailed information on the science behind four innovative drug therapies, the risks they entailed, and the schedules on which they were administered. All four were experimental; that is, they were clinical trials.

Interesting as it was to learn of the risks and benefits of them all, my doctor advised that three of the four clinical trials were inappropriate for our consideration. One was eliminated because the state of my disease surpassed eligibility criteria. The second was untenable because the drug dosage was in need of adjustment, and that would take time—time I didn't have. The third was a month away from starting, and a month was too long to wait. Since that time, so much progress has been made in understanding this lymphoma, and so many breakthroughs have been made in its treatment, that there's no need to provide the details we heard that day.

But I do want to briefly mention the operative drug in one of the clinical trials: Viagra. Yes, Viagra.

There was a study in progress using Viagra, which had by chance shown itself effective in reducing IgM in male Waldenstrom's Macroglobulinemia patients. Taking Viagra presumably either to treat a heart condition or to enhance their sexual performance, they benefited from a fortuitous side effect—their IgM levels decreased, and a clinical trial was born. Women as well as men were participating in the study.

Fascinating, though, how a drug developed and tested to address a specific medical situation might reveal itself effective in others. Initially engineered as a heart medication, Viagra showed the side effect in male cardiac patients that catapulted its name to fame. Now here was another hidden bonus—the potential management of Waldenstrom's Macroglobulinemia.

Could I enter that one? Could I just please stay home, take a pill, and have that count as my chemotherapy?

Again, no. In my case, the cancer was too advanced, and the IgM count too high to qualify me for the Viagra study. Viagra was being tested as a management vehicle, and in me, the disease had passed the point of being readily managed.

Clinical trial number four: alemtuzumab. Dr. Treon explained that, unlike traditional chemotherapy drugs, this drug is designed along a biological model to behave like a natural antibody. Although it's manufactured in a laboratory, not in the patient's body, when alemtuzumab enters the bloodstream it mimics a person's natural defense system and attacks cancer cells. Specifically, it aims for a protein called CD52. Called a synthetic monoclonal antibody, the drug had been FDA-approved for the treatment of chronic lymphocytic leukemia, or CLL.

Since CLL and Waldenstrom's Macroglobulinemia bear some similarities, the researchers reasoned, perhaps alemtuzumab might be effective in combating Waldenstrom's Macroglobulinemia. This clinical trial aimed to find out.

The good news was that the CD52 protein was expressed on my tumor cells. This drug would target them, and its intention would be to kill them. The less good news was that CD52 is also expressed on the immune system's normal cells, so we could expect alemtuzumab to target and kill them, too.

Another piece of good news: this drug also targets mast cells, just recently discovered by Dr. Treon and his team to be key in creating Waldenstrom's Macroglobulinemia. Perhaps we could strike the cancer's source.

Dr. Treon told us he was very happy with results in patients who received this drug as their first cancer treatment. For patients who'd had previous, traditional chemotherapy, the results were less good. Their previous treatments had burned bone marrow, disabling it from producing stem cells and predisposing patients to infection.

Dr. Treon felt alemtuzumab would be validated as a good first line drug. But (isn't there always a but?) very quickly, it can take out a person's T-cells as well as his or her B-cells, rendering the body susceptible to shingles and PCP, the same type of pneumonia to which HIV/AIDS patients are vulnerable. After a few doses of alemtuzumab, no natural defense system would remain in my body. For this reason, as a protective measure, an antibiotic and an antiviral medication were prescribed alongside the drug. As for the logistics of this clinical trial, alemtuzumab would be injected intravenously. As for the time frame, for three consecutive days I'd be given a test dose: first three milligrams, then ten, then the full thirty. Then for twelve consecutive weeks, every Monday, Wednesday, and Friday I'd receive a full dose. That seemed manageable; we could assign an end date to the treatment.

Once the Twelve Weeks concluded, the antibiotic and antiviral pills would continue for two more months.

In other patients the immune system—at least the B-cell section—had rebuilt itself after about a year. If we chose alemtuzumab, that's what we'd be hoping for. In the meantime, since my body would have no natural defense system, my doctor warned that contact with other people would pose a threat.

The presentation was over, and the information was clear. Dr. Treon has a gift of conveying sentiment as well as fact. But I felt my mind rotating dully around the inside edge of a wide, shallow, opaque glass bowl. This day, information brought numbness, not clarity. I heard the words and grasped the concepts, but lost the struggle to think clearly. Even though I'd been accepting, acknowledging, and adjusting to having cancer, this threshold held surprise, and a sense of unreality. How could this be happening to me? How could these frightening choices be for me? But happening to me it undeniably was, and making a choice—soon—was a necessity.

One thing, one fact, opened a brightly lighted porthole of relief for me. My stated goal was to be cured and cancer-free. In the alemtuzumab trial, Dr. Treon told us he'd just seen a major remission of Waldenstrom's Macroglobulinemia in one of his patients. That helped me feel less alone. Someone ahead of me was doing really well; I didn't have to be the first.

In case we had more questions or would like more detailed information—and by now, I imagine Dr. Treon knew we would—he offered to have Zachary Hunter available to meet with us the next day. With appreciation, I accepted the offer. Kindly, Dr. Treon checked many boxes on a phlebotomy order form, and asked me to have blood drawn before leaving.

Overloaded with work, medical information that may as well have been a foreign language, and with worry, Bill declined joining me for the following morning's meeting. When I asked Pat Gratton to accompany me, she graciously agreed.

Choosing the Clinical Trial

The next morning was Friday, September 9th. For the first time, I left Dana-Farber's ground floor clinic level and for the first time, I saw Dr. Treon's office and research lab.

For two hours, Zachary, Pat, and I sat together at a small round conference table. The menu of treatment options this day offered a review of three of the clinical trials along with two traditional chemotherapy options. As Zachary explained them, Pat and I asked many questions and took detailed notes.

On the topic of the alemtuzumab clinical trial, when I heard Pat ask "Has anyone died on this study?" I honestly thought I would die then and there from the shock and audacity of the question. But it's an important question to ask, and important information to know. The answer to the question was yes. Two people had died while participating in this trial. Both women, both older than I, both with pre-existing complications and histories of previous chemotherapies. Their loss was deeply mourned by the medical team.

Zachary repeated what I'd been told the previous day: the drug treatment schedule was intense, specifying intravenous infusions every Monday, Wednesday, and Friday for twelve consecutive weeks. But, honestly, that held more appeal for me than a less intense schedule that stretched out over many months or years. And, as I perceived it, would continue to tie my identity and my family's plans to a chemotherapy ward.

Near the end of the two hours, with so much information before us, Pat asked another key question.

"Which treatment do you think Dr. Treon would recommend for Karen Lee?"

"Alemtuzumab," was Zachary's reply.

"How do you know?" she asked.

"He told me."

Good to know; I definitely registered that.

Before we left, Zachary gave me an information booklet about alemtuzumab and asked if I'd be willing to sign the clinical trial consent form. That way in case I chose it, the forms would be ready to submit to my insurance company.

"What's the cost of participating in the study?" I wondered.

"$186,000.00" was the answer.

It hadn't occurred to me that a clinical trial carried a price tag. How would we pay for this ourselves, if our health insurance wouldn't? As I signed the forms, I intuitively felt myself being moved into the next, new phase.

When Zachary offered to show us the research lab, we accepted out of courtesy more than anything else. I picked up my Propel bottle, Pat picked up her Diet Coke bottle, and we left the office. Just outside the lab's door, Zachary asked us to place our drinks on a shelf, as opened bottles and cups aren't allowed inside the research area. Odd, it seemed, but in time bottles on a shelf became part of the motif of my sculpture "L'Cha'im 2005."

Our tour was brief. I was definitely in the zone that teenagers refer to as "too much information."

It being noon, and our being hungry, Pat and I parked ourselves at the counter of the first restaurant we saw. As we awaited our hamburgers, we did some math. If I started in the alemtuzumab trial in the next week or two, counting forward twelve weeks, I'd be done by Christmas.

We both felt great relief with a targeted completion date that was relatively soon. There was an end in sight. The schedule was as important in my selecting this treatment as the science and promise of the drug itself.

Where did Pat get the nerve to ask about deaths, I wondered? As it turns out, a doctor who's a friend of hers had done extensive research on alemtuzumab. Understanding the explosive powers of the drug, the doctor felt mortality was a clear risk; inquiring about it was a reasonable request.

How remarkable that Pat had taken the initiative to do some research of her own, and to ask brave questions that never would have occurred to me. I was grateful to my friend for standing by me and looking out for me.

That afternoon, I downloaded all the morning's information to Bill, including the not insignificant risk of dying from any course of treatment. The situation was scary, and there were no guarantees. When I stated that Dr. Treon's preference for me was alemtuzumab, with an end-date by Christmas, I could see Bill's relief. Then, he and I decided to take a break from discussing the world of cancer.

And so we made our choice.

Points of View

On Saturday September 10th, I called Dr. Treon for what I expected to be the definitive conversation about my course of treatment.

Regarding the decision to enroll in the alemtuzumab clinical trial, at my mother's suggestion I began to pose the question "If I were your sister or your mother or your daughter, would you feel comfortable with my making this choice?"

Knowing where this was going, and before the question was completed, my doctor's reply was "Yes, with all my conscience."

Knowing my commitment and motivation to participate in a clinical trial, he went on to say there's no right or wrong here. An overarching goal was to do no harm, this in the context of keeping the body intact to accept and withstand future treatments if they were needed. Looking at risks and benefits, as a front-line drug, alemtuzumab had produced some very promising results in some Waldenstrom's Macroglobulinemia patients. Most exciting.

Dr. Treon told me I was very lucky. With no prior therapy, having this drug as my first treatment was my "ace in the hole."

He reminded me that alemtuzumab is a biological agent, not chemotherapy. Designed to behave like a natural antibody, it hits only cells that express its target: the protein CD52. Since most cells and tumor cells—the cells producing the overabundance of IgM—express this protein, the drug would enter my body and aim only for them. Because B cells and T cells also express CD52, the alemtuzumab would destroy them, too. Over time, it was expected that my immune system would come back, but whether it came back with all its original properties intact was subject to debate. Collateral damage caused by typical chemotherapy wouldn't be an issue.

As soon as treatment began my body would be more vulnerable to colds and infections. Due to increased susceptibility, my doctor advised me that everyday activities and normal social engagements could be dangerous. My choices could be a huge help in the treatment's success. I decided on the spot to take myself out of circulation. My doctor entreated me to keep myself healthy, enjoy life, and remember to laugh. My note to myself says: eat breakfast.

We spoke of attitude, hope, and expectation regarding treatment.

"The power of the mind is incredible," Dr. Treon said.

With three treatments a week, alemtuzumab was an active therapy. It was the only clinical trial that was available now, and I needed treatment now. As for the twelve weeks, the first one or two could be rocky, and drug doses might need adjustment. After that, things should proceed smoothly.

After Thursday's session I had told Bill, "As long as I can keep swimming to burn off my anxiety, I'll be all right."

Now I asked if I could keep swimming during treatment.

Probably not a good idea, I was advised.

I'd need to find a new technique to manage my anxiety.

Over the weekend, Pat was uncharacteristically unnerved. When she'd told her neighbors, both doctors, I'd decided to enroll in the alemtuzumab clinical trial, she'd asked them whether they'd make the same choice, if they were in my same situation.

The wife said, "Never."

The husband, an oncologist, said, "Absolutely."

So, there you have it. Terrifying, and promising, both at once.

The following weekend, on Saturday September 16th, as Bill sat with his newspaper, I could feel him fuming. Pushing *The Boston Globe* at me, he jabbed at an article. I don't remember the precise syntax, but two-inch tall letters delivered this message: "Woman Dies from Alemtuzumab." The story said she'd been part of a study, for a disease other than cancer. I recollect she died of complications due to infection.

I took the article as more information on human biology and medicine. It didn't panic me or derail my thoughts on my decision to go with alemtuzumab.

Bill, though, was agitated, distressed, and needing me to call my doctor.

When I reached Dr. Treon, our conversation was calm, and factual. This news didn't change the way my doctor looked at my care. He explained that some drug therapies are borrowed from oncology to treat autoimmune diseases. In his view, with this type of cross-over, the levels of risk-taking increased.

Objectively, he reminded me that drugs for oncology patients all involve a level of risk and, unfortunate but true, a small number of patients succumb. His role was not to advocate for one drug over another. Some outcomes are unpredictable; all have risks.

Given the circumstances of my medical history and state of disease, he thought alemtuzumab represented a balanced risk, and that the potential benefit was worth the risk.

Moving on, my doctor said he wanted to prepare me for some possible developments. Sometimes during treatment, there were setbacks. Unfortunate and unpredictable, they can cost time. Two patients in the study, both with long histories of previous chemotherapies, had been hospitalized. The drug didn't seem to affect men differently from women. Despite setbacks, we have to keep pushing forward, he said. Generally, my doctor believed that we—collectively—are making a difference, and that for treating Waldenstrom's Macroglobulinemia there were now, and would continue to be, many more treatment options than patients previously had.

For the first line of attack—my position right now—he felt, and I agreed, alemtuzumab was our best route.

My reporting back to Bill didn't do much to calm his agitation or reassure him. But, as for me, I was good to go.

Bill was mostly quiet the rest of the weekend. Sometime on Sunday he announced to me "So, there are three things that can kill you: cancer, drugs, or infection as a result of the drug."

Yes, that was accurate.

He dubbed it "Balls to the wall."

Only a guy could dream up that title.

Shopping Without the Spree

With the start date approaching—and with it, my self-imposed house arrest about to begin—I went shopping.

This was no joy-filled spree. There was one item on my list: shoes. Why shoes? I pictured myself sitting for endless hours in an oversized chemotherapy barca-lounger, with the leg support section elevated, looking at my shoes. I might as well have interesting shoes, I reasoned, since I anticipated they'd be my focal point.

At a small local boutique, I bought three sets of footwear. Comfort and aesthetics had equal weight in my selection. Silvery leather flats with a multi-colored, stylized portrait of two women and a man on the top front panel was pair number one. I thought of the people as the three in my family—Bill, Sara, and me. Robed in white, the man represented a healing force. Rubber-soled, the flats were both comfortable and quiet. They became part of my uniform.

Pair number two were funky, orange and brown, cloth and leather, patterned shoe-boots, with leather laces, pom-poms, and leather soles. Noisy when I walked, and not able to be easily slipped on and off, they made it to the infusion room exactly once.

Third was a pair of slippers, moccasin-like, red suede, with black grosgrain ribbon trim. When I was at home, they were on my feet. They were cute and bright and seeing them helped me feel happier.

Back to the Beach

Aware that time was closing down on me, and that life as I knew it was about to undergo a radical change, I longed for a last adventure, and I longed for the sea. Sand, salt, and that clean blue line of distant horizon never failed to open my eyes, my mind, and my heart. With Sara in school and Bill at work, I was on my own. Where to go? I chose a local urban spot, Revere Beach.

I made two trips, a week apart, during the first two weeks of September. Packing a bag with Propel, some fruit, a towel, and a bathing suit, I left home and boarded the subway. First the green line, then the blue line. Arriving at the Revere Beach station, I strained my legs and taxed my overworked heart as I slowly ascended a terrifically long flight of stairs.

It's a gritty kind of beach. Those days it was packed with kids, families, and a few lone visitors like me. On my first beach day, spreading out my beach towel and planting myself on it, I sat self-contained, comfortably isolated in my thoughts.

But life throbbed and jumped around me. Pretty soon, it intruded into my solitude in its most delightful form. Little kids—first one boy, then another; one girl, then another, saw me as a curiosity. This shaded lady under her hat, clothed in long sleeves, seated and still. They'd dart close to me, pose a question, and dart away. I loved their energy and their courage. They made my heart smile. We chatted, in some English and some Spanish. By the time they decided to go into the water, I was feeling pretty warm myself. Although I hadn't particularly planned on swimming, why not at least wade in and cool off? As I stepped into the sea, the urge to proceed and immerse overtook me. Treading water, observing the distant cargo ships and horizon, I felt supported, refreshed, and free. When I related my day's adventure to my family they seemed skeptically surprised.

The next week, Bill suggested I take the car to Revere Beach. Because driving seemed even more taxing than the train ride and the long flights of stairs, I declined his offer. Public school must have started by then, because my little children friends were notably absent. Older people, singles and couples, dotted the sand. As before, I sat, I snacked, I meditated, and I bathed in the salty sea.

Later that evening I told Sherri of my adventure.

"Karen Lee," she said, "you shouldn't swim at Revere Beach. It was closed last month because of hazardous medical waste in the water."

Back to School, Again

With Labor Day past and the treatment course set, Sara was back in school. A week or so into it, I called my daughter's advisor and asked if she'd help me arrange meetings with each of Sara's teachers. She had a better idea. How about inviting all of the teachers to get together with me at the same time?

Early one mid-September morning, I sat in a nondescript high school classroom, on one of those chairs with an attached writing surface. Sara's advisor and all but one of her teachers sat in the same style chair. They sat in a ring on one side, and I sat alone on the other.

At this pivotal moment, my dedication to my daughter's well-being was paramount, and I had to act on her behalf while I was still able. Yes, I made the choice to act, but it was a choice born of necessity; somehow, the courage was there.

I spoke to the teachers calmly, and for quite a while. Factually, I defined the disease I had. I outlined the schedule, the treatment, the risks, and the uncertainties of our family's next three months. Diplomatically, I asked the teachers to be alert to my daughter's behaviors and emotions. Uncompromisingly, I implored them to call home at the first sign of a problem. My words depicted an emotionally charged family crisis, yet my sludge-like blood failed to provide the complimentary emotional rush.

From the teachers, I received empathy for me, and compassion and respect for my daughter. It was an hour extremely well spent.

As great good luck would have it, this was a talented group of teachers who ignited my daughter's intellectual curiosity and creativity. Sara remained engaged and passionate about her studies all year.

With the clock ticking, counting down to September 21st, it seemed appropriate to revisit and review the literature.

Preparing to enter the clinical trial, I went back to another, more personal school: my Waldenstrom's Macroglobulinemia Study-at-Home

School. What else did I need to know? What more could I learn? How better could I prepare? What new questions should I ask?

All of the IWMF pamphlets now joined all of the alemtuzumab literature on the dining room table as I revisited and reviewed the impact I could expect my body to receive from treatment. I thought about precautions I might take to protect myself from germs.

Once again, I generated a list of questions for Dr. Treon, but now my list was short. Some of the literature advised having a pneumonia vaccination and a flu shot before beginning chemotherapy. What did Dr. Treon advise?

Pneumonia shot—it's a protein-based vaccine; yes, definitely have it.

Flu shot—it's a weakened virus. With a week and a half remaining before the first alemtuzumab treatment, injection of a virus in any form was a very bad idea. No, definitely don't have that.

I made two phone calls, one to Dr. Woo to schedule the vaccination, and one to Zachary Hunter. Although I'd told myself I'd never enter the Dana 1 infusion room, in just a couple of days I'd be a patient there. I felt that having a look at it first might make it seem less scary. Zachary kindly agreed to meet me and escort me through it. Our tour was very quick; we literally walked in one door and out another. But that gave me a glimpse of the place and the space, and it was all I needed.

Taking Care of Business

You know that old expression originated by a pop radio station disc jockey, then picked up into common parlance: "And the hits just keep on comin'!"

Here were the hits in the next days up until the first drug treatment.

On Tuesday, September 13th, Dr. Treon called with news, information, and advice.

The news: the September 8th blood test results showed the IgM count had skyrocketed to 4280. Another plasmaphereisis procedure was needed before the treatment began.

The information: Waldenstroms-produced IgM levels trail the disease. Like an airplane's contrail, that cloud of fuel that remains visible long after the airplane is out of sight, IgM cells made by tumor cells could stay alive in my blood for a while, even if the tumor cells had all been killed.

On the bright side, the alemtuzumab would stay in my blood and continue to kill cancer for five or six weeks after the clinical trial had ended. I believe the underlying message was: Be patient. We're in for a long haul.

The advice: Since we knew my immune system would flat-line with the first few alemtuzumab treatments: "Avoid crowds and sick people."

On Friday, September 16th, five days before the first alemtuzumab infusion, I had the fifth plasmaphereisis. As a result of this procedure, the IgM reading was 1910. This became my doctor's baseline by which he would gauge the alemtuzumab's effect.

Also on this day, in the Blood Donor Center of Brigham and Women's Hospital, I signed a healthcare proxy. I named Bill as the person responsible for making life or death decisions on my behalf, with Pat as the alternate. My witnesses were two of the nurses who'd cared for me so well.

Practicality overrode skittishness. No way would I enter treatment without a healthcare proxy, and the people closest to me, in my heart and in the plasmaphereisis room, were the supporting cast.

During

Starting Up

Now my participation in the clinical trial began. The protocol specified one week to adjust to the cancer-fighting drug, followed by twelve weeks of treatment. Every day that I went to the infusion room, my vital signs were recorded as soon as I was admitted, then I was shown to a bed or a chair. I wrote down—in brief—whatever questions or concerns I had that day.

My questions or observations to report to the nurse or Dr. Treon involved the drugs, how I was feeling, what was worrying me, and how our war to kill cancer was going.

Always I had, or made, the opportunity to relay my list, and always I jotted down the responses I got. This became integral to my treatment ritual. No matter how good or how bad I was feeling, no matter how calm or concerned I was, I wrote, I spoke, I listened, and I learned.

Once the day's pre-treatment conversation—or conversations, depending on whether one or several people were attending me—ended, I closed my notebook. Once drugs entered me, all my mental and bodily attention was diverted by them. The notes are factual, succinct, and medical in nature, yet a surprising, upbeat energy drives them.

My experiences during the clinical trial were defined by the habits and routines I developed to hold myself together through everything I endured. The scary parts, feeling bad, the mental focus that sustained my positive energy, the people and the personalities whom I initially feared and despised—just because they were there, and so was I—but grew to respect and to cherish.

Altogether, it is a story of adaptation, transformation, and humanity.

Entry

On the treatment start date, Wednesday September 21st, at 7:30 a.m., a friend delivered Sara to school and Bill escorted me to Dana-Farber. I knew I needed to be there, I'd certainly planned to be there, but oh how I hated it once I arrived.

This day, there was no waiting time. A receptionist checked me in right away. But this reception desk was new for me; it was part of Dana 1 Infusion. Sensing my hesitation, Bill preceded me into the infusion room. After an assistant measured and recorded my vital signs, which I resented and found annoying, she led me to a bed.

A nurse joined Bill and me. Introducing herself as Laura, she presented me with a thick stack of papers, many of which I was asked to sign.

Paperwork? I found that really annoying. I began to bristle, but the nurse held her course and held me to it, too. As I flipped through the papers, feeling more hostile every minute, Bill became sociable. Noticing several credentials on Laura's nameplate, he asked about her training. In oncology nursing, she was a seasoned professional.

Papers signed, Laura asked me to lie down on the bed. I didn't want to.

"I'm not sick," I said. Other than having cancer, I saw myself as healthy. I told her so.

By now I was feeling hostile and expressing it.

"Can I have a chair instead of a bed?"

No, was the answer. The bed was positioned just across from the nurses' station. The nurses had to be able to see me today, I was told.

Perched tentatively on the bed's edge, I looked around. I noticed two types of IV poles. One was simple: a metal stick, really, with branches from which bags of drugs could hang. The other was complicated and scary. This metal stick with branches also had a bulky machine as part of its architecture. The machine had dials and numbers. I hoped I wouldn't be getting that one.

"Stand up. Hold onto the IV pole. Walk around," Laura ordered. There was no denying her, so gingerly and briefly, I did as she asked. I couldn't have imagined how important that simple act would become.

Then Bill and I were relocated to a station with an oversized oncology lounge chair. A patient who'd just been admitted needed the bed more than I did.

As I sat in the giant patient chair and Bill sat in the petite guest chair, Laura gave me a remote control device. She showed me how to turn on the television and how to call for help, should I need it. Since I don't turn on the television at home, and don't ask for help either, I dismissed the device and the information.

Dr. Treon came calling. He made a point of repeating something he'd mentioned in an earlier conversation. Eighty percent of people have a reaction to alemtuzumab, and he wanted me to be prepared. The clinical trial's protocol stipulated that alemtuzumab be given first. If a patient had no reaction, there'd be no need for additional drugs. If a reaction did occur, drugs could be added to deal with it. My mind moved me into the twenty percent of people who would not experience a reaction.

As always, Bill was listening, participating with his presence. As always, Dr. Treon's and my connection and eye contact were full and complete as he spoke. I heard what I was being told.

It turned out to be somewhat like those childbirth classes. They teach you how to control your breathing to modulate the pain. Sitting in a nicely-appointed room, feeling completely normal, you practice, you grasp the concepts, but none of it simulates or prepares you for the dynamic intensity of labor pains, and for me, none of it helped much during labor.

Dr. Treon wished me well and returned to the clinic on the other side of the waiting room.

Laura started the drug. On Day One of dose escalation week, the dose was 3 milligrams. Alemtuzumab needs to be released into the body very slowly, so I was hooked up to an IV pole, the kind with a pump. I noted that and then screened out the information, trying to keep all of it as impersonal and as distant from my consciousness as I possibly could.

Bill sat reading, or doing a puzzle, I'm not sure which. I sat, doing the mental equivalent of twiddling my thumbs. Okay, not so bad, can I go soon?

Then I felt a sensation as if the flesh of my abdomen had rippled into five broad horizontal wave-like folds. They weren't waving like the sea; they were stationary, and they were getting my attention—from both my body and my brain.

"Something doesn't feel good in here," I said to Bill. He kept reading. Perhaps he hadn't heard me. I wanted and needed his help, but I didn't want to ask for it.

I took the remote in my left hand, to call the nurse. This act alone meant I was in trouble. The symbols on the clicker weren't clear to me, and instead of hitting the nurses' call button, I turned on the TV mounted on a soffit in front of me and behind Bill. I was losing my ability to control my thoughts and my actions, but I knew I'd hit the wrong button. Before moving on to try a different button, I made a huge concentrated effort to make my fingers press the button to turn off the TV to save electricity. I did that, and then pressed the help button.

Laura was there very fast. She beeped Dr. Treon immediately. He arrived in ninety seconds.

"You're having a reaction."

I felt awake, aware, alert and completely conscious. Bill tells me I passed out and had a seizure. Speaking was becoming impossible; mostly I was looking and registering the variety of expressions on the faces of the five people ringed around me.

The only word I spoke was "Demerol," repeating the name of a drug Laura was about to inject at Dr. Treon's orders. I repeated the word to be conversational and participatory as the medical team—really Dr. Treon and Laura—were in the process of rescuing me. I remembered Demerol from having heard my mother speak of it often.

Apparently my tone of voice sounded sarcastic.

"Is that funny?" Laura asked.

At some point, she got her face very close to mine, with full eye contact. I heard her say "You're going to be fine."

I tried to acknowledge, "I know."

It took huge mental concentration and physical effort to speak. The two words sounded distant and elongated, like a 45 rpm record played at 33 rpm speed. I never doubted that I'd be fine, but maybe I didn't know how bad I looked to everybody else. I felt calm, but my situation justified panic.

Here's what I saw in the ring of people facing me: next to me on my left was Laura, bent over a treatment table, hands busy assembling drugs, in clear, tight communication—instinctive as much as verbal—with Dr. Treon.

Dr. Treon also on my left, half-kneeling, full attention on me, quietly speaking a few words about the reaction. Dealing with it. In total charge.

Zachary next to and a bit back from Dr. Treon. Extreme anxiety, concern, and distress on his face as he looked at me.

Bill next to Zachary, and further back still. Extreme anxiety, concern, distress, and fear on his face as he looked at me.

A doctor—an oncologist—whom I recognized from the Blood Donor Center at the hospital when I had plasmapheresis. Expressionless. How cold can he be, I wondered.

There was Demerol, Benadryl, and hydrocortisone. So my immune system's violent reaction to the invasion by a foreign fluid programmed to kill cancer cells was controlled. How long this took, I have no idea. I think it was very short, but I was in a state of heightened perception, so everything seemed to unfold in slow motion.

Benadryl and hydrocortisone, along with Ativan, Tylenol, and Tagamet were written into my pharmacy orders as routine predecessors to alemtuzumab.

I have no other memories of that day at Dana-Farber. We were there a lot of hours.

When Bill brought me home, I felt a tad dazed, in a giddy way.

"I'm going to go rest," I said, and went down to bed. It was about three o'clock. I slept.

When I woke up, the fresh blue sky glowed with luminous sun; the clock said six.

Noticing the bright co-flex bandage that covered the spot where the IV needle had been, I unwound it from my arm and re-wound it into a coil. I planted the coil on my blue glass desktop. That became a habit I would continue; eventually, it translated into a sculpture.

I bounded up the stairs. Happy to see Sara at Bill's computer, I greeted her with "Hi Sweetheart. What would you like for breakfast?"

"Mom," she said, "It's six o'clock." In the evening.

That night, both Bill and I were astonished—and mostly sleepless—because I traveled to the bathroom probably two dozen times. All those IV fluids were roughly received.

On Day Two, Thursday, the drug dose escalated to 10 milligrams. Thanks to the battery of premedication, I had no reaction. When a nurse handed me a little white paper cup, and told me to swallow the little white pill it contained, I did it obediently, almost submissively. I who never took pills. When the sodium chloride (for hydration) began to run in my veins, I began to feel unwell. Benadryl made me feel worse. Hydrocortisone confused it all. But the premedication set the stage for the alemtuzumab to arrive and go to work.

On Day Three, Friday, I received 30 milligrams of alemtuzumab—the full dose—and my body accepted it. With dose escalation week successfully completed, the Twelve Weeks—three dozen treatments in three months—could officially begin.

Singing in the Pain

With dose escalation week behind me, on the first Monday of the first real week of treatment, I surprised myself with a totally spontaneous personal gift. It was the gift of singing. Please understand that I have a bad voice and never sing, so imagine my surprise as I spiraled down five flights of stairs, accompanying my steps with vocal melody and original lyrics! Throughout the Twelve Weeks and beyond, I found myself singing to myself. Little ditties, peppy tunes, encouraging lyrics. The songs evolved over time.

As I descended the stairs this first morning, I sang:

Hi-ho, hi-ho
It's off to cure I go.
And soon I will be cancer-free
Hi-ho, hi-ho.

Which I'd repeat and repeat until I reached the ground floor. This particular song became part of the Monday, Wednesday, and Friday morning ritual.

Another that I'd sing during walks in the park, to the tune of *Good Night Ladies*:

Good bye, cancer.
Good bye, cancer.
Good bye, cancer,
It's great to see you go.

One rainy November Saturday, I drove Sara and her buddies to the Cambridgeside Galleria, an indoor mall. For me, the mall was off-limits, so I took the opportunity to walk along a canal that borders the shops. Perhaps football season influenced my musical composition that day. My song took the rhythm and theme of a football cheer, with the revelry magnified:

Go alemtuzumab!
Kill and kill and kill!

Repeated and repeated to the beat of the rain. Violent, you may say. But I was engaged in a battle to the death, and if one of us had to die, I wanted it to be cancer.

Boundaries

"No" is a word I'd never used much. Generally eager to please, help, and comply, I lacked limit-setting skills. Having cancer changed that.

As soon as the Twelve Weeks began, I found I had to consciously care for my body's health and safety, and also be aware and protective of my moods and emotions. Here were some "No's" I established:

No nightly news programs.

No cancer talk after 7 p.m.

No telephone use on treatment days.

On the flip side, on one topic only, I set no limits:

No limits to becoming cancer-free.

Always, I wove this through my meditations and into my feelings and thoughts. I lived by a principle I wouldn't hear articulated until a couple of months after my last treatment. As I watched a television interview with Jeff Skoll, first president of Ebay.com and founder of Participant Media, I heard him say "The power of a vision is that it has to be ideal."

If the physical and mental demands of this time were excessive, the spiritual gifts were abundant. Rejecting everything that was non-essential, I accepted all that the clinical trial demanded. I embraced the medical process because, with all my heart and all my soul, I wanted it to work.

Rituals

On alemtuzumab days, rituals that might otherwise seem foolish grounded me and helped me hold myself steady.

Initially I wore no make-up, so the doctors could see changes in skin tone, which might mean I was in crisis. By Week Two, a bit of mascara helped me look better—at least in my mirror at home.

My clothes were always cotton, always simple, always comfortable. An early fear: what if I go into cardiac arrest? I wanted the staff to be able to get to my heart easily and fast. Afraid of my arms being trapped inside a jacket or sweater by the IV needle and tubing, I'd wear those garments around my shoulders.

As Bill and I left home in the morning and walked to our car, I'd fix my gaze at the top of a very tall redwood tree in the Public Garden. At its tip were three branches, extending skyward. In them I saw the three of us in our small family, alive and growing, all three, including me. To this day I honor this tree and the three top branches, now lush and full.

As Bill drove us to Dana-Farber, my eyes chose not to look forward. My gaze went out my side window.

Riding along the Charles River, MIT's new building by architect Frank Gehry, with its multi-colored facades and undulating roofline, was a visual checkpoint. Riding along the Fenway, the golden bulrushes and marsh flowers were life and hope. Approaching the Dana-Farber Cancer Institute, I couldn't bear thinking I was going to a cancer center, so in my mind this place was called Dana-Farber Cure Institute. And that focused my mind and my body on the transition into wellness.

On the ride home, usually my gaze went straight through the windshield and up to the sky. After so many hours in a blandly painted, windowless place under fluorescent lights, I couldn't get enough of the clean blue skies and white clouds. Even on a gray day, I welcomed the sky.

My identity as a patient existed only inside the cancer center's walls. When each treatment was completed and I exited the infusion room, in the lobby I'd slip off my patient identification bracelet and get it into a trash can. Before I left the building, my arms would go inside my jacket's long sleeves. I wanted the colorful co-flex at my elbow or my wrist concealed from the eyes of my neighbors.

At night as I brushed my teeth, spontaneous dances often occurred. The electric toothbrush provided the rhythm, and humming provided the melody. I'd wriggle and shimmy and shake. Silly? Yes. Absurd? Totally. Light-hearted self-amusement. What a relief, what a wonderful counterpoint to the somber focus and strict discipline of my days. Seeing myself dance in the mirror for just a few seconds, I felt pep and the promise of more of it to come.

In the infusion room, there were rituals, too.

Never did I watch as the nurse installed my IV needle. Always I took a deep breath before, and a very long exhale during. The inhale distracted me, and the exhale relaxed me.

About personal responsibility, Sherri had offered a piece of advice as a banner headline.

"K. Lee," she said, "Always read the bags."

What was she talking about? I'd wondered. She went on to explain it was crucial to check the prescription on every baggie of drugs I'd be receiving, to verify that the prescription was mine. Mix-ups can occur, and she'd often performed this bag-reading service for friends receiving chemotherapy. How brave she is, I thought.

Once I entered the clinical trial and my treatment began, before any prescription drug was connected to my IV drip, the attending nurse always asked my birth date, verified my patient identification number, and verified that both matched the prescription label on the bag. Early on, one of the nurses insisted I learn the name of my drug and made me repeat it as she pronounced it.

"Alemtuzumab. The *mab* at the end tells you it's a synthetic monoclonal antibody."

Most days, I trusted my nurses to read my bags.

Fits and Misfits

Curiously, for many years, as soon as I came home I would take off my shoes and love being either barefoot or in socks. Once alemtuzumab started, right up to today, I feel the need to have a shoe or a flip-flop or something between my feet and the floor.

On Day Three of dose escalation week, I wore a pair of blue leather sandals imprinted with imaginary people and places. As a nurse showed Bill and me to the private room that would be our base camp for the day, she and I noticed we were both wearing the same type of shoe. We chatted about the playful pictures, and it was helpful to my sanity to bond with an oncology nurse over so mundane an item as shoes.

Expecting I'd have plenty of opportunity to read, I'd bought two pairs of funky reading glasses. Why not add some color to the drab beige décor of the infusion room? But I soon found the glasses made my vision seem wavy, and I ripped them off my face. Was it the cheap lenses or the expensive drugs that toyed with my eyesight?

Realizing that each cancer treatment was a multi-hour event, and that Bill intended to stay with me, I told my husband I was excited by the opportunity for long conversations. Instead, as it turned out, he and I were mostly quiet, each coping with the situation as best we could. I had another idea. Why not take along paper and pens—why not use the time to draw? Adding some art materials to my bag, I felt businesslike. I would be productive.

As the drugs began to flow, I began to draw. But my dream ended almost immediately.

The drugs made me feel woozy and uncomfortable. Forcing both my mind and my hand to draw killed the energy and spontaneity that's a hallmark of my work. Stilted line work felt awful to make, and looked even worse. After one sickly page, I stopped.

For me, the infusion room wasn't going to double as studio space.

The First Angel of Death

On Friday, September 30th, the last day of real Week One, Bill and I were shown to one of the private rooms with a bed, in the back of the infusion room. Sensitive to my ongoing adjustment to this place, and knowing better than I did how much time I'd be inhabiting it, the staff wanted me to feel comfortable.

My husband and I were still tentative about settling in, to the room, to the nurses, and to each other. He had his newspapers and a cup of coffee from the urn in the lobby. I had my green loose-leaf notebook, with questions for the day, and the log of caregivers. I wrote in each only at Dana-Farber, and wrote only of the present day—never ahead. I focused on the photos—one of my father and my daughter together, outside in the sun in New Jersey. I next focused on two Xerox copies of color photos of Sara, taken the summer before. The first is the explosion of exuberance, color, and life, as Sara slings her long blonde hair backwards up and out of Squam Lake's clear waters, a rainbow created and flying.

As for the second photo of my daughter: she's wearing a pastel flowered bandana, the Bloomingdale's breast cancer scarf from the previous year, oversized, Jackie Kennedy-style sunglasses, and a huge smile. Behind her is a poster of Leonardo DiCaprio as Romeo, cigarette in hand, looking like he's madly in love with my daughter. What joy for her to set up the pose and ask a friend to take the photo in her bedroom, even though it looks like Italy.

I finished with the photos, wordless mantras of love and commitment to stay alive, inspired by the people I love. I set the photos back into the loose-leaf notebook's sleeve, and turned to the page of questions for the day.

There was a bit of a delay as we sat in the dimly lit room, awaiting our nurse and the initiation of the day's drugs. Dr. Treon and Zachary Hunter came to see us. They seemed to genuinely like my husband and me. Their visits seemed almost social.

Bill posed a question. When he'd picked up the Bactrim and Acyclovir at Gary Drug, our neighborhood pharmacy, pharmacist Herman Greenfield mentioned that the dosage was lower than normally prescribed. Yes, Dr. Treon responded. In this situation, these drugs were under-dosed and intended to act in a preventive, rather than curative, way. I had the feeling that in the drug store, intangible forces were looking out for me and discreetly wishing me well.

When our nurse for the day entered, she was happy.

"I convinced your doctor to decrease your hydrocortisone dose. Why have more drugs than you need?"

That sounded good to me. I sat on the edge of the bed and the ritual commenced:

Ativan, Tylenol, Tagamet, the IV needle, sodium chloride, Benadryl, the lower dose of hydrocortisone, alemtuzumab.

As soon as the Benadryl entered, I tried to lie down, rest, sleep; maybe I stayed in the bed for a few minutes. But a squooshy interior feeling drove me to my feet.

For the first several weeks Bill stayed with me from beginning to end of each treatment. Depending on other patients' needs, nurses' obligations, and the pharmacy's prescription load—plus, of course, variations in my own medical conditions and blood test results—Bill's and my time varied from four hours at the shortest, up to seven or eight. This particular day, I was feeling relatively relaxed. Late in the afternoon, before Bill went to the nearby food court to get himself some lunch, he asked if I'd like anything. Well, here it was, a Friday afternoon, and I more or less was with my husband! It resembled a date! I felt in a party-like mood.

"Chocolate cake and coffee, please," was my request. Although both were delicious, they carried a price. Sugar plus caffeine mixed late in the day with Benadryl, a reduced dose of hydrocortisone, and alemtuzumab were too many chemicals for my body to bear. I felt awful.

At four o'clock, with the day's treatment complete, Bill and I left the infusion room and went home.

Snack. Nap. Dinner. Bed.

In the middle of the night, I got the shakes. Chocolate, caffeine, and hydrocortisone conspired against me. My whole body was experiencing rhythmic contractions that wouldn't stop. It seemed I could handle it, so I didn't wake Bill. The tremors continued through the sleepless night.

Saturday, in the morning, I knew I needed to talk with Dr. Treon. He'd mentioned he'd be going to Europe, but I was hoping I'd be able to reach him before he left. Waiting until eight o'clock, I dialed his cell phone. He answered at once—from Paris! He gave me his total attention as I explained the nighttime tremors. We talked it over ("Any fever?" etc. he posed the standard questions). I explained I felt very weak and not so much shaky, as shaken. I remembered he'd suggested Motrin at some previous time—perhaps after the first day of dose escalation week—and mentioned it. Yes, Motrin would be good to take.

We chatted a bit about the conferences he was attending, France first, Germany next, then said our goodbyes in French.

I took the Motrin. The shaky feeling abated, but the shaken feeling, along with deep exhaustion and weakness, stayed. I wore my nightgown and bathrobe that day, and spent most of it draped over the big white chair with the big white ottoman. Next to it was our bird cage in front of the west-facing French doors with Bert, a big blue parakeet, and Bonita, a smaller green parakeet.

I meditated in the chair. Inside my closed eyelids, a brilliant green image came. Something like a vertical rectangle, but the corners weren't there; it was sculpted somehow. The color and the image wouldn't leave. At the time I couldn't identify the source, or the meaning.

I drooped in the chair, hung my arms over its arms, rested my head, and listlessly watched the birds. Listened, too. They were noisy that day.

I passed the day and night in weakness. I knew I had to get through it, and I did.

The next day, Sunday, I awoke, went upstairs, and made coffee. The moment I sat in the white chair, I knew something horrible was happening in the birdcage. Bonita was lying on the floor trying to lift her head, trying to move, but losing her grip. I looked inside.

The food dish was empty. Urgently I filled it, put Bonita's head near water, and tried to give her food. I watched her and focused on her recovery over the next twenty minutes. I was sure she could eat and get strength and revive. She died.

I'd been too weak the day before to fill the food dish, and too preoccupied to notice that it needed filling.

When Bill and Sara came upstairs, I told them the parakeet had died.

When it was time to bury Bonita, Sara chose not to join Bill and me. My husband and I went down to our building's courtyard with the bird's small body wrapped in a white paper towel, like a Jewish burial shroud. With a tablespoon, I dug a hole for her under the tree nearest our elevator entry. She joined Ruffles the hamster, and Bobo, another parakeet. It was sad, but I was somewhat dulled to emotional pain. I didn't yet know Bonita's death was a premonition.

So ended Week One.

After my shaky night, I swore off sugar and almost all white flour products, and limited coffee to pre-drug hours on alemtuzumab days. Dr. Treon restored the hydrocortisone dose to its original strength.

The Second Angel of Death

Week Two.

Thursday evening, I was meditating in my bedroom. I sat on my side of the bed next to a window. The room was dark; a lamp in the far corner was switched off. It's a tall crystal lamp with a golden base, etched spheres, and dangling, elaborately carved crystals.

I remember the day it came home. I was five, or maybe six. One late summer afternoon, the lamp entered our living room and was enthroned on a leather-topped mahogany coffee table. My mother regarded it with reverence. To her it represented culture, and beauty, and wealth. There was an air of awe.

Behind the lamp was a trio of windows, which would have admitted luscious western sun, except that the drapes were permanently drawn shut. "We don't want people to look in and see what we have," I was told. Maybe once, maybe twice in thirty-three years, I opened the drapes, sunlight rolled in, and the lamp's prisms shot out their rainbows.

I honestly didn't get the beauty in the lamp that first afternoon, or pretty much ever. Nonetheless, decades later when my mother sold her

medical practice and my parents sold the house, the crystal lamp was one of the few items I chose to keep.

So it came with me to my loft in New York, and it came with me to Boston when I married Bill. Sometimes it was in our living room, but lately, as it lost a crystal here or there, or the improvised paper clips my father had used to reattach fallen dangles over the years looked too shabby for a public room, the lamp had migrated downstairs to the bedroom.

This evening as I meditated with closed eyes, I saw a neon-orange light. Not vague, not in rays, but in two or three clear forms. Roughly elongated rectangles, jagged edges, unparallel sides, stacked roughly.

A few moments later, orange light again.

I opened my eyes, just to be sure.

A few moments later, a third brief appearance of brilliant orange light.

I got up and walked diagonally across the room to the crystal lamp. "I hope it's not my mother," I said.

I checked the light bulb and screwed it in tighter. I checked the plug, and pushed it in tighter. I played with the switch to be sure the lamp was turned off.

"I can't pull the plug," I said.

Back on the bed, I completed my meditation.

The next day, being a Friday, was a Dana-Farber day.

That evening at around 9 o'clock, I left the living room and telephoned my parents from Bill's office.

I liked to hear my parents' voices and keep them informed of my medical situation. Since July, my mother's medical problems had been intensifying, so checking in on her was another reason to call.

My sister-in-law Lorraine answered the phone. She loves both my parents deeply, and her tone was unprecedented. Pretty quickly she said, "Let's put it this way. If there's anything you want to say to your mother you should say it now."

It didn't take long for me to ask, "Is she dying?"

The response: my mother might die that night, and I should stay in touch.

East coast to West—touch isn't easy.

I told Bill, who had trouble believing it.

Sara was watching TV in the kitchen with her friend Liz Iannuzzi.

When I told my daughter the news, she let out a kitten-like "Oh—." She was empathic and very sad.

In a while I called back and spoke with my brother Larry. My father was distraught, unable to talk with me.

"What would you like to say to Mother? She can't talk to you, but I'll tell her."

"Tell her I love her."

The next day, Saturday, I spoke with my family more than once. My mother was dying. My father, my brother, and his wife were all with her. Myra wanted to die at home and had made that clear. She didn't want a rabbi and had made that clear. My family could no longer carry her, so they'd brought in round-the-clock-professional help.

My brother assured me that my mother's wishes were all being met, and that when the point came that she was in pain, the pain would be relieved. He told me that my father had called him Friday morning, making it clear that something had changed severely, very much for the worse, and that my mother's condition was very bad. He said the change happened Thursday evening, but my father hadn't wanted to bother my brother at night.

I know the change happened at exactly the moments that the brilliant orange light came to me through my mother's crystal lamp. My mother came to me to say good-bye.

That Saturday in Boston the air was charcoal gray, and it rained like it can in the West: thick, incessant.

I was plenty weak by this time, with plenty of alemtuzumab in me. I remember being alone at home, sitting on the sofa in the back of the kitchen, looking at the moon calendar, feeling sick that my mother had seen her last set of full moons. I remember going out onto the fire escape with a jar of soap bubbles, blowing bubbles up into the sky, and watching rainbows swirl within them. I remember imbuing each shimmering bubble with a wish of hope for my mother's life and spirit, and watching them stay alive for very long times.

"Breathe," I whispered to her. "Keep breathing."

She did.

Bill and Sara, along with Sara's friends Liz, Lindsay, and Becca had ventured out into the rain and came home with a new parakeet. Tiny, a baby really, the girls had created a big name for him: Je m'appelle Claude Jennifer Bombay. He joined Bert in the birdcage.

We stayed in touch with my mother's dying. When we went to bed she was still breathing in her bed.

The next morning was Sunday, October 9th. With the three-hour time difference, it was too early to call the West coast. I called my dear Sherri, who's had more experience with funerals than anyone I know, and who's Jewish like I am.

"What do I do?" I asked.

Sherri told me that any Jewish funeral home would have yarzheit candles and prayer books to use while sitting Shiva. Bill and I went out to buy groceries and get some mourning materials.

The air was gray, the rain thick. When Bill went into the market, I sat in the car for a while, then took a walk and discovered a playground and park. I thought so hard of my mother. I sent her my love. I sent her my tears.

At Stanetsky's Funeral Home in Brookline, Bill, my Catholic-raised husband, went in while I stayed in the car. He returned with an armload of material—prayer books, black mourning ribbons, a calendar with every Jewish holiday. He said the people couldn't have been kinder.

The car radio played that delicious song that mixes "Somewhere Over the Rainbow" with "What a Wonderful World" by Israel Kamakawiwo'ole. It moved me so, and still does. I felt how happy my mother would be when she flew over the rainbow.

Back at home I tried to rest and be patient, but finally around 1:30 I said to Bill, "I can't take it any longer. I have to call my family."

My brother told me my mother had died at 10:10. He wanted me to know she had no pain, and he was with her when she died. My father wanted to talk with me.

Noah got on the phone. His voice was gruff, as if from sleeplessness, grief, and worry, but his words were loving and reassuring.

"I told mother you love her—I told her we all love her. She knows. We made sure she didn't feel any pain. Now, Karen Lee, you need to take care of yourself."

How bizarre, how final, to have a parent die. In the dining room, I gathered my little family. I told them the news, and we lit the yarzheit candle. We all mourned.

Over the course of the next few days, my brother said, "We always thought mother's heart was the problem, but I can tell you, it was beating really strong."

My father devolved into wordless grief.

My brother told me he'd gone for a walk, and in the sky was a glorious rainbow in all the colors my mother loved. One bird flew through it; he knew it was she, and she was pain-free.

My dining room table became an altar in honor of my mother. An orchid plant bloomed—six white flowers. Photos congregated of my mother and our family at many ages, through many stages.

The yarzheit candle burned for ten days.

In my bathrobe, in my weakened state of body, I mourned and remembered.

The next day, October 10th, was the official Columbus Day holiday. It being Monday, Bill and I went to Dana-Farber. The building was very quiet, and the lobby uncharacteristically deserted. Ahead of us, at the elevators, we saw one person: Dr. Treon.

As we greeted each other, Bill said, "Karen Lee's mother died yesterday."

Dr. Treon and I embraced. He was so compassionately sad. I told him what a great fan of his my mother was.

Truly, shaken with the events of the dying and in grief with the death, what are the odds that on a holiday, the one person Bill and I would encounter would be Dr. Treon?

He was emotional, he was kind. I got my alemtuzumab. I wanted it, and my mother would have wanted me to have it.

Happy Birthday

Wednesday, October 12th was the real Columbus Day, Sara's 17th birthday, her day to take the PSATs, Yom Kippur, and a Dana-Farber day. It was Week Three, real dose number eight.

By now, I had my food, my medications, my hygiene, and my prayerful icons in place, and I was feeling slightly stronger since my mother's death. So the morning rituals were all enacted as I prepared at home, as

Bill drove me to Dana-Farber, and as we readied ourselves to enter the infusion room.

My chair this day was in the back corner of the second biggest infusion room—the only chair on that side of the room—and I liked it for its relative isolation and privacy. Bill and I settled in—he in the small guest chair, I in the oversized patient chair. For the first time since the first day, Laura was my nurse. I felt myself pull back; I felt intimidated.

Bill quickly told Laura, "Karen Lee's mother died Sunday."

Laura became transformed with empathy and compassion. Her care and concern for me, living through my cancer and my mother's death, was very strong, and forged a powerful bond among Laura, Bill, and even me. I say "even me" because I was still experiencing a physical drain from the emotional strain of death, as well as the biological response to the assault of alemtuzumab and its host of companion drugs. Bonding wasn't my strong suit just then.

The nurse leaned close to me, as she had on that very first day, and spoke with Bill and me almost intimately, as a friend who had my best interests at heart. She inquired about my experience in the clinical trial thus far. Rigors is the name for the seizure-like reaction I'd had on Day One, and again at the end of Week One, she said.

"Are you sleeping?" Laura wanted to know.

"Not really. But I have Ativan."

"Ativan's not designed as a sleeping pill. I'll call Dr. Treon."

She was very concerned that I wasn't sleeping. She knew well that my body was under attack; yes, by cancer, and yes, by a drug that was hammering at the cancer with explosive force.

"Nutrition, hydration, rest," Laura said.

She said it so simply, so clearly, and so seriously, that this phrase became a mantra to me. It guided my thinking, my actions, and how I took care of myself throughout the clinical trial and after.

We talked, the IV needle was installed, and Laura called Dr. Treon. As was my wont, I pulled the privacy curtains part-way, turned off the fluorescent lights, and created a more private ambiance.

By now I'd convinced Bill that it was okay for him to leave me. Reluctantly, he did, for just an hour or two at a time.

Mid-morning Dr. Treon's office assistant entered my dimly lit, somewhat personal space, bearing a prescription for Ambien. She'd had some experience with this drug, and repeatedly suggested I start with just half a pill. I appreciated her visit and the prescription, but in my Benadryl-induced groggy state, the advice about taking half a pill didn't stay in my mind.

Laura administered the drugs: Ativan, Tylenol, Benadryl, hydrocortisone, and alemtuzumab. I switched over from the big patient chair to the guest chair Bill had vacated. The smaller chair was much better suited to my body's size and much more comfortable for me. Also, choosing to sit there helped me feel like a person, not a patient.

Laura asked me to let her know if I was feeling any anxiety or an elevated heart rate. If I did experience this sensation, she'd want to check my blood pressure. At some point, I mentioned that I felt my heart rate picked up as soon as the IV started running.

This day, the IV drug routine moved along smoothly and was completed fairly early, Around 2:30, Laura pulled the needle. As I sat in the little chair and waited for Bill, I felt pretty good and decided I could have some normal time. Why not relax and read? I opened John Milton's *Paradise Lost* and read a section of Book II.

I read about Satan's return visit to Hell. There he encounters Sin and Death, and learns that Sin is his daughter and Death is his son. I read hideous, horrifying details of their births and their job descriptions.

The birth of death. My mother was an obstetrician. My mother had just died. I saw it all too graphically. I felt it all too viscerally. My heart rate skyrocketed.

Uncharacteristically, I reached for the nurse's call button and asked for Laura. She took my blood pressure, which was elevated, and asked me to stay until it normalized.

Bill returned to find me agitated, and not yet able to leave with him.

That was how I experienced the power of literature as an active, physical force.

When Bill and I returned home, Sara was there with Liz.

"How were the PSATs?" Bill inquired.

"Fine," was our daughter's brief response.

As was our custom, we had tickets to attend Yom Kippur Kol Nidre services at Harvard Hillel with our friends the Goldklang family: Becca, her brother Jake, and her parents Cilla and Ira. Clearly I couldn't go this year, so we invited Liz to accompany Sara and Bill. Being Catholic, Liz hadn't yet been to a synagogue. Being a history buff interested in world culture, she welcomed the invitation.

Earlier in the week I'd called Harvard Hillel, and, without explaining that I had no immune system, I said that, for health reasons, I couldn't attend services but would love to borrow a prayer book to help me observe the holiday at home. The rabbi's assistant couldn't have been kinder, and said that my family could bring a book home for me.

When Bill and the girls departed, all three looked beautiful in their schul clothes. I had a peaceful time at home in the dining room with the yarzheit candle, the white orchids, and the photographs that comprised the altar in my mother's honor.

After Kol Nidre, Liz went home. Bill and Sara exploded into the house in an ebullient mood.

"We saw Laurie Bayliss. After the service she came up to us and asked us if you were dead. We stood up during the Kaddish, and she said a husband's supposed to stand up only if his wife died, and a kid's supposed to stand up only if a parent died."

Bill explained that it was my mother who had died, and that he and Sara stood in her honor and her memory. Apparently, Laurie reprimanded them for their misbehavior.

She later emailed Bill, who reassured her that I hadn't died.

A second amusing event transpired after the service.

It seems that both Bill and Sara sequestered prayer books under their jackets to bring home for me. Somehow they figured out the duplication before leaving the church building where the Jewish service was held, and only one prayer book came home. It was a treasure for me.

As the time approached 10:30, Sara's birthday celebration began, just we three. It was a joyous time. My daughter sat on the dining room floor, her back against the mirrored oak chest with the sculpted griffins, her long lovely legs extended in front of her, and her presents around her.

There were just a few presents, and my daughter appreciated each of them. The one that stays in my mind is a tall glass tube with floating, colored glass bulbs inside, that move in response to barometric pressure. Bill and I bought it at the Dana-Farber gift shop.

The Dread Becomes the Dance

In the first eight weeks or so of the clinical trial, after each alemtuzumab treatment I'd come home and head straight to bed. For an hour or two, or three, depending on the physical and mental trials of the day, I'd sleep. Generally, this sleep was a dreamless escape. One day, it became a joyous engagement.

In the early days, I dreaded everything and everyone, including the nurses. But a subliminal shift began to take place. As I paraded around with my IV pole, on two separate afternoons, two separate nurses asked me what drug I was getting. When I answered "alemtuzumab," each literally lit up.

"People get wonderful results with alemtuzumab," each of the nurses said.

My mind received this dully as encouraging but impersonal news. Good for them. What about me?

"Would I like to meet some patients getting alemtuzumab?" I was asked.

"No."

That was too personal, too risky. It felt as if I already had plenty of information to deal with. I felt the process for me had to be solo, not social.

Through the nurses' professional efficiency and demeanor, warmth was coming to me. As my consciousness surfaced from one afternoon's nap on the edge of waking, the dread became a dance. My dream showed me a ring of nurses holding hands, dancing in a flowing circle, bathed in the glorious light of a New England autumn afternoon. Seeing them, I felt happy.

I woke up smiling, and another shift propelled my thoughts to replace fright with trust.

In the last four weeks or so, the steroids in my blood increased my sense of hunger. My pattern changed, and a substantial snack preceded the retreat to bed. The scale eventually registered a thirteen-pound weight gain.

As we monitored decreasing IgM counts and a shrinking M-spike, the dream of being cancer-free held steady.

Unspecial

Hearing, seeing, listening, observing, taking in so much around me. Input and compassion. No judgment.

Staying very much to myself, and keeping very private, I spoke little, but took in a lot. It took weeks before intuitive understandings formed themselves into concepts, and even more weeks until they took shape in words.

When I sat in the infusion room, as I paced through it, cancer was there in men and women, young and old, black, white and Asian, showing itself through pain and scars and needles. Cancer dissolves barriers of class, race, money, and everything else. It builds community, uniting its victims in struggle, frustration, terror, and sometimes, hope.

To Bill, I eventually said, "I am so unspecial."

Cancer teaches humility, and humanity.

Trick or Treat

In 2005, Halloween fell on a Monday, an alemtuzumab day. It was the start of Week Six.

The previous week I'd heard some of the nurses chatting, almost giggling, about the upcoming holiday. Not wanting to intrude, and cognizant of keeping my mind in the present, I asked only a mild question, like "Oh, will something be happening here?"

The answer came back: oh yes, Halloween was a special day here, and there was a tradition of acknowledging it.

As I was checking in with reception before Bill and I entered the infusion room, not only could we feel the buzz, we also caught sight of pink—lots and lots of pink—beyond the door.

Entering the clinic, we found ourselves in a tropical wonderland, albeit a very pink one. Tropical birds, cavorting fish, fluttering palm trees (made of paper, glitter, feathers) lined the hallways, animated the nurses' stations, and transformed a visually somber space into a delight-filled play land. On the counters that delineated the nurses' stations, big bowls overflowed with colorfully-wrapped candies.

The staff and the nurses had been hard at work, both planning and installing this magical setting after Saturday's shift ended and before this morning's shift began. Bill's and my spirits were lifted and transported with wonder and appreciation. I'm sure all the other patients and their companions felt the same way.

One of the volunteers, a tall, older man who enjoyed pushing the newspaper and magazine cart through the ward, had dolled himself up as a clown! A curly ring of orange hair, a big bowtie, a real circus clown outfit, oversized, flat-footed shoes—the patients were a bit taken aback, but he was utterly delighted with himself. No matter how much privacy I or any other patient may have preferred, we couldn't possibly ignore this jovial volunteer on this particular day.

And the nurses—this serious, efficient, professional group—even they dolled up a bit, some wearing pink-hued Hawaiian shirts over their lab coats, others choosing pink plastic leis.

It was all so out of character; it utterly transformed the experience of the place.

Once my vital signs were checked and recorded, Bill and I were escorted to our station. With the IV in, sodium chloride running, Benadryl, then hydrocortisone administered, and the alemtuzumab drip begun, Bill thought he might leave and go to his office for a while. But we'd been told that at some point a parade of children would come through to trick or treat.

Interested and curious, Bill hung around. He was next to the main entry door when his attention was captured. We were mesmerized.

Sometime around noon, the parade began. And what an extraordinary parade it was.

My IV pole and I were standing near the central nurses' station and opposite the main entry door.

As the door opened, I was totally unprepared for what I saw. Kids, lots of kids. But these kids were in wheelchairs, on crutches, or cradled in their parents' arms. The kids were cancer patients, too, in costume, or wearing a token decoration. Some were bald, some were pale, some looked very weak. Most registered some form of smile or happiness, responding to the festival. Others were unable to register much.

I don't know what I was expecting, but I wasn't expecting this.

The parade of kids, and their assisting adults, headed straight toward me, turned to the right, then turned back toward the door, collecting candy and treats from nurses and patients along their short route. The patients in our unit who were able to stand lined the kids' path, clogging up the halls.

What rose high, and did some clogging of its own, was emotion. How moving to watch these sick kids come to have some fun, and to give so much joy to us. How horrible that they were so young and had cancer. You can imagine the mix of emotions I felt. Happy, uplifted, surprised, stunned. The parade didn't last long in real time, but it will last forever in my mind.

For the adult patients, too, there were goody bags. Jane Moss, a volunteer who befriended my husband and me, came by with a small goody bag for me.

"What's this?" I'd asked.

"It's a gift for you from The Friends Committee."

What a surprise! People were looking out for us patients, offering kindness and offering gifts. In the bag were some lemon candies, a small statue of a Halloween witch, and a very small book called *Words on Courage*.

It was a day that felt like floating, in the infusion room.

"Germ of the Month"

When I was a kid, pharmaceutical companies sent my mother monthly magazines. One of them featured on its back cover the "Germ of the Month." Magnified to six inches square, the germ was always grotesquely colorful, and it was always utterly ugly. My brother loved making hideous faces as he imitated the germ of the month. He made me laugh, but we both knew there was nothing funny about the disease-bearing germ.

After the first couple of alemtuzumab treatments, exactly as Dr. Treon had predicted, my body's immune system flat-lined. From a Dana-Farber administrator who'd had her own experience with cancer, from my nurse Suzanne, and from my father, came warnings about those ever-lurking germs and ways to keep them from doing me harm.

The administrator told me about life without an immune system, once chemotherapy destroys it. For the first time, I heard about and began to think about the supreme importance of personal hygiene, when one's immune system goes missing.

After Suzanne, my primary nurse, told me many kinds of bacteria that normally live on our skin could now be a threat to me, I was careful to keep my hands away from my mouth and eyes. I'd observed various staff members using the wall-mounted Purell pumps to clean their hands, but I assumed that was for them, not for me. When I saw Dr. Treon use the pump and the Purell, I became an instant convert. It was as though his example vetted the value of the antibacterial hand gel for me.

Sometime later, as my IV pole and I paced, I stopped to chat with a medical assistant. Her pushcart was stocked with bottles of Purell, which she was distributing around the ward. When she offered me one, I accepted. She told me when I used that one up, she'd give me another.

"When I'm through with this, I'm through," I said.

My intention was to make use of this bottle while I was immune-deficient, and to have the cancer gone when the Purell was.

Punctilious, almost fanatic, hand-washing, laundering towels and sheets often, never touching one's fingers to one's mouth—why would I ever have been aware of any of this before?

And then there's the original Mr. Clean: my father. After World War II, his first business was laundromats. His second was manufacturing cleaning products. Our home was immaculate, always.

When I told Noah that personal hygiene would be important to my avoiding infection, he gave me his lecture and explained his rules.

In public bathrooms, he said, germs are rampant. Always line the toilet seat with a liner or with toilet paper before sitting down. When you flush a toilet, or touch a faucet, a doorknob, or a door handle, always have some paper between your fingers and the object.

It all sounded obsessive and compulsive, which it is, but it's also common sense.

These clear, matter-of-fact guidelines became inviolable routines that I adhered to both at home and at Dana-Farber.

Taking Dr. Treon's advice to heart, I avoided contact with other people as much as possible. Even a visit to the hair salon was out of the questions, and ironically, this had a silver lining.

About eight years earlier when I began a career of sorts as a model, I'd followed the advice of a make-up artist and had my hair cut very short.

Now, during the Twelve Weeks, and for a couple of months after, my hair grew, uncropped. Curls and waves returned.

Ironic that my biology-based cancer drug caused no hair loss, and in my case led to a new, softer look.

Thanksgiving

Typically for Thanksgiving, our family hosted a festive dinner. A dozen people would join us for food and fun that lasted all day. This year was different.

The holiday fell during Week Eight of the clinical trial. My being was suffused with drugs, and with hope. Home, Dana-Farber, and public parks were my domains. No shops, no restaurants, no friends' houses, and very few visitors to our home.

Bill was doing all the shopping, cooking and caretaking for our family. Although he never mentioned the strain, he needed a break.

For Thanksgiving, he arranged a special favor from the chef of a nearby restaurant. Although it wasn't her habit to provide take-out meals, when she heard Bill's story she agreed to package three dinners for him to pick-up.

In quiet and calm, our party of three felt most thankful to be together.

Personal Shoppers

With no immune system, I strictly adhered to my policy of self-imposed "house arrest." Going shopping was out of the question, but I found there were a few items I needed. Although I wanted to keep my daughter as far out of the loop as possible—meaning as insulated from my medical process as possible—I enlisted her as an ally to do a little shopping for me.

In late September, Sara bought me a dozen white washcloths at Marshalls so I could use a washcloth only once, and then launder it.

In late November, as my cotton tee shirts wore out, she and her friends shopped for me at their then-favorite store, Old Navy. The girls came home with several long-sleeved, colorful cotton tees, in an array of rose and blue-green shades that were perfect for me.

I believe they had pleasure shopping for me, and I had pleasure seeing their thoughtful, loving choices.

Home Alone

Twice during the Twelve Weeks, knowing that Bill and Sara could use a break from my routine, I encouraged them to go away for the weekend. Both Fridays that they were away, Pat picked me up and drove me to Dana-Farber. She stayed with me through the intake procedure, and joined me at my assigned seat. But since my being there was largely an internal experience, not a social one, and Pat respected that, we kept her visits inside the infusion room brief and she didn't stay long. When treatment was completed, either Pat or Sherri came to collect me in front of the building and take me back home.

Those two weekends, home alone, I was productive. My main activity during the first was to finish reading *Paradise Lost*. Much of it I read aloud, which really helped me hear the meter and the rhyme. Even though Adam and Eve were being expelled from paradise, sent to a world fraught with disease and finalized by death, the scenes held radiance and a sense of calm. Reading, I felt peaceful.

During the second weekend, I painted small pieces with watercolor and glitter. Signs, really. Here's what they said, which I'd seen on a decorative blanket displayed in the Dana-Farber lobby, made by kids with cancer:

Yesterday is history
Tomorrow is mystery
Today is a gift.
That's why we call it the present.

Two Worlds

The trials of this time were excessive, but the gifts were abundant. Rather than being preoccupied with sickness, I lived in awareness of

health. The long-term objective was to achieve cancer-free good health; the immediate requirement was to stay grounded, alert, and aware in the present. Taking one day at a time, one moment at a time, to move through sickness, to endure through treatment and, to tolerate both.

As medical as the situation was, as scientific as the clinical trial was, the Twelve Weeks was at its core a creative process. Not unlike my most productive times in my art studio, I let go, and experienced a type of free-fall. Trusting my doctor, relying on my husband, I felt safe. Worry had no place in my thoughts. Caution, however, most certainly did.

Inside the time capsule that was the Twelve Weeks, I needed coping mechanisms. The plunge into cancer treatment and the impact of cancer drugs had their own writhing life. Within it, I had to find a way to stay sane, hold my focus on the return to cancer-free good health, and keep my body well enough to survive the process.

Thanks to the previous six months of meditation and self-education, I established and maintained two worlds, two separate ways of existing that supported each other and me. In a culture which has historically separated our mental life from our body's well-being, it may seem that my framework would hold conflict. But just the opposite was the case. Grounded in meditation and living mindfully in each moment, World One thrived within the creative privacy of my mind. Rooted in awareness of my physical vulnerability, World Two revolved around taking care of my body. Each world anchored the other; together they kept me as sane and as well as possible, given the circumstances.

Physically restricted by exhaustion and socially restricted by the absence of an immune system, in the privacy of my mind my thoughts roamed freely. World One pulsed with vitality and awareness. Over the months my meditations evolved as medical circumstances changed. Inside the Twelve Weeks, the meditations' content and process experienced a sea change. As Benadryl, hydrocortisone, and alemtuzumab ravaged my body at forty-eight hour intervals, more or less, the shock waves rode one upon the other. As the drug stream co-mingled with my bloodstream, my choices were limited to one: my brain and my body had to "go with the flow."

Unless an aberrant situation like the rigors event made it impossible, my habit was to meditate every morning and every evening. The foundation remained vocal, with the morning "Ah" and evening "Om" sounds. But the twenty minutes sometimes became thirty or forty, and long silent periods became filled with what I can only call prayer. Along with the over-arching vision that I was healthy and cancer-free, my favorite equation ever stayed in my mind: Belief = Hope+Expectation.

As I meditated, my thoughts were pure optimism, pure love. I saw and felt myself totally healthy and cancer-free, as if that already existed, now, in the present. I could feel all my cells smiling along with my thoughts.

When a person believes he'll get better, and expects he'll get better, the body systems get that message from the brain. It makes a huge positive impact on health and healing. In my father's words, "The brain influences the chemistry of the body."

I included love, appreciation, and prayers for the good health of Bill, Sara, all my family, my doctor and his team, my nurses, their families, and their teams, and my widening circle of friends whom I knew were all praying for me. I say widening circle of friends because, although my ring of confidents remained small, Bill reached out to his friends. In return, he received tremendous compassion and support. These sustained his strength in his solitary role of caring for Sara and me. As for those who'd discarded me when they learned I was sick, we never missed them.

Thanks to my positive outlook and the love and support of family, friends, and my medical team, Dr. Iannuzzi's Intangibles accompanied my family and me with powerful spiritual energies.

Mainly, I meditated at home. But on my walks along the river or in the Public Garden, aware and mindful of birds, flowers, leaves, trees, in all of it I saw life, and symbols of my own healthy, ongoing life. Truly noticing and appreciating everything—because I was aware that I was alive and able to do so—was life-affirming.

This type of moving meditation slid into my treatment time. Around Week Eight or so, pacing with my pole through the infusion room, I silently spoke to the alemtuzumab, urging it to target and annihilate all the tumor cells. My images were violent; they had to be. It was war: cancer, or me.

Because the alemtuzumab infusion was regulated by a pump and the full dose required exactly two hours, the nurses knew exactly when a treatment would be completed. Typically, Bill would accompany me into the infusion room and stay with me most of the day. If he left for his office, he'd return a few minutes before I was able to leave. Typically, and understandably, at the end of each treatment, the instant the IV needle was pulled, all I wanted to do was get out of the infusion room and out of the building as fast as I could. Almost always, Bill was already at my side. I'd bolt, take the lead, and out we'd go.

About two thirds of the way through treatment, I surprised myself with a shift in attitude, timing, and locale.

It happened one early winter afternoon, by chance, because Bill's arrival was delayed. My treatment completed, free of my IV needle and tubes and pump, I bid good-bye to my nurses and, for the first time, walked out of the infusion room alone.

Having just done a few hours of moving meditation, that is, pacing and praying within the ward, I felt filled with love for all the staff who helped me so. And my disease was diminishing. This place had become for me a safe haven, and a wellspring of health. Exhausted, of course, seeking anonymity, of course, I found myself in the lobby, and chose a seat facing the wall near the gift shop.

As I closed my eyes and relaxed my arms, meditation came. It was peaceful, and it was beautiful. What a transformation of attitude, to find myself comfortable and at ease in this place.

After this experience, I'd sometimes intentionally ask Bill to come a half hour later than I'd be free to go. Sitting alone in the waiting room, I felt the alemtuzumab charging through me, keeping up its cancer-killing momentum. The cycle of cure continued.

I felt so close, so connected emotionally to my nurses and their support staff, I included them in my prayers. To meditate, to pray, in Dana-Farber's lobby, just a few yards away from my medical team and place of healing, I remained physically and spiritually connected to and embraced by this great ring of health. It was a time of thanksgiving, a transition from hospital to home.

At home, within meditation, from time to time my eyes would open. Sometimes I'd mentally control my gaze and refuse to be distracted by moving objects, like airplanes or birds. Holding steady was a sign of strength. Other times, I'd delight in following the travels of the airplanes or birds. Moving with them was a sign of living.

Symbolizing freedom and life, birds became immeasurably meaningful. When two appeared, they'd symbolize Bill and Sara, living in health.

Would I be alive and with them? I'd search for a third bird. Invariably, it appeared.

Occasionally as I meditated, I'd feel my head lower and sense my chin close to my chest. Not the traditional yogi pose, you might say. But because it felt right at the time, I'd hold that posture for as long as it was needed. Three and a half years later, my yoga teacher asked the class to lower our heads in this way, saying the position opens the way to honesty and humility. Both of which dwelled in the core of my being during the Twelve Weeks.

As for World Two, I became scrupulous about taking care of my body. The discipline helped buffer the unpredictable effects of the drugs and helped keep me grounded within routines.

About that concise mantra offered by Nurse Laura—nutrition, hydration, and rest—in caring for myself, for the first time in my life I became absolutely compulsive about establishing and adhering to rules about them. I added hygiene to the list. Thanks to Maggie Trichon's advice, food came with me to the infusion room. Offered a meeting with Dana-Farber's nutritionist, I accepted. At least it would help occupy the time, I reasoned. She counseled eating foods high in immune boosting nutrients. As for fruits and vegetables, I applied the same guidelines advised for travel in developing countries: if you can peel it or cook it, it's safe to eat. Avoiding germs and bacteria was the goal.

On alemtuzumab days, I'd have two breakfasts at home: first cereal, then an hour later, eggs. I'd routinely eat a sandwich and an orange before the alemtuzumab infusion began. I felt the food braced my body to receive the drug more easily. Maybe activity in my digestive system would set a good example for alemtuzumab's activity in my circulatory system.

In sickness as in health, we need to keep our bodies well-hydrated. As I've mentioned with blood thickened by Waldenstrom's-generated IgM cells, Dr. Treon advised I drink a Gatorade-type beverage. His guideline for hydration was simple: clear urine means the body is hydrated. Yellow urine color means hydration is needed.

Hydration took two forms: Propel, which Bill bought by the case at Costco, and sodium chloride, the potion the nurses ran continuously during treatments. For the first seven weeks, I drank two bottles of a vitamin drink every day. When lab tests showed elevated liver numbers, Dr. Treon cancelled Tylenol, and I asked if all the other pills—Ativan, etc.—could be eliminated, too. The drugs were pared down to the minimum: sodium chloride, hydrocortisone, Benadryl, alemtuzumab. I decided to cancel the vitamin drink, too. Sometimes, there can be too much of a good thing.

Rest was a necessity. For the first time in memory, rather than push myself, I learned to just stop, and simply rest, without feeling guilty or ashamed. This alone was an important life lesson.

Disease and drugs created exhaustion and fatigue, not intermittent but constant. There was no choice but to slow my pace to almost a standstill. On Tuesdays, Thursdays, Saturdays, and Sundays I did what I could. The bills got paid. Daily, I napped. Lethargic on the outside, mind and anatomy were in high-gear on the inside.

Even as I rested, my mind tuned in to the feelings of my body. I visualized alemtuzumab circulating, moving, roving through my blood and bones, detonating on contact with cancer cells. Over time I began to see first my blood, then my bones, healthy and clean and cancer-free. I saw a normal lymph system, and an untaxed, healthy heart.

And I felt it as if it were already true.

Taking my doctor's advice literally—"Avoid crowds and sick people"—I placed myself under what I called voluntary house arrest.

As for excursions, and friends, and shopping—no, no, no. The only public place I went to during the three months of treatment, and for three months after it was completed, was Dana-Farber. On the days I didn't go to Dana-Farber, I walked in the Public Garden or along the river only if I had some energy. No stores, no friends' homes, no nothing. My domains were: home, Dana-Farber, public parks. Period.

When I asked even my closest friends to please stay away if they had cold or flu symptoms, they understood the reason.

Most, if not all, anti-cancer drugs suppress or kill one's immune system. Why expose yourself to germs when your body has no defense? Better to postpone those parties, and then really enjoy them once you're well.

About Time

Having cancer set me into a curious style of time travel. Unlike the traditional sci-fi methods, which either fling a person back into the past, or catapult her far into the future, time travel for me meant being fully, and almost constantly, in the present. Because there was no script prepared for me, and no time machine to "Beam me up," my journey into the present was gradual.

Pain—first in my hands and legs, a few months later in my screaming, locked knees—acted like a brain magnet. When all you can think about is the pain you're feeling, your mind is quarantined in the present. Cancer, the diagnosis, was next to bind my attention in the present. Once diagnosed, cancer rooted in my thoughts like the most vicious poisonous vine. It choked off my future; it strangled my past.

Throughout the diagnostic process, like a numb automaton, I existed unhappily in the present. "Go here, go there, have this test, have that." Why think about the future? Why anticipate meaning? It was too scary, the waters too murky.

I was living fully in the present, but it was a bad, bad scene.

In March, a shift began with my New York City visit and meeting Dr. George Wong and Helen Marx. A couple of months later, when Dr. Treon advised me to enjoy every day, my initial reaction was indignation. Was he patronizing me with trite advice? Quite the reverse, I'd soon realize.

By early summer, a deeper shift occurred. Ongoing twice daily meditations pinned me in the present. I became mindful of it, and felt calm living in it.

With the start of the Twelve Weeks, and my initiation to the rigorous routine the clinical trial prescribed, my time travel narrowed. To stay sane, I needed to stay in the present. Looking back, thinking about why I was sick, had no upside. It distracted my energy, and I needed to harbor all the energy I could. Looking ahead was too demanding, too hard. To contemplate Twelve Weeks of drugs was too taxing, too frightening. The only way to get through this was in small chunks of time.

For example, I was given a booklet: *Alemtuzemab For Injection Treatment Diary*. There were five categories:

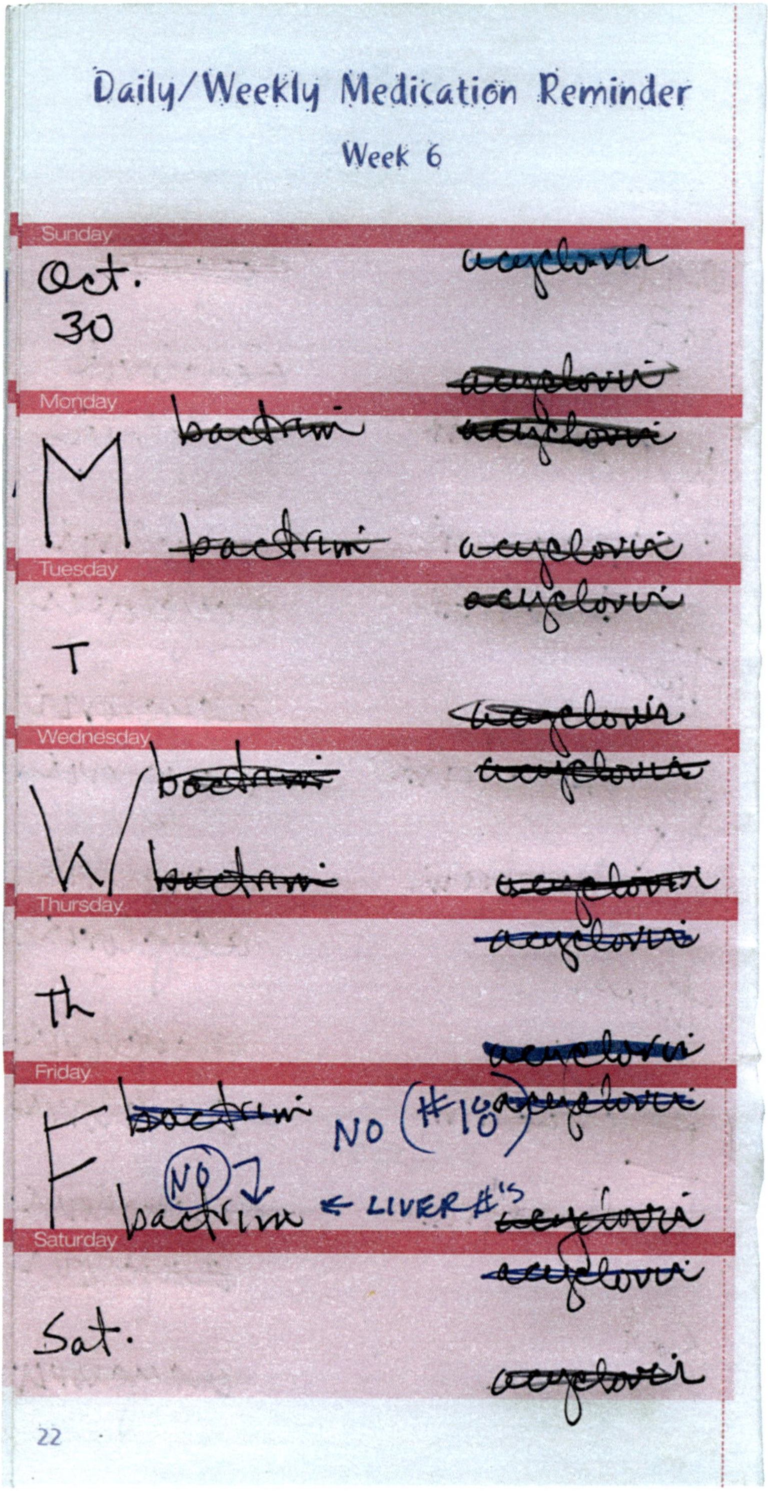

Daily/Weekly Medication Reminder

Week 6

Sunday

Oct. 30

~~acyclovir~~ ~~acyclovir~~

Monday

M

~~bactrim~~ ~~acyclovir~~

~~bactrim~~ acyclovir

Tuesday

T

~~acyclovir~~

~~acyclovir~~

Wednesday

W

~~bactrim~~ ~~acyclovir~~

~~bactrim~~ ~~acyclovir~~

Thursday

Th

~~acyclovir~~

~~acyclovir~~

Friday

F

~~bactrim~~ NO (#10) ~~acyclovir~~

(NO) ↓ bactrim ← LIVER #'s ~~acyclovir~~

Saturday

Sat.

~~acyclovir~~

~~acyclovir~~

22

Tracking Progress,
Medications to Take,
Blood Count Tracking,
Appointment / Treatment / Symptom Tracking Calendar, and
Daily / Weekly Medication Reminder.

Just reading the titles was jarring. For each category, there were pages of charts, fill-in-the-blanks as you go. Twelve weeks worth of charts, day-by-day, blow-by-blow. Way too overwhelming, and far too intimidating a set of calendars. I was willing to be meticulous, but not obsessive-compulsive about cataloging my medical records. The only section that I employed, and relied on, was the last: *Daily / Weekly Medication Reminder.*

For dose escalation week, no supplemental drugs were prescribed. On the Sunday before Week One began, Dr. Treon asked that I take Acyclovir, the anti-viral drug, morning and evening. Starting on Day One of Week One, I'd be taking two Acyclovir pills every day, and two Bactrim antibiotic pills every Monday, every Wednesday, and every Friday—alemtuzumab infusion days.

To keep the timeframe narrow and my mental commitment focused, I filled out and set up the drug reminder page one week at a time. Every Sunday during the Twelve Weeks of the clinical trial, and for an additional eight weeks after, I carefully wrote the names Acyclovir and Bactrim in the appropriate calendar boxes. A seven-day plan I could manage; a twenty week plan intimidated me.

Forgetting to take the pills wasn't an option, so I set up a drug station on the old oak chest, the one with the mirror, in our dining room. I chose a strategic position for the weekly chart and the two pill containers—the corner of the chest closest to the kitchen. Methodically, I took the pills and crossed out their names each day.

At Dana-Farber, I embodied the motto: "One day at a time." With a sophisticated, mathematical mind, Bill has a natural ease with numbers. As Week Three concluded, he said, "We're one quarter through." I heard, but blocked out the statistic that represented a milestone of sorts. As Week Four ended, he said, "We're one third through." I appreciated Bill's tracking time, but getting through each single day was the only accounting method I could handle.

My particular adventure in time travel became a rich gift. Preoccupied with plans, or anxieties, or worries, for much of my previous life, this cancer experience helped free me from unhealthful habits, and permit me to see, hear, and feel the present.

I trained myself not to look at my watch or at clocks. In the infusion room, what was the point? The flow of drugs from the pharmacy was only loosely predictable. Some days, my nurses received my bags of drugs at perfect intervals, with each appearing precisely when the one preceding it had emptied its hydrating or anaesthetizing contents into my veins. Other days, depending on the number of scheduled appointments and emergency admissions, and the complexity of other patients' prescriptions, a delivery of my medications could be delayed for hours.

Precise timing set the pace for the preliminary drugs I needed to have before my body could tolerate alemtuzumab. Once alemtuzumab arrived and the clock and pump on the IV stand were set, scheduled to release the 30 milligrams dose during two hours exactly, time took on a different persona. At rigid intervals, two drops of alemtuzumab exited their bag and began the slide down through yards of clear plastic IV tubing. I noticed them, I watched them. From my heart and soul, I talked to them, cheering them on to attack, defeat, and conquer the cancer.

When alemtuzumab's biological weapon was released and its baggie arsenal drained, the pump sounded an alarm. Once Suzanne caught on to my wandering ways, she taught me how to read the machinery so I'd know when the infusion was almost complete. Usually, the nurse or assistant would ask me to be back at my seat when the alarm was due to sound. He or she would meet me there, and "pull the needle." Occasionally, we'd make a deal to meet at a certain spot in the ward, near the nurse's desk, for example, and the needle would be pulled right there. It gave me some responsibility, and I liked being part of the team.

When Suzanne mentioned we wanted to get the last few ccs of alemtuzumab into me for good measure by letting the IV run for a few more minutes after the timer beeped, that became a mission for me.

Some days unexpected events seemed to stop time. "Code Blue: Dana 2" over the loudspeaker always grabbed my attention and rallied my compassion. A platoon of nurses racing out of the ward, only to return flanking a stretcher with a patient in distress, embodied emergency. With renewed respect for the medical team, and prayers for the patient, my heart and soul extended beyond me.

At night, I'd awaken often. Here, too, I trained my eyes to avoid the clock. Seeing the time only made me feel anxious—it was late, it was early, would I be unable to fall asleep, unable to get enough sleep. Ignoring man's measure of time removed one source of stress and let natural processes take the time they needed.

Devoted Doctor

As high as my respect and as deep as my trust was for my doctor prior to the Twelve Weeks, both intensified during them. In treatment he represented to me all hope and all health.

The Twelve Weeks were punctuated by mostly unplanned encounters with Dr. Treon. Always, Bill and I greeted him with pleasure, respect, and optimism, as he greeted us. When he gave us updates on my medical progress, he was informative and frank. As he began to see indications that the signs of disease were retreating, his support and encouragement buoyed my spirits and sustained my commitment to be cancer-free. Whether he was present in the infusion room or not, he was my lightning rod of trust and hope.

When my body ran into trouble—rigors the first day and again at the end of Week One, elevated liver enzymes at the end of Week Six, a violent rash when the clinical trial was through—Dr. Treon knew what to do and how to fix it. Either in person or by phone, he was always in touch.

In the infusion room, Dr. Treon would stop by to see Bill and me to say hello and to monitor my progress. He listened, educated us, and kept me and my treatment on track.

But it was our chance encounters that fanned the fires of my belief in being cured.

Preferring to stand in the hall rather than sit in the waiting room, Bill and I bided our time on Monday, Wednesday, and Friday mornings until my name was called and we entered the infusion room. Often, as he moved quickly between the clinic and the treatment area, Dr. Treon would spot us and stop to talk. He'd give us his total attention along with a progress report. Invariably, the news was good, the disease was declining, and his excitement was palpable, as was his support and appreciation for Bill's and my efforts to keep the positive trend going.

On October 17th, Dr. Treon told us he'd checked on my IgM. The numbers showed the disease was already in major remission. They looked "super," and he would reschedule the next six weeks of treatment for a total of twelve.

A month later, my notes say:

16 Nov. Dr. Treon

I was just looking at your #'s. 568. In addition to IgM, there's something we call the M spike, and yours is starting to go down. I just told Suzanne there's a good chance you can extinguish the entire clone. Keep up the good work.

Dr. Treon told us the M-spike characterizes tumor-made IgM. A decreasing M-spike indicated declining tumor activity. We were striking at the cancer's lifeline!

The M-spike currently registered 2.62. In my mind's eye, I saw it decline to zero. I pictured the entire malignant clone utterly gone, and my blood and body totally cancer-free. I saw it and I felt it as if it were already the case. My doctor's phrases of encouragement buoyed my spirits. I shared them with my nurses and incorporated them into my meditations as mantras.

Even if Dr. Treon and I exchanged only a look or a quick greeting, his presence elevated my mood. During long days, as I walked the length of the treatment area, my body was restricted to stay within its bounds, but my gaze and my thoughts were free to roam. In the intake area, or in the kitchenette, I'd stand still and look through the vertical glass panels in the exit doors. In the waiting room, or beyond it in the clinic area, I'd occasionally catch a glimpse of my doctor. For me, he was hope and health personified.

He still is.

In this deadly combat, this football game from hell, my doctor was my medical coach, quarterback, and cheerleader, and I was the front line. For the same support and more, on the emotional and daily survival fronts, my husband's devotion and constant hard work enabled me to stay in the game.

Super Spouse

When conversations around me triggered my anxieties, or nearby patients' IV needles were being installed, flight was my defense. Up I stood, and off I went, abandoning Bill as I sought self-preservation.

Stalwart and still, Bill sat. Pen in one hand, newspaper in the other, he worked puzzles. A devotee of crossword puzzles since his college days, he finds relaxation and pleasure in solving them. In August, I'd spotted a new puzzle form in *The Boston Globe* and had set it on Bill's book table where it remained unnoticed. During the second of the Twelve Weeks, as he perused a newspaper at Dana-Farber, he discovered this puzzle form himself, solved it, and showed it to me with delight. Its name was Sudoku. From that day on, Sudoku became an anchor in Bill's daily routine.

Concentrating, silent, his mind managed the anxiety-provoking activities and conversations swirling around him. Months later, it occurred to me that Sudoku was one of my husband's forms of meditation, and a screen to keep him grounded and sane in tough circumstances.

Just as Propel, oranges, and peanut butter and jelly sandwiches became my steady diet on alemtuzumab days, Bill, too, had his comfort food. For him, it was a Subway sandwich, purchased at the food court and eaten as he sat with me.

In the unpredictable environment of a infusion room, being able to count on something—even if it's your sandwich—is a beautiful thing.

Through it all, Bill was truly the "Super Spouse." Respecting my needs and wants, but never intruding, he cared for Sara and me tirelessly. As his waves of energy kept us afloat, at one point I told him he was the Energizer Bunny, in real life.

Doctors, nurses, all the staff, and many patients valued Bill's presence and upbeat attitude. During baseball playoffs, he talked Red Sox with the most devoted fans among the staff. As football season rolled along, he talked New England Patriots with them.

Late in the Twelve Weeks, Bill had to leave the infusion room to attend a meeting. My assigned station that day was deep inside the largest room, my least favorite. My chair was next to the nurses' station about as far away from the entrance as it could be. With a wet cold running through me, I ran through boxes of tissues. I worried that the nearby nurse was annoyed with all my noisy nose blowing. I worried more that she might catch whatever I had.

As Bill stood to go, I said "Good bye, Bill."

As he left me and walked through the ward, passing a couple of other nursing stations on his way, I heard a melodic chorus rise and float back to me. "Good bye, Bill," spoken by dozens of voices, rose to greet him as he passed by. Voice after voice, some overlapping, some solo, expressed comradeship and appreciation to my husband.

What a beautiful song!

On the Move, or, I Know Why the Polar Bear Paces

In the infusion room, I had some social—or really, antisocial—reactions that soon became automatic. I'd scan the area, swiftly and thoroughly registering the other patients and their companions. I'm tempted to say sidekicks, since always guest chairs are placed to the side of the patients' chairs. In addition to the obvious—sex, age, nationality, color—over time, it became relatively easy to pick up on a patient's degree of distress, discomfort or anxiety. This done, I would pull my attention back to my own small circle of space. I found it essential to keep my mental and emotional resources within myself.

Hearing a doctor or a nurse ask another patient detailed questions, listening to a patient's graphic language about cancer history or current pain, or drug reactions, or emotions, had the ability to distract, unnerve, and upset me. In dire straits myself, I couldn't afford those liabilities.

So I would leave. Escape. Literally. As best I could. If I hadn't yet seen my nurse or begun receiving drugs, I would stand up and wander away to a quieter spot. If my IV was running, I would take my pole with me and walk away. Bill seemed to have the self-possession to stay put. At the time I assumed he screened out other people's conversations. Over time I've come to believe he heard them all, and somehow managed to cope.

Amid the tumult of other patients' settling in, and the physical and mental control I needed to exert over myself, there was neither time, energy, or desire for my husband and me to talk about our respective experiences. Always, as I abandoned my station and my husband, I admired his staying power and felt a pang of guilt for stranding him. But strand him I did.

There was a second situation that got me on my feet and on the move. It took a good eight weeks before I could articulate this to myself, and finally to Bill.

"The drugs make me feel lousy."

In the first instance, I moved to escape from other people. In the second, I moved to escape from myself.

Every single day I would open a book, perhaps a novel, or Spanish grammar. Every single day I would tell myself this day would be different, this day I would relax, sit, and take it easy. Always tired, I would tell myself this day I would nap. Once the drugs started running, reading was good for fifteen minutes, max. Napping, or trying to nap, had the same narrow time slot. Discomfort drove me to my feet. A groggy head and a blurry abdomen would seize my awareness as I sat. On my feet, on the move, I invariably felt better. I told myself my body's movement facilitated almetuzumab's circulation through it.

In my observation, most patients stay seated and stay still. As they receive chemotherapy, people read, snooze, chat, and watch television. In the first few days of walking the ward, I was self-centered and sometimes felt myself intruding on the nurses' turf. As my IV pole management skills improved and I was better able to modulate my body's movements, I learned to defer to the nurses' right of way. The last thing I wanted was to be a nuisance.

My route was fixed, determined by the ward's layout. From my seat, be it in a large area, a small alcove, or a private bedroom, depending on the placement of the day, I'd enter the main hall, the spine that connected the infusion bays. With my IV pole in my hand and by my side, I'd walk from one end of the infusion room to the other. Again and again and again. When I reached the hall's end, to reverse direction I'd pivot to make a turn, clockwise if the IV needle were in my right arm, counter-clockwise if it were in my left.

Although my route never varied, I was never bored. The nurses fascinated me. Watching their patterns of movement—to the patients, to the pharmacy, to their desks—was intriguing. In silent observation, I picked up on personalities, personal styles, and person to person relationships. Trying to stay out of their way, hoping not to be a bother, I found I earned the nurses' interest and respect. Beautifully, in time, this blossomed into friendships. Sometimes, if a nurse had a few moments between duties, and my IV pole and I happened to be near her, I benefited from profoundly encouraging and enlightening conversation.

For instance, on two different days early in the clinical trial, two of the nurses, Carol and Natalie, expressed interest in the drug I was getting and enthusiasm for the wonderful results they'd seen other patients get from alemtuzumab.

Another example is a conversation with a nurse named Rosemarie, she of the colorful sandals imprinted with images of exotic people and places, the sandals similar to mine. On Day One of Week Four, Rosemarie happened to have a few free minutes. When I encountered her on my stroll, she asked me how it was going. I told her both the excellent news—that alemtuzumab was beating back the cancer—and my vision: that I'd be cancer-free and healthy. With generosity and enthusiasm, she supported my vision.

Immediately after Rosemarie and I spoke, I returned to my chair of the day, uncharacteristically opened my green loose leaf binder, and recorded our conversation. My notes say:

17 Oct. 05 Rosemarie

Hindus believe: power / influence of the mind.

Have to visualize the full process:

see the alemtuzumab going to the cancer

see it destroying cancer

see body cancer-free

see body rebuilding / healing / healthy

Ok— in fact necessary—to admit the negative—part of the process—normal part—not natural to not allow it in.

Being happy all the time is manic—causes disease.

Thank you Rosemarie

Rosemarie's philosophy was so visual, so comprehensive, and so vibrant that it immediately became a core component of my meditation. As a result, I embraced the alemtuzumab and cure in an even fuller way.

When I noticed an extra large bottle of Propel on Nurse Marissa's desk, she and I bonded over our beverage of choice.

And Laura! My assigned nurse for only two days of forty—the first day, and Columbus Day—Laura monitored my progress religiously. Out of the blue, she'd comment on my steadily declining IgM. Her demeanor was reserved, but her eyes shone with excitement.

Catching the drift of my drifting, Suzanne cued me in to the timer on my IV pump. Many days she'd confer with me, and make a plan for me to either be in my seat or meet up with her when it was time for a change of drugs, or when the alemtuzumab dose of the day was finished. It gave me some responsibility, and we were a good team.

One day Suzanne turned from her desk and said she knew I was coming because she could feel my warmth as I approached. A ray of sunshine, she called me. What a compliment!

Oncology nurses work hard, and their energies and attention are with their patients. Over the course of the Twelve Weeks, separate from our primary focus on my care, my medications and my well-being, Suzanne and I found moments here and there to exchange thoughts about our children, our families, and our lives. Picturing her kids playing soccer or performing in a concert lifted my thoughts out of the cancer zone and humanized the experience of being confined there.

Another group that caught my attention were the young science investigators. While making his rounds during Week Two, Dr. Treon introduced me to two young staff members who were part of his research team. Emanating youth and health, Chris Patterson and Jake Soumeri made a point of checking my chart and checking in with me. Seeing them automatically raised my spirits and helped me feel better.

My gentle guide, Zachary Hunter, would swing by the infusion room from time to time. Behind his nonchalant manner, he was a creative and dynamic researcher. Publicly he came to chat, privately he monitored my progress. His presence became a touchstone of friendship for my husband and me.

Acknowledging their dedication, Dr. Treon calls his group "The Mighty Team."

In the infusion room, intangible forces were at work.

As I walked, a conundrum appeared. To make eye contact, or avoid it? So much emotion was expressed in patients' eyes, but how to make meaning of it? If I smiled, would I seem arrogant? If I kept a stone face, would I seem heartless? Remember, I had a plethora of my own feelings—emotional and physical—in play all the time, too. Unsure, I took a neutral course, looking straight ahead, avoiding eye contact with other patients as best I could.

But I'm no iceberg. Very early on, as I sat in my big chair in a small bay, I observed a beautiful young woman talking with a nurse. With curly blond hair, blue eyes, and porcelain skin, she seemed like a cherub who had come to grace the infusion room and show the rest of us a picture of health. I assumed she was a visitor. Wrong. She was a patient, and she was in pain. Neuropathy in her legs rendered her near tears. I saw she had a cane, which she leaned on heavily.

There was a couple, Rob and Maggie. In their early sixties, they were a unit. He was the patient, she held his hand. She told Bill and me Rob had liver cancer. His doctors had said he'd be dead a year and a half ago. But here they still were, coming for periodic chemotherapy, seeing that as a small and manageable price to pay for the privilege of his being alive, their being together, and having time to enjoy with their family.

One Friday, seated in the chair I had on October 12th, was a young man. Maybe thirty. Blond, virile looking, with a sweet disposition. A truck driver. Why was he here? In three months time, he was hoping for a liver transplant.

One time I observed a lively, almost raucous group. An older man and woman, a young man and woman. As much as I thought I'd abandoned preconceptions, I was taken aback to see that it was the robust young man who sat in the big chair. It was he who had the cancer. The laughing, loving, caring group around him formed a ring of security that was tangible.

A different day, as I sat in the largest section of the infusion room, a doctor delivered the best news to a young African American woman. A PET scan showed that her cancer was gone! Preoccupied and tormented by pain in her feet, the patient was unable to share her doctor's joy.

Another woman, Josette, I'd seen once or twice before. During Week Ten, we were seated side by side. She had breast cancer. She'd had previous rounds of treatments. She was expecting to lose her hair, again. She and her husband disagreed on wig style, but Josette planned to stick with her favorite. She told me she'd take the opportunity to sleep while she received her chemotherapy, then she'd return to work. Remarkable. After my treatments, I could barely function.

Week Eleven. An elderly, elegant European couple shared my bay. He was the patient, and he needed the bed. He was experiencing intense pain. Talk of kidney problems, and the mention of my doctor's name, led me to conclude the gentleman and I had the same disease, but he had a long and troubled history with it. Despite his agony, he and his wife maintained an intimate, almost passionate rapport during several hours. Eventually, drugs reduced his pain. His relief was tangible. Relaxation emanated from him and his wife.

Week Twelve. A Vietnamese man, along with five female relatives, shared that same bay with me. He was the patient, and this day he needed the bed. Although I didn't understand his language, his screams were pain personified. He seemed to feel isolated, alone, desperate for help. It took a long time, but he too was eventually relieved from his suffering.

Also during that last week, I saw my first private party. A woman, fifty-something, was completing a chemotherapy cycle. But she was worried, and repeatedly raised questions and concerns about ongoing symptoms and recurring disease. When a group of nurses delivered a cake and non-alcoholic wine to her, a gift of congratulations of sorts, her worry left no room for acknowledging the milestone she'd reached.

In a single treatment center, patients' cancers, their treatment cycles, and their scheduling have a great deal of variation. On any given day I was receiving my treatment, the mix of patients would be random. Even so, there were three women whom I saw repeatedly. Each in her own way became significant for me. With each I formed a bond, one in silence, two in friendship.

With the first woman, I never shared a word, or even eye contact. She was tiny, middle-aged, and simply seeing her broke my heart. Roundish, raw-looking wounds splattered over her neck, her face, and her head. Always, she was accompanied by a tall, handsome young man. Always, she needed the back bedroom. Always, she moved toward it silently and slowly, but with determination, in the lead as the young man trailed behind.

To me she looked very, very sick. I guessed her pain to be unbearable, and her prognosis grim. I suspected this is what Kaposes Syndrome looked like, and I assumed she had the type of skin cancer associated with HIV/AIDS.

Over the course of seven or eight weeks, I probably saw this pair sporadically five or six times. Toward the end of my Twelve Weeks, as I stood in the outer lobby, I was astounded when I saw them again. The woman's scars were completely healed; her complexion was flawless. Still in the lead, she carped shrewishly at the young man. What a transformation of physique and behavior. I marveled at the miraculous change.

With Tanya, the second woman, I developed a bond and a friendship. Both extended to her husband Tad. It was she who made the first overture.

On October 12th, as Bill and I sat in our station awaiting my nurse and my IV needle, I reached in my bag, extracted John Milton's *Paradise Lost*, and began to read.

"You must be a high school English teacher."

The statement came from Tanya, seated opposite me and to my left. Her husband sat at her side. Both were about my age.

No, I explained. My daughter was a high school student, and I had the privilege of being introduced to this epic poem thanks to her.

We four exchanged pleasantries then fell silent, awaiting the main event: chemo for her, alemtuzumab for me.

Over the next few weeks, from time to time I'd see Tanya and Tad when her treatment days coincided with mine. Circulating through the ward, I'd sometimes stop to chat with this amiable and devoted couple.

As November ended, our two main topics were history and literature. History because my daughter was immersed in researching the 1970 murders at Kent State, and Tad was both knowledgeable and passionate about the event and the era. Literature because Tanya, a college professor, knew I'd forged my way though *Paradise Lost*.

During one extended chat, Tanya and Tad urged me to sit and join them at her chemo station. That being more commitment than I could offer, I declined and took off to continue my walk with my IV pole.

There came a day during Week Eleven when Tad and I encountered each other in the hall near the kitchenette. Feeling a connection of friendship, Tad spoke to me of his wife's condition. Her cancer was a fast-mutating sarcoma that adapted quickly to chemotherapies. There were only four drugs available for this sarcoma. The first three had failed; she was now receiving the fourth, and last. Even more than his words, Tad's face and his voice conveyed despair. Of course I listened and took in the information, but it was very difficult for me to bear. Confiding in me as a friend, Tad seemed to brush aside the fact that I was a cancer patient, too. As soon as I could, I excused myself and fled.

Single-minded as I was about my drug's outsmarting my cancer, Tad's information opened a door I didn't want. For Tanya, her cancer was outsmarting her drugs.

As for the third woman, I met her by official introduction. During Week Three, Dr. Treon respectfully asked if I might be willing to talk with a new Waldenstrom's Macroglobulinemia patient whom he was about to give alemtuzumab. Patient privacy laws and medical ethics prohibited him from speaking about me or my case to others, but no such restrictions limited me. Especially in the early days, chatting with patients took me out of my comfort zone, but saying no to my doctor wasn't an option. My IV pole and I followed him to the new patient's station.

Dr. Treon introduced me to Lianne. She and her companion listened attentively as I told about alemtuzumab making inroads into my disease, and my declining IgM counts. My story was factual, and the facts were encouraging. Alemtuzumab was showing itself effective in beating back my lymphoma. As the same drug dripped into us both, Lianne's expression brightened with hope that it would also beat back hers.

Although she offered me a seat next to her, my IV pole and I chose to remain standing, so I could make a quick getaway when the conversation became too much for me. Telling Lianne what I'd learned about the importance of staying hydrated, I offered her a bottle of Propel. She appreciatively accepted.

In the infusion room, anyone's success gives everyone hope.

Television became a companion of sorts, or at least a diversion. Never a big fan of TV, I rarely watch it. But as I walked, I'd sometimes pause and observe the action on other patients' TV screens.

Baseball and football game highlights, Meredith Viera's fabulous cheekbones, vintage cartoon shows. For a few moments here and there, they'd hold my attention and add color, action, and distraction to my time.

Instead of sitting still and staring at my colorful shoes for endless hours, as I'd imagined I would, I walked endless miles in them. At first, my steps were small and my pace slow. As the weeks progressed and the treatment began to beat back the cancer, little by little walking became easier and more normal. Eventually my pacing pattern elicited unanticipated reactions. From their chairs patients would nod their encouragement, or gaily say things like "It's great that you walk. I should do it, too."

Many, many months after the Twelve Weeks ended, a realization came to me. In the 1970's, living and working in Manhattan, I'd often pass through the Central Park Zoo. I found one of the polar bears mesmerizing. Too big for his man-made domain, confined beyond reason, this bear paced in perpetual motion. His path was always the same. The rhythm of his steps, and the pattern of his turns, never varied. I wondered how he did it, why he didn't go insane.

In my Twelve Weeks, in my place of confinement, repetitive motion helped me stay sane.

I know why the polar bear paces, and why I did, too. We did it because we had to. It was automatic, and it was necessary. For us, moving affirmed living.

Symbols of Hope at Home

I lived in two opposite universes, parallel and intertwined. One involved the rigor and discipline of the clinical trial, receiving an experimental drug for a disease termed incurable. The other centered on my conviction that, as a result of the clinical trial, I would become cancer-free and healthy. Always, I had to keep both universes in balance.

In my dining room, just opposite my medication station, stands a fish tank. Inside is one fish, a goldfish. Ten years ago my daughter named this fish Goldie. As Goldie grew, we replaced small tanks with bigger ones; she's now almost eleven inches long. From time to time, we'd pulled her back from the brink of death. Frolicking when we passed by, slurping noisily at the water's surface when she wanted food, Goldie behaved more like a puppy than a fish.

During the Twelve Weeks, whenever I passed the fish tank, or even as I sat in the dining room, I'd fix my gaze on Goldie and see in her a vital life force that reaffirmed my own. If the goldfish had defied death and won, what an inspiration for me!

In the botanical realm I found more symbols of life and hope. Two hibiscus trees stood in our living room, in the back corner where Bill likes to relax, read, and do puzzles. As long as I could see one flower in bloom on one of the trees, I saw a continuum of life for me. The trees never failed to flower.

Through October the evenings were warm. With sunset being my favorite time, if I had the strength on non-alemtuzumab days I'd walk along the banks of the Charles. In the white sails of boats, I saw white blood cells—mine: IgM—too much of it. As the light dimmed, fewer and fewer boats remained on the water. Their diminishing numbers symbolized my diminishing cancer. As I watched until the last boat docked and its last sail furled, I pictured the last of the cancer cells disappearing forever.

Symbols of Hope at Dana-Farber

Because my mind was set to think positive thoughts and to see positive signs, these came to me even within the cancer hospital. Alternately standing and pacing just outside the reception area, waiting for a nurse's assistant to call my name and escort me into the clinic, I happened to glance down the wide hallway that connects the Dana building to the Mayer building. At the far end I saw a large rectangular fish tank. Intrigued, I went to check it out. Three fish inhabited the water. Two were sunshine yellow, the same color but different species. The third was much larger, and deep black. Black—the traditional color of death. But I needed a positive spin here, so I created a positive symbol for myself. In this black fish, and his quick, agile shifts of direction, I saw alemtuzumab as it zeroed in on my cancer cells and exterminated them. The fish symbolized an angel of death, but in a good way, because what was dying was cancer.

As for the yellow fish, they were sunshine and silliness. Curiously, I felt each of the three to be extremely lonely.

Down this same hallway, on the floor, an equally powerful symbol lay. Just about the time my M-spike was registering 2.62, I discovered that the hallway's floor depicted the route of the Boston Marathon.

The starting point, in Hopkinton, was closest to the fish tank. Its mile marker: 26.2. The finish line, in Boston, was closest to the infusion room. If that mile marker were noted, it would read: 0.0.

As I noticed the coincidences of the numbers, my own mental mini-marathon was born. Walking the path of the floor's graphic marathon route, from start to finish, I visualized the 2.62 M-spike diminishing steadily until it became 0.0.

Zero cancer. Zero monoclonal gammopathy.

Good Vibrations

To help reduce my overall anxiety, I'd stopped watching the nightly news and reading the daily newspaper. But, as often happens, I made one exception and that exception opened the way for a new dimension of complementary or holistic integrative medicine to join my process.

On Thursday, November 24th, a day off from alemtuzumab, I took a look at the "Styles" section of *The New York Times*. An article titled "What's the Buzz? Sound Therapy" caught my eye. It spoke of Dr. Mitchell Gaynor, a New York City oncologist, who'd been introduced to Tibetan singing bowls by a patient, himself a Tibetan monk.

Over time, Dr. Gaynor came to understand the power of sound vibration as a healing tool, even for cancer patients. Intrigued by the article, I ordered his book, *The Healing Power of Sound*. According to laboratory research with cancer cells and clinical observation of patients, sound vibration can have a profound influence on cell health, as well as disease. According to one of the book's main premises, cancer cells can't tolerate dissonance, and break apart when subjected to it.

Well this was big news! Weak as I was, I leapt into action. Only a couple of apartments abut ours, and assuming my neighbors were out, I planted myself at the piano. Banging and barking, yowling and howling, I pictured the cancer cells cracking up under the aural assault.

Just reading *The Healing Power of Sound* set up waves of optimism within me. My mind seemed brighter and my body, lighter, as if my cells were already vibrating at a higher, healthier frequency. Very much alone at this time, still respecting my rule of self-selected house arrest, and further limited by the strange cold, I felt the need to reach out and try to connect with Dr. Gaynor. Locating his New York City office phone number, I dialed.

When I told the receptionist I'd just finished reading the doctor's book and was interested in the singing bowls, she offered the name and number of the bowls' distributor. She also mentioned that Dr. Gaynor had made a cassette tape that incorporated sounds and music. For twenty dollars, that definitely held appeal.

A few days after I'd mailed my check, the tape arrived. A few days later, I listened to it. Since it was a cassette tape, once again my antique portable Panasonic Walkman cassette player from 1984 became my companion.

Lying still, weakened by alemtuzumab, and worried by the strange cold, I listened. As I listened, sound and imagination carried me above my preoccupations with my varied bodily conditions into a larger, more peaceable realm. Along with musicians and non-Western healers, Dr. Gaynor had created and recorded a series of meditations; some guided by his voice, some wordless vocalizations or pure music. While I had some familiarity with guided meditation from DMA and my own evolving daily meditations, much of the sound and music was unfamiliar. Otherworldly sounds, rhythms, pacing, and flow—all became calming. For two or three weeks in the final phase of the clinical trial, imagining myself free and well, listening to the tape became a physical and mental refuge.

Weird and Wet

On December 7th, the Wednesday of Week Eleven, a bit of a scratchy throat began. By Friday, more cold-like symptoms appeared. Suzanne told me this was more or less normal and of no real concern. If fever or chills developed, well, that would be a different story.

A weird combination of symptoms evolved, and I found myself coughing a wet, almost incessant cough, and running through a box of tissues every day. I took to wearing a mask during my treatments, not to protect myself from germs, but to shield other people from my germs. Behind my mask, as my IV pole and I paced, I hummed roughly to myself, employing Dr. Gaynor's dissonance principle to break up my cancer cells. When I realized other people could hear my humming through the mask, I ceased the practice. No need to be annoying.

At home watching Bill's and Sara's concerned expressions, I worried that they were worried about me. Sleeping became even more minimal than it already was, as I coughed through the nights. But it never crossed my mind to stop getting the drugs.

#39, and Prudence Visits

December 16th, the day of my next-to-last treatment at Dana-Farber, was the day of my friend Dan Miller's first treatment there.

Eighty-four years old, Bill's colleague had been diagnosed during my dose escalation week with lung and liver cancer. Dan had decided to go ahead with treatment in the hope of extending his life. Prudence King, Dan's soul mate of twenty-eight years, accompanied him to Dana-Farber, but took a break to visit me.

Prudence and I spoke every week, so she knew I was fully enlisted as a cancer patient, and I knew Dan's health had been steadily deteriorating.

Feeling optimistic about Dan's treatment, Prudence came to me in a positive mood. That particular day I'd been assigned to a back corner in a big space. It had a bed, but I preferred to perch on the small guest chair. Looking around, Prudence remarked that the infusion room upstairs was more pleasant, with windows and fancier furniture.

Hearing about my role as a patient was one thing; seeing me in it was quite another. My normally composed friend was visibly rocked by the sight of me tethered to my IV stand, yards of clear plastic tubing, and drugs. She chatted brightly, but she was thrown off-balance by the scene. Our visit was warm, awkward, and short. Close as we were as friends, and with all that she knew about my situation, she was clearly startled to see me replete with IV apparatus.

And of course we were both aware that a few floors above us, Dan, too, was hooked up.

#40, and a Moment of Math

To keep the record accurate, here's a moment of math; that is, a tally of the infusion room visits and treatments.

	Infusion Room Visits	Treatments
Dose Escalation Week *Wednesday, Thursday and Friday*	3	3
Twelve Weeks *Monday, Wednesday and Friday*	36	35
One aborted treatment due to liver function concerns, so this treatment took place at the end.	1	1
Totals	40	39

At the final infusion room visit, the alemtuzumab prescription was delayed for hours. Eventually, close to one o'clock, we learned that the pharmacist, adhering to the protocol of the clinical trial, had been refusing to fill the prescription. As he saw it, there had already been 39 appointments, and the alemtuzumab prescription could be filled only 39 times.

Behind the scenes, unbeknownst to us, Dr. Treon had been working to convince the pharmacist that in fact only 38 doses of the drug had been administered. On November 4th, when blood test results had shown troublesome abnormalities in liver function, Dr. Treon had chosen caution, cancelled treatment, and sent me home. I received no alemtuzumab. By the following Monday, liver function tests indicated a stable situation, and treatment was resumed.

Today's treatment might look like number 40 on the calendar, but it was number 39 in the IV tube. A "makeup dose."

Truth won out, and eventually the pharmacist filled the prescription.

As the alemtuzumab dose traveled its regulated course at its regulated speed, from its bag to my blood, I alternately paced for a while, and then sat for a spell in a small guest's chair near my oversized patient's chair.

Toward the end of the treatment, as I rested and sat, Suzanne and six nurses appeared in front of me. One held a white cake box, one a bottle shaped for wine.

Smiling, beaming, they sang to me. Although I don't remember the song, I'll always remember their happiness. I felt self-conscious as I smiled and accepted the warmth and respect these extraordinary women gave so generously.

I was anxious, antsy, really, to have this treatment routine over. I received #40, and completed the clinical trial.

Yet I felt uneasy amid this fond farewell.

I remembered my mother's advice when she knew my treatment would be starting soon: "Trust your doctor" and "Pretend it isn't happening to you." The first was a given, and indisputable. The second was more subtle.

Altogether there were forty appointments at the infusion room. Each day, before I checked in at the reception desk, in a public restroom I'd brush my hair and apply lip gloss. Only once during treatment did I glance in a restroom mirror inside the infusion room. It was the last day of the clinical trial. The act surprised me, and I realized I'd been intentionally avoiding seeing my reflection there, concentrating instead on looking at my hands, the soap, and the paper towel dispenser. Anything but my own face.

I later learned this might be what psychiatrists call dissociation. By not seeing my face reflected in the mirror, I was able to maintain some

measure of psychological distance from my placement in the infusion room.

A second distancing instinct also became habit. Centrally located within the infusion room, a white marker board showed the number of each patient station. As each patient arrived throughout the day, his or her name along with attending nurse's name, was recorded in black marker on the board. Early on, a quick glance revealed the nature and purpose of this daily calendar. From then on, although my mind would register its sober presence on the wall, never did my eyes rest long enough to read the names, or to locate my own. Like seeing my reflection in the mirror here, seeing my name on the board would have identified and fixed me in that place. I needed to avoid feeling attached to it in any permanent way. To me, the mirror and the marker board were fixtures, and I was just passing through.

After

Rash

By December 19th, the day of the last treatment, my notes say that a bad mucous cough had joined my scratchy throat and running nose.

The clinical trial was finished, but this strange cold wasn't. It stayed with me, becoming a burden. Little did I know that the cold would soon become the least of my worries.

Although potent doses of alemtuzumab were no longer being injected into my veins, those I'd already received would continue to circulate through me for several more weeks. My body still churned from intravenous infusions, and the bizarre cold wouldn't quit. The clinical trial's home medication protocol continued. For two more months, the antiviral medicine Acyclovir was required twice a day everyday, and the antibiotic Bactrim was required twice a day, three times a week. Both were prophylactic, as my immune system was non-existent.

On Friday, December 23rd, my patience with the wet cold ran out. Calling Dr. Treon, I described the white water rapids of clear mucous as gurgles. Basically, I begged for an antibiotic to squelch it.

"Levaquin should get it," Dr. Treon said, and called in the prescription.

When I reported an itchy rash between my shoulder blades, the doctor advised me to keep an eye on it, and reminded me I was doing well. Lacking eyes in the back of my head, I relied on an adjustable mirror to follow my doctor's advice.

By December 29th, with seven of the ten Levaquin taken, I called Dr. Treon and was surprised to find him at the lab. I reported that 95% of the mysterious cold was gone. Once or twice each day I'd have a coughing spell and a fluid feeling remained in my chest, but the nose no longer ran like a broken faucet. But the rash now stretched across both shoulders, reached over my collarbones, and slid along the sides of my ribcage. Red skin showed bumps. Christmas had been an emotional time, and occasional palpitations bothered me.

To quell the rash, a couple of days of twenty-four hour Claritin, plus 1% hydrocortisone cream were suggested.

About the palpitations, "Don't work yourself up," Dr. Treon advised. "Among all the people on the study, you've done the best. You're the flagship."

What an encouraging image! Visualizing myself as the sculpture on the bow of a ship, back arched, hair flowing, gaze lifted to the sky, I felt happy, and stronger.

In addition to this personal lift, there were broader words of encouragement.

"The reason we're here at the lab today, a vacation day, is because we're really committed to keep working until we find a cure."

As 2005 faded and 2006 dawned, the rash became ruthless. By January 2nd, it blanketed most of me, but stopped at my wrists and knees. Delicate but angry red, web-like lines played connect-the-dots with red bumps on my breasts.

Believing Dr. Treon to be out of the country on holiday, and not wanting to intrude on his vacation and privacy, I scheduled an appointment with the covering physician. On Monday January 3rd, two weeks after we thought we'd said good-bye to Dana-Farber for a while, Bill and I were back in the clinic. I felt dazed and amazed. But even so, I was alert and aware enough to know I had to continue to pay attention to my body and advocate for my health.

I briefed the doctor on the alemtuzumab experience and told her I was currently taking Acyclovir, Bactrim, and Levaquin. Because the wet cough was back, she ordered a chest X-ray, to be sure there was no pneumonia. She sent me to the phlebotomy lab to have blood drawn, and suggested I see a dermatologist.

Calling the skin doctors whose names were provided, I was offered appointments several weeks into the future. Instinct told me this situation couldn't wait. With the help of Dr. Treon's secretary, I found a dermatologist who could see me in three days.

On that day, Bill delivered me to a low building not far from Dana-Farber that houses medical offices.

I soon found myself in a large, dark examination room, theatrical almost.

"The rash is impressive," the dermatologist said. The good news was she saw no signs of cancer. Skin cancer, that is. Feeling emotionally numb, I mentally checked out and gave in when the dermatologist's nurse prepped my arm for a skin biopsy. In about one week, the lab results would tell whether the rash was a drug reaction—but not which drug was the cause. In two weeks, I'd need to return to have the stitches removed.

In the meantime, I should monitor the rash to see if it spread. A prescription cream should relieve the itch and reduce the rash. Benadryl capsules would relieve the itch and make sleeping easier. Or so went the theory. On our way home, Bill stopped at Gary Drug, and as I waited in the car, the prescription was filled.

That same evening, I saw one of the signs that the rash continued to spread. The next day I called the doctor with the news: there were now red spots on my face, too.

Even as the skin situation worsened, the cancer news was very good. On Friday, January 6th, Dr. Treon's assistant told me that blood test results from January 3rd reported an IgM count of 168 and an M spike of .24. Three weeks earlier, on December 19th, the IgM count was 290, and the M spike .3. The alemtuzumab continued its work, and the cancer markers continued to diminish.

Although I applied the skin cream carefully and diligently, it was useless. The rash spread steadily, and irritation escalated to pain. On Saturday afternoon, while Bill took Sara and her friends on an adventure, incessant burning pain on my ears and hands made it impossible for me not to scratch constantly. As much as I hated to disturb a doctor on the weekend, I called the dermatologist. She had sympathy, but no suggestions.

That same day, Zachary Hunter and I spoke at length. I learned more about the cancer, and got a clue about the rash. During alemtuzumab treatment, he said, some reactions, such as rash, were suppressed by intravenous steroids and hydration. Once treatment stopped, the reactions sometimes reappeared.

Sunday everything exploded. My eyelids swelled. The rash seared my scalp, fell below my knees, and fondled my feet. Red dots were everywhere. The dermatologist's advice that night: apply the skin cream sparingly and with caution.

Monday morphed the dots into a near-continuous mass of welts. My skin became leathery. On a different front, Monday brought a piece of good news: the chest X-ray was normal, showing no evidence of cardiac or pulmonary involvement.

Throughout the many months of living with the knowledge I had cancer, and the many weeks of receiving alemtuzumab, meditation had been an anchor. With a still body and a calm mind, I'd been able to ride through pain, fatigue, and fear. Now, the skin situation kept my body jumping and my mind reacting. Meditation was out of the question. My private emotional mooring had come undone. Pain was in charge, and I had no means to manage it.

In high school biology, we learned that the skin is our body's largest organ. It still seems odd to me to consider skin an organ at all. But with almost all of mine inflamed, it provided the most dominating and incessantly torturous pain I'd ever experienced.

Searing physical pain and the mental preoccupation it demanded nailed me to the present. I couldn't even entertain the thought, "Enough already. Can I please be done now?"

Ruthlessly, relentlessly, the rash spread its territory and its terror. Like an evil prima donna, pain demanded center stage in my mind as my skin burned and swelled. Dr. Treon would soon be back.

On Tuesday, January 10th, at 5 o'clock, shaky, beaten down and close to broken by pain, I called him and described what I was experiencing. He mentioned a systemic steroid might be needed, but dermatology reactions were hard to predict, and could have many causes. He'd seen rash reactions in a couple of other patients.

When he asked me to come to the clinic the next day at noon, the thought crossed my mind: "How about now? Right now?" But politeness overrode pain, and I stayed with the next day's appointment.

My family had of course been watching me, and their faces registered their worry. With my skin screaming, my restlessness was palpable. Unable to sit for more than a few moments at a time, unable to bear the touch of all but the loosest clothing, unable to sleep altogether, I was becoming crazed.

By Tuesday evening my face was so badly swollen that my eyes were half-shut. Seeing the anxiety and concern on my daughter's face, I put on sunglasses, and wore them for the rest of that January night.

Somehow, I made it until noon the next day.

On Wednesday, January 8th, Bill and I returned to Dana-Farber. I had become the person I dreaded most: the one wearing dark glasses to hide the ugliness and the pain, the one sitting because she's too weak to stand, the one who appears to be in Big Trouble. I was the pariah: disfigured, disgusting, disguised.

As always, I chose seats at the edge of the waiting area. This day, Bill and I sat next to the path from the infusion room to the clinic. At one point, Suzanne hurried out of the infusion room on her way to the clinic. Spotting Bill and me, she of course paused to greet us. She was surprised to see us; just three weeks earlier, on December 19th, she'd administered my final alemtuzumab treatment and we'd bid each other a fond farewell, deep with mutual affection, friendship and respect. We'd not expected to see each other again so soon. Standing to greet this wonderful nurse, I lifted my sunglasses. Through my swollen eyelids, I saw Suzanne's usually composed face register shock. With care and concern, she listened to my brief summary of the rash, and wished me well with Dr. Treon.

Clinic was busy that day, as it is every day. Beyond weak, my body was limp with pain. My brain told me I was sinking. Towards the end of our forty-five minute wait, I whispered to Bill, "I hope Dr. Treon gives me intravenous antibiotics." Imagine—me, who had hoped to avoid drugs altogether, now craving an IV, seeing it as the only way to pull back from the edge of disaster!

When a clinical assistant called my name, she led us to a tiny examination room. As we waited, I alternately stood and perched on the edge of the examination table.

When Dr. Treon entered, just one look at me led him to utter "Oh, Sweetie." The spontaneous expression of concern, as well as the expression on his face, matched Suzanne's for surprise and dismay. Examining the now-stinging rash, Dr. Treon categorized it as an allergic reaction precipitated either by a drug, or by an interaction of drugs. Wasting no time he said "Let's get you into the infusion room for some steroids."

Bill and I were ushered across the hall where I was immediately checked into the infusion room. At 12:45 Dr. Treon made sure I was placed in Suzanne's care. Seen from the outside, my appearance, posture, and pace must have read like the weakest of ambulatory patients. Felt from the inside, only mental force kept me upright and moving. I felt myself fading, too weak to think about hope or fear.

The back bedroom was free, and assigned to me. With determination, I aimed myself toward it and led the way. Bill and a nurse's assistant trailed me. The promise of care kept me from collapsing. When I reached the room, I was grateful for both the privacy and the bed. For the first time in this cancer experience, I lay down, and I lay still. Bill sat, vigilant, no doubt worried.

As the Prednisone began to flow with my blood, I felt gratitude to my doctor. I had no sense of time. Perhaps the infusion lasted an hour or two, perhaps it lasted all afternoon. Dr. Treon sent us home with a prescription for Prednisone and Prilosec. Thanks to Bill and Gary Drug, the steroid pills would continue to corral the runaway rash, while the Prilosec pills protected my stomach from being pitted by the steroid. One Benadryl tablet every twelve hours completed the menu. Apparently I wasn't done with specialty drugs after all.

I had a 1:45 appointment scheduled with the dermatologist that same day. Instead, I lay still in the infusion room, welcoming the IV steroid. Hospital records list me as a no-show for dermatology.

As for the skin cream—worse than useless. Back at home, I threw it out.

The next day I called Dr. Treon as he'd requested. From him, I heard something that surprised me. He said he'd been "horrified yesterday." He went on to say "I didn't know if we could fix it."

As for me, I'd not for a moment doubted that he would.

We spoke about drugs. Acyclovir, yes, keep taking it twice a day. Ativan, yes, take it for anxiety. Bactrim—should I perhaps take a different antibiotic now? No, better skip antibiotics altogether until the rash was gone, which the doctor anticipated should be early the next week. Although I'd be "a little exposed" without an antibiotic, and we were "taking a bit of a risk here," given the circumstances, it was the right decision.

In parting, I heard these words of support and encouragement from my doctor: "You're the beacon. Keep up the good work. We want to make you healthy."

The image of light breaking up darkness penetrated my dim mind and refocused me on cancer-free good health.

A year and a week after I took the last Prednisone Bonnie Bermas had hoped would reduce the high sedimentation rate and cardiac reactive protein level in my blood, Prednisone was back in my life. Dr. Treon's prescription aimed to reduce the rash and its debilitating manifestations.

The steroid went to work, but the rash raged. Abdomen, back, arms, legs, the backs of my hands and the tops of my feet. Face. Ears. Curiously, my neck was spared. I was grateful for that.

Fatigue became lethargy. Time lost meaning. If I moved, it was in slow motion. Resting by necessity, by late afternoon I made an effort to shower and dress before Sara came home from school and Bill came home from work.

Five days after I'd been in the clinic, I called Dr. Treon to check in, and by then I was able to report good progress. The rash had lost its itch. The itch had become more like sunburn. Still sensitive to light, my eyes were more open and less puffy. At its edges, the rash was starting to break up. Some normal skin was showing.

Without the Monday, Wednesday, Friday routine, and the steady infusions of alemtuzumab, daily structure vanished and the accumulation of drugs inside me knocked me into a state of physical and mental lethargy. The rash continued to harass me.

Now I began to realize that a clinical trial doesn't end with the last dose of experimental drugs. Like any scientific or creative endeavor, it's a process. How a patient responds, how his or her body reacts, in the aftermath of treatment, is a crucial component of the dynamic of that treatment. My role, and my value, as a lab rat—and I use the term in its highest sense—continued far beyond the Twelve Weeks themselves. And my relationship with my doctor became one of the dearest I have.

On January 17th, through exhaustion and rainbows of red and purple skin, I received calming words from Dr. Treon. He assured me I was doing well, improving, turned a corner. He told me a lot of hope was invested here. To him, all facets of patient care mattered. To him, we're all part of the same family.

In any case, each day the rash's pain lessened and its territorial spread ceased. But my tender skin hurt all the time. If wearing clothes had been painful, it became near impossible. Once again tank tops and the colorful three-tiered Express skirts—one hot pink, the other acid green—became my favorite outfit. In fact, being the only clothing that was non-abrasive to my seared skin, it became my only outfit, a uniform really. The red slippers with the black grosgrain ribbon clashed violently with both skirts. One afternoon, as I retrieved the mail from the hallway outside our front door a neighbor caught sight of me, in mid-January, decked out like a middle-aged Bohemian hippie. Her widening eyes expressed surprise as she viewed what could only be some alter ego I confined to my home and concealed from the public.

Like the aftermath of an extreme sunburn, my skin peeled for days. It occurred to me that I was literally shedding, like a snake. Perhaps my body needed to rid itself of cells that had harbored so much disease, and so many drugs. Perhaps I needed a new skin for a new life.

Singing Bowls

A year earlier, through January and into February, so many late afternoons were punctuated and defined by telephone conversations with my internist. If those days had seemed dark gray, these days, the rash days, seemed black. During the Twelve Weeks, alone at home with hydrocortisone, Benadryl, and alemtuzumab dulling my vitality as they did their work, I'd felt generally calm and composed. Now, alone at home with Prednisone and Prilosec trying to quell the rash, but the rash still raging, I felt isolated and on edge.

The most recent blood tests showed both the IgM and the M-spike continuing their decline. The cancer had decreased dramatically, but it wasn't yet gone. Through the rash's painful fog, I knew it was important to re-connect with my vision to be healthy and cancer-free.

The idea of Dr. Gaynor's singing bowls attracted me, and I eventually mustered up the strength to make a phone call. Calling the number Dr. Gaynor's receptionist had provided in November, I learned to my surprise that singing bowls come in different sizes. Their tones include the full range of the musical scale, and their vibrational frequencies match those of our bodies' chakras. Who knew?

It seemed like a good idea to have a set of bowls whose range encompassed the musical scale and, not coincidentally, the principal chakras. That would be seven. Diameters ranged from ten inches for the heart and throat chakras, to eighteen inches for the solar plexus chakra. Overwhelmed by the information, I thanked the man who'd educated me, and set my potential shopping list aside.

A week or so later, I called back. This time I was referred to a retailer and told it would be better to buy my bowls through her. Dialing her number in the Berkshires, I had the good luck to make the acquaintance of Andrée Clearwater.

Andrée taught me more about the singing bowls, and played a heart bowl for me to hear through the phone. She also told me of goji juice, a healthful beverage made from Himalayan goji berries. A few days later I ordered singing bowls, and signed up for monthly juice deliveries.

When I mentioned goji juice and its purported healthful properties to Dr. Treon, I gleaned new insight into the protocol of a clinical trial. My doctor said he couldn't bar me from drinking the juice, but if a food or substance had proven to be effective in combating Waldenstrom's Macroglobulinemia, a patient couldn't use it while participating in a clinical trial. The clinical trial is a controlled experiment; breaking protocol by introducing additional elements would corrupt the process and invalidate the results. To his knowledge the juice had no proven anti-Waldenstrom's properties, and I could drink it if I chose.

The January days remained dark, the rash maintained its presence, and lethargy sustained its hold on me. When the bowls were delivered early one afternoon, I, in my bathrobe, was utterly overwhelmed.

Seven singing bowls arrived in five gigantic cardboard shipping cartons. The largest carton, housing the solar plexus, "E" bowl, stood higher than my waist. Together, the cartons filled the elevator hallway. Just looking at them tired me out. Opening a box I faced pools of Styrofoam bubbles and forms. I had to dig deep to locate a bowl. The big one was heavy. The physical effort was too much. As weak as I was, how could I cope with this mass of material?

Calling my father, I explained.

"Send them back," he said. "The hell with it."

His advice made some sense, and I considered it.

In a panic I called Andrée.

"Keep them, try them," she advised. I could return them later if need be.

Slowly, over the course of the afternoon, I unpacked the bowls. As I waded through the plastic packing materials, glimpses of creamy, opaque glass appeared. With a texture like a medium grade sandpaper on the outside, and smooth as milk on the inside, the unboxed bowls became slightly less intimidating. Unpacking took most of the afternoon, and all of my effort. At the inside center of each bowl a colored paper label named its musical tone, and the vibrational frequency of the corresponding chakra. To "play" the bowls there were wands wrapped in white leather. To separate the bowls from the floor or table, and protect the integrity of their vibrations' flow, there were thin rubber black rings to rest them on. I set the bowls around the perimeter of our downstairs hall. They were pretty, but intimidating.

Despite printed instructions, I didn't know what to do with these bowls. With Andrée's help, I learned of a healer whose principal tool is sound, and invited her to teach me how to play the bowls.

At the end of January, with Bill away on a business trip and Sara studying for her Chinese mid-term exam, Heather Hood the music healer visited our home. With her vibrant voice, she sang. With her agile arms, she played the bowls. The motion of the sounds penetrated my pain, at least for the moment.

My daughter later told me that waves of sound had billowed up the staircase and filled our home. Concentrating on Mandarin, itself a language of sound, had been a real challenge.

A day or two later, I gingerly approached the bowls. A pamphlet mentioned that if a person had a sickness, it was advisable to move the wand counter-clockwise. Soon a daily ritual developed.

In the late morning or early afternoon, assuming my neighbors were out, I'd move the bowls to the center of the hall. Generally, I organized them according to the order of the chakras. Always I followed Dr. Gaynor's "prescription." He'd found in the lab that cancer cells were most consistently destroyed when three elements were combined: the music and vibration of the bowls, the sound and vibration of one's voice, and the power of one's intention.

First I'd concentrate on my intention: "I am cancer-free and healthy."

Then, as I rubbed the leather-covered wand around the outside edge of the bowls, I'd sing, or howl, or hum, or buzz, or use whatever sounds my body felt like making.

Once the bowls got vibrating individually, they'd pick up each others' frequencies and new rhythms would result. Often I'd lie on the floor in the midst of them, letting the vibrations wave through me. I'd lose track of time.

Often lasting up to forty minutes, the singing bowl sessions became the next phase and form of meditation. Always I visualized the demise of all the cancer, my cancer-free good health, and the health and happiness of my family, my friends, and my medical team.

As for the goji juice, a couple of times a day I'd slowly drink a couple of ounces. Always, a L'Cha'im, a prayer for life, preceded the drink. Although I can't say that the juice helped kill the cancer, I can assure you that the power of my intentions definitely lifted my spirits, and I believe my cells' spirits, onto a healthful plane and made them open and receptive to being cancer-free.

Winter Into Spring

For close to a year, I'd been talking to my body with my soul's voice. The unvarying, underlying theme was clear and concise: I saw and felt myself healthy and cancer-free, in the present, as if it already existed.

Initially my dialogue was a general statement. Over time, it evolved and became more specific. During the Twelve Weeks, it focused on individual cells—I visualized cancer cells exploding as the alemtuzumab targeted them; I visualized healthy cells replacing the deadly ones.

In January, under the guidance of Dr. Gaynor's book, I pictured the cancer cells self-destructing as my vocal gyrations and the singing bowls' vibrations fractured their drive to survive.

As January ebbed away, strength imperceptibly seeped back, but fatigue remained my pervasive state. During an afternoon phone call with my father, I mentioned that although I was exhausted, I seemed unable to settle down and rest.

"Is there a radio in your bedroom?" he asked. "Why not try some classical music. It may help."

And it did. For the first time in two decades, I listened to music every day. Then it was rock 'n roll, now it was classical, jazz, blues and Saturday afternoon opera, "Live from the Met."

With the assistance of my father and the radio, I relaxed, rested, snoozed, and recharged. Another form of vibration was helping me heal.

In February, I visualized my bone marrow being clean and clear of cancer. My mental gaze penetrated bone, looking through it to pure, healthy, disease-free marrow. Seeing this in my mind's eye, I felt it in my spirit.

A Very Different Birthday

A year earlier in 2005, my birthday was saturated—infused—not only with sickness, but with the knowledge of sickness. A confirmed cancer diagnosis. It was sickening.

Now, a year later, I'd completed the Twelve Weeks, and weaned myself off Prednisone for the second time. Having a few questions, I called Dr. Treon. I was pleased to tell him I was feeling much, much better, and in two days I'd take the last Prilosec. Since this was Week Eight post-alemtuzumab, might I stop taking Bactrim and Acyclovir? Yes, I could stop taking Bactrim, but he asked me to finish out the week with Acyclovir.

When I mentioned that today was my birthday, I told Dr. Treon of the contrast between last year's birthday and today. With his distinctive enthusiasm, Dr. Treon told me his birthday was very close to mine: February 12th, "President's Day."

Although I was thanking my doctor, he instantly began thanking me. My role in the clinical trial helped pave the way for some very important next steps, he said. The data showed some unexpected good results; the immune system seemed to be restoring itself, which opened the way to make new leaps forward for treating people.

Over the phone, my doctor embraced me so warmly with genuine affection that he created a new and very personal bond between us, our birthday bond. He answered my questions and assuaged my concerns, and as I was wont to do, I focused us on ending the disease.

Signing off, he said, "We're fellow Aquarians. We fish stick together. We will celebrate many, many, many happy birthdays together."

I received these words as a gift, an assurance, and a promise: my doctor knew something. He knew I would live for a long time; he knew I'd be healthy to live for a long time. Also, I now realize he knew we would become very special friends.

Ecstatic, I said good-bye. In joy, I flew upstairs and relayed the conversation to Bill.

Cognizant of my lack of an immune system and making every effort to avoid getting sick, I donned my warmest coat, wrapped a big scarf around myself, added boots, gloves, and a hat, and set out for the block-long walk to the Public Garden. In the bitter air and ice-crystal sunlight, I might have seen two or three other people in the frozen park that day. With a light step, and feeling a lightheartedness that had been absent for a long, long time, I circumnavigated the frozen lagoon, counter-clockwise.

From my ebullience, a life-affirming new song came:

Happy Birthday to me,
I am cancer-free,
Happy Birthday,
Happy Birthday,
Happy Birthday to me!

The cancer hadn't totally flat-lined yet, but I never wavered from the belief and the conviction that it would.

There was a variation to this song, which I continued to sing long after my birth date.

I am happy and I am healthy and I am cancer-free,
I am happy and I am healthy and Happy Birthday to me!

What a sea change, from feeling I'd soon be dead, to feeling happy and comfortable that I would have a future! If my oncologist saw me living on, to celebrate birthdays—plural—and have a future—what more assurance could I possibly need?

There was a tangible gift too. I could officially retire the little booklet with the medications chart. The vials of Bactrim and Acyclovir could go away. My family and I no longer needed to see these constant reminders of cancer and treatment.

Sometimes, absence is a great present.

At one point, much to my surprise, I felt a brief whirlpool of creative energy. Almost on autopilot, I went to my studio. Working on instinct, I created one painting. Again, a new color palate appeared. White mostly, some black, slashes of red. Reflective of the process of cleansing blood and clearing disease, perhaps. Other than that one canvas, I needed to concentrate my limited pep on rebuilding my depleted body.

White Ducky

February brought bitter cold, but also brilliant sun. With a modicum of energy back in my body, most afternoons I encased myself in warm clothing and walked to the Public Garden.

As it had been in Mexico, at Squam, at the Charles River, and in the Public Garden through the past spring, summer, and fall, nature's beauty and richness captured my attention and elevated my spirit. Frosted leaves against clean blue skies looked glorious. I noticed and marveled at detail and grandeur in equal measure.

As I circumnavigated the lagoon, usually traveling counter-clockwise, I might pass only one other person. The footpaths were heavy with ice and empty of people, but my heart felt light with health and full of joy.

Not utterly alone, I had companionship in the flocks of ducks huddled together on the ice, or in the few pools where ice had melted. As winter temperatures in the northeast had grown increasingly milder and the winter season shortened, the ducks had ceased to migrate south. They'd become year-round residents. Although I mourned the implications of global climate change for us all, I must admit I enjoyed the ducks' company.

One duck in particular grabbed and held my attention. Among flocks of gray, brown, and green feathered friends, this duck's feathers were the purest white. To me, he symbolized pure good health, a clean and cancer-free body. He had two steady companions, a mallard and a female. I was glad he had company; he was different, but he wasn't an outcast.

For a full year, each time I stepped into the Public Garden, my first impulse was to locate my "white ducky," my wild and living embodiment of hope.

Luminous

About six weeks into the New Year, with the rash cleared and the accumulated drugs in my body declining, Dr. Treon and I agreed that I could begin to re-enter slightly more public places.

One bitter cold morning, fortified by layers of warm clothes topped by a wide-brimmed hat, I ventured outside. Taking a radical departure from my dogmatic routine, instead of heading right, to the Public Garden, I headed straight—up to Charles Street.

There was little need to fear germs. Probably they'd all frozen to death. And the sidewalks were almost empty. Walking on a commercial street for the first time in six months, I delighted in the colorful window displays. I felt giddy.

Glancing up past my hat brim, I saw a man and a woman approaching. To my surprise I knew them: Tono and Diana Hixon, a couple I like very much for their empathy and their warmth. When we reached each other, wordlessly I wrapped my arms around Diana in a full-body hug. She received it and reciprocated.

Through the grapevine of kids and parents at my daughter's school, she'd heard that I was very sick. Months ago she'd sent me a greeting card, with glitter on a beach. If I ever wanted a simple walk near the ocean, just let her know, the message said. It was just right—generous, caring, leaving the offer on the table and the initiative to me. I never acted on it, but I appreciated it.

This day Tono and Diana had decided to take the train from Cambridge to Boston and explore a bit, just for fun.

Observing me closely, Diana remarked that I looked luminous.

"I had an unplanned chemical peel," I said.

Despite its tiny scale, impromptu and intimate as this gathering was, it felt like my coming out party.

Red, raw, angry skin was replaced by the soft, clear skin of a newborn. It was a marvel, but I don't recommend alemtuzumab as a beauty aid.

Thrilled with this newfound loveliness, I decided to support it further. Recalling that the gel of the aloe plant soothes and heals irritated skin, I called a couple of florists, located an aloe plant, and drove to Chestnut Hill to buy it. This being my first foray to a store since the Twelve Weeks began, and my immune system being non-existent, I'd asked the florist to meet me in the parking lot with the plant. I accepted the plant, she accepted my credit card, and home I went.

For a couple of days I applied the gel straight from the leaf to my skin.

Then my dear friend Yolanda Ramirez, well versed in the medicinal properties of plants, told me the aloe would be more effective if I heated the gel.

"But," she warned, "you must refrigerate the extra boiled aloe between applications."

Why not try this method, if it enhanced the aloe's powers? For months now, I'd only used the stove to boil water for coffee or to make scrambled eggs, but I now cooked up a batch of aloe, applied it to my skin, and all was well.

Until one evening when I'd failed to refrigerate the potion, and found myself too tired to hike up the stairs for a fresh leaf, too stingy to throw out the cooked but unrefrigerated aloe in the bathroom, and too obsessive to skip the treatment and just go to bed.

Spreading the nearby aloe potion on my skin that night was an unfortunate choice. It triggered a new rash reaction, and resulted in yet another Prednisone cycle.

Sometimes, a person just has to know when to stop.

The So-called Kiss of Death

On March 1st, as Sara's spring break approached, I asked Dr. Treon whether it might be possible for me to travel. Someplace warm, someplace where our family could relax and recharge after the grueling months of cancer treatment. Was it safe for me to be on an airplane? In a crowded public place?

Dr. Treon's response was a qualified yes. Despite the absence of my immune system, Dr. Treon felt we could take a trip. But there were two conditions: at our destination, hygiene standards had to be impeccable, and we needed to be in close range of one of Dr. Treon's hematology/oncology colleagues and a major hospital.

Although he felt there was low probability I'd require a physician's care, "Cut me some slack on this," my doctor said.

In case I needed medical attention and care, my doctor wanted to be certain it would be readily available.

Given this stipulation, as far as the Caribbean went, we had exactly one option: Puerto Rico. San Juan housed both a trusted doctor and a major hospital. Bill began the planning, and we were delighted when our niece Michaela agreed to join us.

Given the medical and emotional build-up leading to the Twelve Weeks, and the intensity of the treatment, it never occurred to me that the cancer would need to be monitored after the clinical trial ended. Now I learned that follow-up would include a clinic check-up and blood tests at three-month intervals. The first appointment was March 6th.

Dr. Treon, Bill, and I chatted about the upcoming trip to Puerto Rico. Swimming in the sea would be fine, but cleaning my goldfish's tank was still off-limits. As for swimming in a pool, might my now sensitive skin have an allergic reaction to chlorine? Test it with one foot first, my doctor advised. I'd have Cipro with me, just in case a flu bug bit.

As he checked off boxes on the phlebotomy list prior to having my blood drawn, Dr. Treon asked if I'd mind his tracking my CD4, a term used to denote mature T-cells.

The CD4 count would be a good marker of whether my T-cells, annihilated by alemtuzumab, were coming back. Of course, I agreed. What were two more vials of blood, to help aid this gifted physician and researcher unravel the mysteries of Waldenstrom's Macroglobulinemia, track the fallout from alemtuzumab, and help future patients?

After Dr. Treon examined my throat and abdomen, I inquired, "What did you feel?"

"Nothing."

Three days later, the blood test results were back.

Zachary Hunter sent Dr. Treon a note: "Did you see her data!"

By phone, my doctor delivered great news.

The IgM count was 114. Since a normal IgM count ranges from 30 to 240, 114 was a beautiful number! As for the M-spike, the marker in IgM cells that says they were made by tumor cells, it showed up only as "a faint little band that can't be quantified anymore." It was too small to measure! Telling me the M-spike was almost extinguished, Dr. Treon said he was ecstatic.

"My goal in life is for you to be ecstatic," I replied.

"This is about as good as it can get," my doctor said.

Of course, this progress and this news were thrilling. "But," I said, "We need it to go away completely."

During a brief pause, I sensed my doctor considering that thought.

"Well," he said, reflectively, "alemtuzumab is a biological drug. We didn't drop the atom bomb. And there is the so-called kiss of death."

Given more time, those long-lived IgM cells made by cancer might die altogether. All signs of Waldenstrom's Macroglobulinemia might disappear.

And now I had a new image for my meditations: the kiss of death. In my mind, I saw the last traces of alemtuzumab sucking the life out of the last vestiges of cancer. I watched as that faint band flattened to a skinny line, and vanished, completely and forever. The way the sun vanishes at the horizon, and day becomes night.

This kiss of death became my new best friend.

Singing in the Sand

Singing bowls were now at the heart of my daily meditations, but transporting even the smallest glass bowl made no sense. Perhaps for our trip I could locate a metal singing bowl, the kind Dr. Gaynor's Tibetan monk patient had initially mentioned? As luck would have it, Charles Street is home to a shop named Tibet Emporium. Calling the shop, I learned that yes, singing bowls were in stock. How unexpected, in this neighborhood.

Visiting the shop, I soon learned that all singing bowls are not alike. Tibetan bowls contain seven metals. They're hand-hammered into shape, and it's said that each blow of the hammer is accompanied by a prayer. Depending on its size, and a thousand unquantifiable variables, the tone, resonance, and vibrational frequency of every bowl is unique.

In the back of the shop, the owner, Kelsang Sangto, patiently tested many bowls with me. She taught me how to revolve the wooden wand, and how to hear the different rhythms and ranges of sound that play simultaneously. Each singing bowl has its own personality, and eventually, I chose the bowl that was perfect for me.

As my family and I boarded our flight, the metal singing bowl nestled in my suitcase along with newly-purchased sun-protective clothing. Dr. Treon had given me billboard-size advice to keep the sun off my skin. His concern was melanoma; however we would learn that even a small amount of sun exposure triggered a rash reaction. Sunscreen stayed home.

After the aloe fiasco, there was no way I'd put any topical agent on my skin for fear of re-igniting the rash.

Passionate about the beach and the sea, I always find it soothing, invigorating, healing, and inspiring. Now I mobilized all the resources I had to propel the healing and expel the disease.

At the beach, I was clad in white from neck to ankles—the outfit was a long-sleeved shirt with drawstring beach pants, or a ghost-like, hooded poncho, plus a hat, and sunglasses. To avoid strong sunlight, I tried to restrict my swimming to either early or late in the day. The hat swam with me. Ocean swimming only; I was concerned that a pool's chlorine would aggravate my skin.

For long stretches of time, many times each day, outfitted as I just described, I would sit below palm trees, or walk along the shoreline, or, toward the end of the week, perch near the pool where Sara and Michaela bathed. In one hand was my Tibetan singing bowl; in the other was the wood wand used to play the bowl by setting its vibrations in motion, into audible range. I meditated aloud—chanted, really—as I sat or strolled. Simultaneously I tuned in to the sounds and rhythms of the sea and bird songs, as well as the majesty of palm trees, waves and sky. I was determined that the decline of cancer continue until all of it was gone.

It was peaceful. It was wild. It worked.

However, I must add: Thank God Sara, then seventeen, accepted what had to appear as eccentric, if not bizarre dress and behavior on her mother's part, with a detached and sly but affectionate sense of humor. Light-hearted, we enjoyed a wonderful week.

In New York City almost exactly a year earlier, on St. Patrick's Day, on Madison Avenue, the rhythms and sound waves of teenagers' voices and trumpets and drums had managed to penetrate my thickened blood and set my heart to singing. Two months later, in May, the ancient meditation method mobilized my voice into a personal marching band. Morning "Ah's" and evening "Om's" radiated positive, audible, palpable energy from my voice box to and through all my cells.

In September, I began singing spontaneous little songs to myself. In November, Dr. Mitchell Gaynor's book set me howling and slamming the piano. Let's break the cancer cells' aggressive rhythms, the death march they'd orchestrated for me!

Two months later in January, mind, body, and home reverberated with sometimes harmonized, sometimes cacophonous waves of music. The trio: singing bowls, my chanting, or humming, or growling voice, and the power of my intention to be cancer-free and healthy. And now, two months after that, in March once more, in a setting of sand and sea and sky, with the love of my family, nature's music supported and augmented the vibrations of the metal singing bowl, the freedom of my voice, and the dream of my heart.

Precautions notwithstanding, sunlight found its way to me and a small rash reaction followed me home. When I reported in to Dr. Treon, I described my happiness at re-entry into society after months of being sequestered.

The doctor said my call made his day. "Our purpose in life, our combined work, our joint effort, is to make progress thanks to folks like you."

In parting, he offered three pieces of advice: hydrocortisone cream, avoid sun, enjoy!

Dan Dies

As I recovered, Dan Miller lost ground. Two types of chemotherapy failed to slow the progress of his lung and liver cancer.

Wanting time with Dan and Prudence, Bill and I made a breakfast date with them.

On April 4th, a gray and drizzly morning, we picked up our friends in front of their home near a monastery in Cambridge. Leaning on a cane and looking thin, Dan was in high spirits. His restaurant choice was a diner straight out of the 1950's. His food choice was his favorite cornmeal pancakes. Dan's animated replays of his life in the theater, and in the Israeli army, entertained and moved us. With glee, he spoke of his recent passion for writing poetry. He'd composed a near-epic poem that proposed a brilliant solution for peace between the Israelis and the Palestinians.

Leaving my home that morning, I wondered what gift I might bring Dan. What would have meaning to a dying man? The metal singing bowl, the one I'd bought on Charles Street and taken to Puerto Rico, came to mind, and it joined Bill and me in the car. After breakfast, we felt Dan needed rest. The four of us stood along one side of the car, preparing to say good-bye.

Taking the singing bowl in both hands, I was ready to offer it to Dan. As I extended my arms toward him, his arms reached out to me. As though by magic, the bowl left me and settled on Dan's upturned palms. There was a magnetic attraction. The bowl needed to go to Dan, and Dan knew it. Not a word had been said.

Later that day I explained to Prudence how to use the wand to set the bowl singing. She and Dan used it everyday for the rest of his life.

On the evening of April 13th, I called Prudence only to learn that Dan had been taken to hospice a couple of hours earlier. When we heard her cell phone ring, we said a quick good-bye. Through her cell phone came the news. Dan had just died.

The singing bowl lives on with Prudence.

The Finish Line

Only the Commonwealth of Massachusetts celebrates Patriots Day. As the Boston Red Sox play their first home game of the season, thousands of runners converge to participate in the world's most prestigious marathon.

With the monoclonal gammopathy a no longer quantifiable "faint band" and IgM at a perfectly normal 114, Monday, April 17th, 2006 presented ideal conditions for sports, and for me. Sunny but cool, spring had sprung. When a friend invited us to join his picnic on the roof of the Lenox Hotel, Bill and I happily accepted.

Located on the marathon route two blocks from the finish line, the hotel's roof is the perfect perch. Standing on the east side, looking down at Boylston Street, I saw two gigantic yellow numbers laid out on the black asphalt: 0.0. To the runners, 0.0 meant the end, and victory. To me, 0.0 meant zero cancer, zero monoclonal gammopathy, and another type of victory.

Riveting my gaze on that giant 0.0, I willed with all my being that I'd reach my goal, and the last trace of Waldenstrom's Macroglobulinemia would vanish.

Soon it did.

With another appearance of rash, I called Dr. Treon on April 19th and found him as he made hospital rounds during one of his semi-annual clinical rotations. He asked me to have blood drawn on April 28th so we'd have the lab results for May 1st, the date of my next routine appointment. The previous IgM count had been 114, a perfectly normal number, and the M spike had registered as a faint band, too small to be quantified. Now my doctor would be looking for no monoclonal gammopathy.

"Since no M-spike had shown on the March 1st blood analysis, we already have a complete remission by the old definition," he said. "But I want to 'go by the book' here."

The next day, I called him again to report a rising rash. Again, I found him as he made rounds. More Prednisone and more Prilosec were prescribed.

Knowing his compassion for patients and his commitment to care, I asked "Are you enjoying your time in the hospital?"

"Enjoy isn't the word I'd use," he said. "Being here makes it so obvious. Good health is so important. Everything else is trivial. I can assure you of that."

Car Chants

Freed from the rigorous schedule and released from the rash, I enjoyed taking my daughter to school in the mornings and picking her up in the early evenings.

For my impaired immune system, the car became a germ isolation bubble of sorts. For my singing spirit, it became an unexpected sanctuary. Lining Memorial Drive, ancient sycamore trees formed a welcoming arc of protection for my car and me. What a change from the days I'd dreaded driving.

On the way back home one morning, rather than flip on the radio to hear the news, I began to hum. It was the morning "Ah" meditation, with the tones and rhythms that naturally arose to modulate it. In the privacy of the car, I could be loud. Liking this use of my time and the lack of restraint, I made this return trip my new morning meditation slot.

During one such session, my awareness awakened to a new depth. As my voice reverberated through me, I experienced a new sensation. Deep inside my core at the base of my spine, I felt rotating vibrations in my sacral chakra.

It was exquisite, as though the innermost cells and energy center were harmonizing with my voice and my being.

And a new height, or depth, of meditation was born.

After my daughter finished her demanding school day and strenuous crew workout, I liked to be ready and waiting in the school parking lot to carry her home. Invariably, crew practice ended later than it was supposed to, but again I found privacy and a meditative atmosphere in the car. Tuning the radio to a classical station, I'd allow my voice to flow along with or in opposition to the music. Time didn't matter. Musical meditation became my vehicle for transition from day into dusk.

Happy Anniversary

Social seclusion was getting old, and Bill's and my eighteenth wedding anniversary was upon us. Beyond thrilled that the cancer was dramatically diminished, and profoundly grateful to my family and our closest friends for their physical and emotional sustenance throughout the past, hard months, I suggested we host a dinner party. Bill reserved a room at a neighborhood restaurant and we invited our closest friends to join us. We had much to celebrate.

For the occasion, I bought myself a present, a new pair of shoes: high heels! Red satin with black and silver flowers, open toed. Two years ago, when cancer first gripped my legs in a crippling way, I could barely stand in low heels. A few months later, when it mangled my knees with pain, I'd sadly resigned myself to never be able to wear high heels again. As cancer left, it took the pain with it.

Saturday, April 29th was a stellar spring day. When Mary Ting and Todd Springer arrived at our home, my bowls' pulsating singing mesmerized them.

Around six, Mary and Todd joined Bill, Sara, and me for a stroll though the Public Garden. Honoring our tradition, we paused to enjoy our weeping Japanese cherry tree and take a few pictures.

Stepping from sidewalk sunlight into a wood-paneled bar, we saw most of our guests chatting. As happy as I was, and as well as I knew them all, I felt startled and shy. Being in such close contact with so many people, in a party atmosphere, felt strange to me. I suspect seeing me in that context seemed strange to our friends, too. People hugged me, but delicately, as though I might break. Some looked at me with reserve, or was it disbelief? I probably looked like the proverbial deer-in-the-headlights. I certainly felt that way.

Once we threaded our way through the bar, a gracious room welcomed us. One large table with vases of floral fireworks seated us all. Most of our guests had been friends of Bill's and mine before we married.

Donny and Barbara Levine had been man and matron of honor at our wedding. Duncan and Pat Gratton had raised their children side-by-side with our daughter. My college friend Dr. Lili Gottfried joined us. Prudence King was there, and we felt Dan Miller's presence, too.

Sara's buddies Lindsay Rabkin and Becca Goldklang came in their spring party dresses, as did Becca's mother Cilla Lavin. Although Sherri Mahne and her son Thomas couldn't join us, we felt their ongoing love and support. Sherri's research, and her image of my reaching for a different branch of treatment had been so important, as had her encouragement during and after the Twelve Weeks.

Filtered daylight entered through a wall of windows, and the light of friendship entered our hearts. Between courses, I stood near Bill and paid tribute to each person present, interconnecting them and their contributions to our family. Naturally, I dedicated my final words of gratitude, along with dessert, to my husband and my daughter.

About those red satin high heels. When my legs lost their pain and regained normal use, my hands did, too. Healthy blood with normal viscosity flowed easily through me. When cancer engorged my blood and strangled my body, I'd resigned myself to living with physical limitations. Now I was overjoyed that I didn't have to.

On a notepad, I wrote "Cancer Cures Arthritis." But I didn't have arthritis, and cancer's not a cure I recommend.

The Best News

On May 1st, Bill and I saw Dr. Treon in Dana-Farber's clinic. The blood test results were in: the IgM count was 159. Good, healthy IgM cells were coming back, and they were free of the monoclonal protein that identifies tumor-made IgM.

The best news! My blood showed no evidence of cancer! We were thrilled!

Dr. Treon went on to tell us the blood analysis yielded more information. As for my immune system, there was little evidence of that. A low CD4 count indicated I was "still in the doghouse" as far as my body's natural defenses were concerned.

Although the blood counts remained "in the basement," they were swinging up. The doctor predicted it would take twelve to fourteen months, post-alemtuzumab, for the immune system to reconstitute. In the meantime, if I ran a fever, or even had a sniffle, I was to call him right away.

Telling Dr. Treon that my father would be coming to visit in early June, I inquired again about my being in public places.

"Avoid crowds and sick people for the first two years," was his advice.

With a swollen splotchy face from yet another—this time minor—recall rash, and a heart racing but full of gratitude, I asked how I could help with my doctor's research. His response: more clinical trials need to be approved and implemented to advance the science of combating cancer.

As we parted, Dr. Treon reflected that although there hadn't been a lot of disease in my bone marrow, it had made a lot of IgM—enough to be deadly.

On May 3rd, Zachary Hunter told me "We're absolutely, totally thrilled. Our goal is to see you, but to never have to see you at Dana-Farber again."

Round Three

Just as several diagnostic procedures had located and identified cancer sixteen months earlier, those same methods would now be used to verify its absence.

Proceeding "by the book," following the protocol of the clinical trial, Dr. Treon ordered three procedures. A CAT scan, the third, was scheduled for May 11th, and a bone marrow biopsy, the third, was set for May 15th. Both would be done at Dana-Farber. An endoscopy, also the third, was slated for June 6th at the Brigham.

For the CAT scan I felt impatient, and a little bored. During the two hours required to slowly imbibe two bottles of the special drink, I spent most of my time and energy in the wide hallway that connects the reception area to the procedure rooms. I paced in a pattern resembling a racetrack oval. I meditated on results showing I was cancer-free. When the time came for the scan, I was calm, and it seemed routine.

As soon as he received the results, Dr. Treon called to tell me where swollen segments of the upper stomach had once housed lymphoma, there now was no evidence of cancer. Terrific news.

He went on to say that the CAT scan was a critical event, "to match things up." But I heard some cautions, too. Regarding the upcoming bone marrow biopsy, my doctor presumed he'd get a good sample, but "If we can't find tumor cells, it doesn't mean there aren't any." Even if we verified a complete remission, he didn't want me to think it's a cure.

My doctor explained that the term "complete remission" was based on the best clinical abilities to look for residual signs of disease. Even though blood tests, a CAT scan, and a bone marrow biopsy might show no evidence of cancer, the disease might still be present at the microscopic level.

"Think of it this way," he said. "It takes a billion cancer cells to form a tumor the size of a pea. If only a few cells remain after treatment, and even if our diagnostic techniques can't detect any sign of it, the cancer is still there."

Believing this to be true for every cancer, Dr. Treon made the distinction between a complete remission and a cure. Cure would be defined as the total absence of cancer cells.

I reported that I felt worn out and was advised that even if anemia from Waldenstrom's Macroglobulinemia were resolved, fatigue persists.

Anemia and fatigue. I'd been living with both for a long time. Fifteen months ago, lymphoma depleted my red blood cells much faster than a diet of lamb and lentils could rebuild them. Now, tests were showing no signs of cancer, and alemtuzumab no longer pummeled me three times a week. Still, exhaustion prevailed. This, too, was important information for my doctor's research, and for me.

I'd have to be patient and take it easy for a while longer.

Sunday, May 14th was Mother's Day. Calling Dr. Treon to report a wet cough that wrenched my chest, I found him at the San Diego Zoo. He'd just completed a round of lectures in Philadelphia, Princeton, New York, and San Diego.

Anticipating our clinic date the following day, the doctor wished me Happy Mother's Day and said, "We want to keep things going in the right direction."

On May 15th, while Bill waited in the reception area of Dana-Farber's Gosman Adult Clinic, I had what I hoped and expected would be a definitive bone marrow biopsy—one that determined all cancer was gone. Heart racing, nose running, coughing from time to time—it was all minor compared to our big goal of being cancer-free.

In a large procedure room, I stood as I waited for my doctor. When he arrived, his mood was joyful. He told me I was the first person with a complete remission from a synthetic monoclonal antibody.

Rolling up his sleeves and spreading his arms wide, Dr. Treon announced, "Today we're reconfirming a complete remission."

What a positive pronouncement from my experienced, cautious doctor! His optimism flooded me with renewed faith that the cancer was gone.

During the next half hour or so, as he anaesthetized my left hip area and extracted marrow from the pelvic bone, I heard my doctor say, "I'm not worried."

And that's all I remember about the procedure, that day.

When the results came in, there was no sign of Waldenstrom's Macroglobulinemia.

None at all.

"We have a lot to celebrate," my doctor said.

On June 6th at the Brigham, for the third endoscopy, I was calm and composed. This time my upper body was raised to about a sixty-degree angle, a near-seated position, almost no anesthesia was used and the procedure seemed easy and fast. The examination showed all was normal, and this time, it was.

On my way out to meet Bill, I stopped in at the Blood Donor's Center to report the great news to my plasmaphereisis nurses, and again thank them for their kindness and their care. I'd survived the cancer treatment, and my healthcare proxy hadn't been called into action.

Holistic Healing

Free of prescription drugs for the first time in six months, I wondered whether traditional non-western remedies might again be useful. For many years, my brother and his family had relied almost exclusively on homeopathy and naturopathy. My elderly parents' medical problems had been either stabilized or significantly improved by these means.

I called my family's key practitioner, Joe Kassel, a gifted naturopathic physician and healer. From Joe I received guidance about foods to help rebuild my immune system, and tips on hygiene to practice until the immune system returned.

All of these suggestions helped, but my progress was slow. Fatigue and weakness continued to dog me and drag me down. One dull spring day, May 30th, I must have looked particularly puny to Bill.

"Why don't you take my appointment with Judi Piani today?" He offered.

Well, why not? At least it would get me out of the house for a while. Never could I have guessed what a momentous turning point this encounter would be.

A Reiki master who draws on many traditional non-Western healing techniques, Judi Piani had come to Bill with an impressive reference. A colleague of Bill's, a young man in his mid-thirties, had a ruptured meniscus. His activities were so restricted, and his knee pain so severe, that he'd set the date for knee replacement surgery. At his mother's suggestion, he booked a few sessions with Judi. As a result of those sessions, his pain dissolved, his knee returned to normal good health, and his surgery was cancelled. Impressed by this story, Bill had seen Judi a few times himself. He drove me to Judi's house, introduced us, and left to make phone calls from the car.

Beautiful, sensitive, and near telepathic, first Judi listened. I told her of the cancer, the alemtuzumab, and the clean blood test results. She marveled at the miracle.

"Your contract's not up," she said. I wondered what she might possibly mean. "You're still here," she said. "You have work to do."

And that set me on the launching pad to gather strength. From the perspective of having survived Waldenstrom's Macroglobulinemia, I was free to decide—or perhaps intuit—why I was still here and what I was supposed to do. What was my unique contribution, to benefit other people and give happiness to myself? The kaleidoscope's lenses began to shift focus once again.

Judi spoke of universal life energy and described how Reiki practice helps restore natural, healthy energy flow in the body.

Ephemeral and visceral, the images and metaphors appealed to me. Exhausted but receptive, I began to relax as Judi began to work. My body felt lighter and my spirit brighter. She sent me home with encouragement, and a sheet of paper containing a list of mantras she'd created for physical, emotional, mental and spiritual health.

As I began employing Judi's daily mantras, my meditations and visualizations expanded. Now the health and well-being of the endocrine system, the immune system, and the chakras joined the cells and bones and marrow in my picture of good health. Since, in my case at that time there was no immune system, my meditations, or prayers if you will, had to be adapted to fit my personal profile. In addition to concentrating on "balancing, strengthening, and renewing my immune system," I concentrated on recreating it.

Vocal and visual meditation, spontaneous singing, singing bowls, classical music—vibration in many forms had supported and sustained my optimism for more than a year.

With a rhythm of their own, each entered my life exactly when I needed it. Each enhanced and enriched the others. Together they became a kind of free-form symphony.

I placed great faith and trust in powers and forces that we can't see or touch. Open and receptive, I welcomed and accepted Judi's unwavering commitment to healing me with invisible sources of energy.

Cyber Prayers

Prayer groups can take many forms. For me, it was a private congregation of one. For Mrs. Ting, it was the small group of friends, meeting each Tuesday night, joining their souls for peace and for health. For Bill, it was a network of family and friends, communing through the invisible universe of e-mail.

During the Twelve Weeks, from time to time Bill would tell me "Arman prays for you in church every day," or "Chuck sends you good wishes." Not until the Twelve Weeks were long past, and we received the fantastic news that the cancer, too, was gone, did I realize how extensive Bill's support group really was.

As messages of happiness and congratulations rolled in through the computer, Bill told me about them and invited me to read them. Seated at his desk, I saw dozens of names on my husband's computer screen labeled "Karen Lee Update" list.

I understood that Bill, seeming solid, stolid, and solitary through those difficult months, had been nurtured, supported, and reassured by a large and loving circle. More Intangibles had been pulling for me than I realized.

Invisible energies have power.

Simple Gifts

As I recuperated from cancer and cancer treatment, walking in the Public Garden remained a life-affirming pleasure. Always I'd pay homage to the paper bark maple, the three dawn redwoods, and, of course, my white duck. I discovered new gifts, fresh affirmations of life. Ducklings! I watched the smallest over many weeks, as they learned to swim and to dive for food. When the first groups grew into the duckling equivalent of teenagers, their antics took on different charms as they flapped their wings and learned to fly. As new batches of ducklings hatched, overlapping circles of duck families animated the lagoon's waters and its grassy shores.

Circling the water, I'd often hum to myself, one of my meditation forms. Nature's life cycles seemed to support my own. Growing, exploring, and gaining strength. The ducklings and I had much in common.

The first weekend of June brought special gifts in human form. My father, Noah, and his youngest brother, Uncle Jack, came to see us. Ninety at the time, Noah made the cross-country trip to see for himself that his daughter was okay. From the west coast, he flew to New Jersey. There he reunited with many of his nieces and nephews. Then he and Uncle Jack boarded the Amtrak Acela Express and headed north to Boston.

Damp weather had no power to dampen our excitement at being together. On Friday afternoon we all exalted in Sara's happy school news:

an A+ on her math exam! On Saturday morning, we sent her off with love to take the SATs. Sitting and chatting around the dining room table, we savored pastrami sandwiches from a nearby deli.

Being together was the only activity we wanted. Outside entertainment seemed an unnecessary distraction. It was a life-affirming time for us all.

Meeting the Mighty Team

As Judi Piani's Reiki treatments unclogged my internal energies, they uncorked my creative energies too. With the Twelve Weeks long over and the lymphoma over too, the colorful stack of co-flex bandages still inhabited a good piece of territory on my desk. My mind's eye began to play with them. The result was a sculpture I named "Clinical Trial 2005."

Pleased with the sculpture, I was eager to present it to Dr. Treon. His assistant suggested that an appropriate time would be just at the conclusion of the research team's weekly meeting.

Nine months earlier, Pat Gratton and I had spent the morning with Zachary Hunter, on the fifth floor of the Mayer Building learning all we could about my treatment options. We'd briefly stepped inside one of the labs where young people were hard at work. Now, I returned with Bill and waited outside the conference room until the technical portion of the meeting concluded. When it did, we were welcomed in.

Around a long rectangular conference table sat fifteen young people. As Dr. Treon introduced us, we learned that this was a truly international group. Italy, Greece, Georgia—the Russia Federation variety—were all represented.

The sculpture, a wooden yardstick with dangling trios of colorful co-flex, displayed medical bandages in an unorthodox manner.

My doctor asked if I'd mind telling his team about the piece, and about my Waldenstrom's Macroglobulinemia experience, and my alemtuzumab experience, which of course I did. People listened attentively. I realized they were hearing something new.

Here's the gist of what I said:

"In my case, 'watch and wait' lasted less than five months. When retinal hemorrhages appeared we had to act.

Brookline, MA

"I was extremely fortunate to have a choice about my treatment, and even more fortunate to be able to enroll in a clinical trial. My family, my doctor, and I chose an aggressive option, although, really, every cancer-fighting drug has to be aggressive. Together we analyzed, evaluated, and selected a clinical trial that we hoped would achieve my goal. My goal was to be cured and cancer-free. The drug was alemtuzumab, a synthetic monoclonal antibody.

"The time frame was compact. During dose escalation week, I received alemtuzumab on Wednesday, Thursday, and Friday. For the next twelve weeks, I received alemtuzumab every Monday, Wednesday, and Friday. September 21st, 2005 was the start date. December 19th, 2005 was the end date.

"For reasons I didn't know at the time, during the Twelve Weeks of treatment, I saved every piece of co-flex that came home with me, on either my right arm or my left, depending on where the IV needle had been that day. Little stacks of the randomly colored bandages dotted my desk, one stack each week. After the Twelve Weeks were over, and after I'd regained some strength, these bandages became a sculpture.

"The thirty-six inches of the yardstick represent twelve segments of three inches each, or twelve weeks with three alemtuzumab infusions each. At one end is the co-flex from dose escalation week. At the opposite end, atop the yardstick, sits a lone piece of blue co-flex. Following the last dose of alemtuzumab, I developed a violent rash. On January 11th, 2006, intravenous Prednisone stemmed its tide. This last piece of co-flex came home on my arm that day."

When I concluded my doctor thanked me. For people who spend their days and nights in a laboratory, he said, meeting a patient and hearing about the clinical side of cancer care added the human dimension. It provided validation for their work, and assurance that they were making an important contribution, a significant difference. I appreciated the opportunity to be useful, and publicly expressed my gratitude to my doctor and his team.

Surprised and delighted with the artistic journal, Dr. Treon asked if I'd hold on to it for the time being, and present it to The Bing Center officially at a conference scheduled for November.

Of course I agreed.

The PET Scan

The CAT scan, the bone marrow biopsy, and the endoscopy all confirmed the blood test results: there was no sign of cancer, the standard used to define a complete remission. But when Bill and I saw Dr. Treon in the clinic on August 7th, he told us he wanted one more look, and one more confirmation. A PET scan was scheduled for August 9th.

Positron Emission Tomography. Only once before had I heard the term PET scan. On an alemtuzumab day, about halfway through the Twelve Weeks, I remembered hearing that this test could confirm that cancer was gone. Now, as I heard the term for the second time, a PET scan was being scheduled for me August 9th, 2006, at 1:30 in the afternoon.

As is my wont, I called ahead to learn as much as I could. Here's what I heard: a PET scan is done on the same machine as a CAT scan, but the test is more sensitive. While a CAT scan looks at structure inside the body, a PET scan looks at metabolic activity. It highlights tumor cells' activity.

To prepare for the test, after 7:30 the previous evening, I could have plain water only, and no exercise except walking. When I reported for the scan, there could be no metals on my clothes. I'd be given a "small bit" of radioactivity, and sit alone for one hour. During that hour, I could read, listen to music, and watch TV. I was instructed to bring Ativan.

As soon as Bill and I arrived at the hospital, we were separated. No wait time, no preliminaries. A nurse led me to a space so small that the oversized, over-upholstered lounge-style chair filled it. The nurse advised me to settle into the chair and find a comfortable position, one that I'd need to remain in for a full hour. She gave me a beverage containing a radioactive tracer. The idea was to drink the chemical, then remain motionless as it spread and circulated through my body. Closing and sealing the door, the nurse left me alone with the drink and my thoughts.

For all the weird diagnostic tests and treatments I'd been through, and the otherworldly places in which they'd been performed, the PET scan experience set a new standard for physical and emotional separation.

This place, too, felt like it belonged in outer space. I was so isolated and so disconnected from other people—by necessity and by design, to confine the radioactivity to me, and to shield others from it. Feeling alien and alienated, I perceived the room as one of those escape pods ejected from a doomed spaceship.

Holding my body immobile—which you know isn't my normal state—I kept my thoughts focused on cancer-free good health. Periodically, I'd glance at the small clock in the room. After one hour exactly, the nurse came to fetch me, I slowly unraveled myself from the chair, and we went together to the PET scan examination room. Once again, I was positioned center-stage, lying on my back inside the machine, alone with my body and my thoughts.

The scan would take thirty-five minutes, during which I must remain perfectly still. Knowing the importance of the test, and wanting with all my soul to have this confirmation of cure, I maintained a steady breath. I thought of a clean, cancer-free picture, I thought about time passing, I thought about nothing at all. I knew I could get through it, and I did.

The scan completed, checkout had its own set of rules.

A nurse advised Bill and me that, over the course of the next twenty-four hours, the radioactive material in my body would gradually dissipate. During that time, I should avoid close contact with others. Hugging and kissing babies was forbidden.

As after the first plasmaphereisis, I felt a foreignness inside my own body, new, strange, separating me from everybody else. I again felt unable, or perhaps unwilling, to speak. And I felt hunger.

Gesturing to Bill, I led the way to the food court in the Dana-Farber/Children's Hospital complex. Famished and needing food fast, I went for fast food. McDonald's had a new menu item, a snack wrap. Crispy chicken in a soft taco shell. Ordering two, I ate in silence.

That night, our family was invited to Donnie Levine's birthday dinner party. Knowing this would be a large gathering of warm and friendly people, as well as many young children, I fashioned a sort of nametag for myself. On a heart-shaped piece of pink paper I wrote:

I love you

BUT

Air Hug – Air Kiss

Thanks to Bill's e-mails, some of the guests had kept pace with my medical hegira, but to most, it was news. As briefly as I could, I explained why I wouldn't be hugging and kissing that night.

Two days later, our family was back at Squam Lake, renting the same house as the previous summer. In 2005, so much information and support from my mother, my doctor, and the Blood Donor Center, had come to me through the phone lines. So much more had come to me in person, as family and friends traveled to the lake with love and encouragement for Bill, Sara, and me. As I'd hydrated my body with Propel, I'd nourished my spirit and nurtured my optimism with meditation and nature's beauty. Feeling lousy and limited in my physical being, my mental being had managed to hold steady and maintain a positive outlook.

Now, in 2006, when the telephone rang, we had a joyous surprise. We'd been told it would take several days before we'd have the results of the PET scan, but here was one of Dr. Treon's assistants calling.

"Great news!" he exclaimed.

His report was exhilarating. The PET scan results were in: nothing was found. He told me Dr. Treon's main concern had been any thickening in the stomach or esophagus, or any transformation to a higher-grade lymphoma. If they were present, these would have shown up on the PET scan: but they did not.

Instantly, with joy and gratitude, I relayed the fantastic news to my husband, my daughter, and the family and friends who were with us.

Then I began the round of phone calls to the small circle of people whom I'd kept informed of developments along the way.

When I called Beverly Woo, she'd already reviewed the PET scan results. "This is the best," she said. "This brightening experience helps everyone. You had to look it right in the eyes."

When I called Bonnie Bermas, she was thrilled. Glad things had worked out, she wished my family and me a nice, relaxing summer, and thanked me for following up with her.

Calling one of my New York City touchstones, Helen Marx, I told her the wonderful news.

"Fantastic!" she said. "I'm thrilled."

And, of course, Dr. George Wong, my other New York City touchstone, was most pleased as well.

On August 10th, when Dr. Treon and I spoke, he said, "The news couldn't be better."

Blood test results from August 7th showed no monoclonal gammopathy and an IgM count of 147.

If there were Waldenstrom's Macroglobulinemia cancer cells to be seen, the PET scan would have shown it as a "smoking gun." But there was no smoking gun. Dr. Treon said he was ecstatic with this exciting result. With it, he said, the sun shined on a lot of people, oncology professionals as well as their patients. When patients in the clinic experience success, research fellows in the laboratory receive validation, confirmation, and encouragement for their work. The urgency of helping patients was a reality that my doctor told me he never forgets.

Gratitude and appreciation for cancer-free good health are a reality for me, which I always remember.

Friday, November 4th, was the date set for The Bing Center's symposium on Waldenstrom's Macroglobulinemia. Connected both to Dana-Farber and the Longwood Medical Area food court, a large conference room was the site of lectures and lunch. Listening to the presenters, I recognized many as members of my doctor's team. Chatting at lunch, I learned that some of the guests were patients.

That evening, at the Harvard Faculty Club in Cambridge, Bill and I had the pleasure of sitting with the young members of the research team. We enjoyed their vivacity, and we made friends.

As dinner concluded, I was invited to speak. With outstretched arms and upturned palms supporting my sculpture's wooden yardstick, I was a wide load. Unable to fit behind the podium, I stood and spoke directly to the group of seventy doctors, scientists, patients, family, and friends. I spoke from my heart, in my own, unamplified voice.

Briefly, I told my story. I had the privilege of publicly thanking my doctor and all the Bing Center team for banishing my cancer. With gratitude and respect, I officially presented the "Clinical Trial 2005" sculpture to Dr. Treon. With humility and sincerity, he accepted it.

Mounted on the wall of the Bing Center for all to see, the sculpture reminds us that together we can conquer cancer.

Zero—Zero

Monday, November 6th, brought Bill and me back to the Dana-Farber clinic for a routine three month check up.

We met with Dr. Treon, then I went to phlebotomy. As my blood was pulled into many vials with many different colored tops, my gaze and my thoughts focused on the wall calendar. 2006. To me it read "I have zero cancer, and zero monoclonal gammopathy."

A few days later, when Dr. Treon called me with the lab results, he left this message: "Hi, its Steve Treon calling. Hope you're all doing very well. Just to let you know, no monoclonal gammopathy, one of our favorite things. I want to congratulate you again and wish you well. All the best wishes, bye-bye."

Spontaneous Art

In January, I felt capable of making a public appearance at a New England Aquarium board meeting. When the president asked how we might further engage the public in our work, I thought, "Why not bring sea animals to the cancer ward."

Flipping over the agenda sheets, I surprised myself with the two drawings I made.

When a neighbor invited me to join her painting class, I accepted happily. When we arrived in the classroom, there were a few things I wasn't used to. The model wore clothes, yards and yards of them, which totally obscured the shape of her body. Everyone else planned to work on a single image, on a single canvas, all morning. Not my style.

I positioned myself at the edge of the room, and it's a good thing I did. In a group of artists who worked in oils and approached their canvases slowly and seriously, I was odd-girl-out.

The others set their canvases up on easels; I laid my big pad of paper flat on a table. With watercolor paints, pastel sticks, and calligraphy ink arranged at my right hand, I wanted to make the most of this opportunity and this two-hour period. I didn't want to waste most of it "warming up."

Ripping a page of paper from the pad and unscrewing the cap from the ink bottle, I outlined my first image with a generous splash that spanned the paper's width. That gesture unleashed energy. I worked fast, and I worked free. As I finished a page, I dropped it on the floor to dry. Ripping, splashing, and dropping, I was the noisiest person in the room. Despite my unorthodox behavior, the others were extremely nice to me. Some said they admired the abandon with which I worked. From this class and another the following week, two dozen paintings emerged.

A couple of weeks later, I carted them to Judi Piani's house. I was glad to be painting again, and I knew Judi would be glad for me. As we looked at the work together, a realization came. On the pages, I saw myself and my spirit. The setting, as I'd interpreted it, depicted the isolation I'd felt as a patient in the infusion room, and the feelings of the experience. Although I hadn't been aware of it, I'd interpreted the studio models and the setting as a series of self-portraits during the Twelve Weeks.

"L'Cha'im"

Now we come to February 6th, 2007. As Dr. Treon had predicted, I was alive and well on my fifty-ninth birthday. Cancer-free and healthy, I felt energetic and creative.

For a long time, say fifteen months, I'd been keeping, not recycling, a few plastic bottles from the range of beverages I'd imbibed during the course of this Waldenstrom's event. I had a sculpture in mind, a memento, a physical journal to document and remember the journey. Its name would be "L'Cha'im 2005." In Hebrew, "L'Cha'im" means "To Life."

At one point last spring, I'd organized the containers sequentially, as I'd needed them. Over time, I set them up on a board from a demolished cabinet, but couldn't commit, couldn't glue them in place. The bottles went back into a paper shopping bag. Once during the summer, I thought of throwing the empty bottles into a picnic basket and delivering it to Dr. Treon along with "Clinical Trial 2005." Another time, I thought of throwing the bottles out. Something told me not to.

Saturday, February 3rd, 2007, was the time to make the piece, and I did, completing it on Sunday, February 4th—Super Bowl Sunday.

Here's how the bottles sit, from left to right:

Ginger ale, given when a person wakes up from the anesthesia following an endoscopy; Canadian Club, self-administered to invite numbness and shield the shock of knowing there's cancer inside; Gatorade, thanks to Dr. Treon's knowing, at the molecular level, that Waldenstrom's challenges normal hydration; Propel, my Gatorade substitute; and finally, water, because that's all a person with normal, healthy blood needs to drink.

Nail polish drops, representing blood, begin almost purple, become denser, change to a brighter red, and evolve to a clear, pure, luminous red. There's a chaos of white netting from a Christmas tree, tent-like, entangling all but the water bottle. There's co-flex, the bandage used to wrap a wrist or an arm after the IV needle is pulled. And there's a timeline, a seamstress' measuring tape, glued along the board's bottom edge, wrapping three of its four sides. Sixty inches, and just about sixty weeks, from January 1st, 2005—when diagnostic tests were about to begin—to February 12th, Dr. Treon's birthday.

On the back, the side that didn't have the tape measure glued to it, I wrote:

"L'Cha'im 2005," a.k.a. "It's So Great." For Dr. Steven P. Treon and your Mighty Team.
"We will celebrate many happy birthdays together."
SPT, MD, PhD. Karen Lee Sobol 6th February 2007.

Monday, February 5th, was the date for my three-month check-up.

For every post-alemtuzumab, post-rash visit to the clinic, I'd brought Dr. Treon something. Goji berries, goji juice, the "Clinical Trial 2005" sculpture. What could I offer him now? Of course—the new sculpture! But—I'd be clear that while I wanted him to see it, Dr. Treon didn't have to keep it if he didn't want to.

To transport the sculpture and to conceal it, I encased the "bookshelf" in a white plastic trash bag and bound it with white string.

As was our habit, Bill and I went together to Dana-Farber. Bill dropped me, and the large package—forty inches long, eight inches wide, sixteen inches high—at the main entrance to the Gosman Adult Clinic. I entered happy—no trepidation, no anxiety—smiling at people. But as usual, I took the least populated route through the lobby, and I took note of the blank look of pain in some people's eyes.

12 13 14 15 16 17 18 19 20 21 22 23 24 25 26 27 28 29 30 31 32
41 42 43 44 45 46 47 48

Calmly, I checked in, recited my date of birth, and extended my right hand to receive my bracelet. I found the waiting room relatively empty, and chose a small seating alcove with a table. The table received the bundle of sculpture. I sat—a rarity for me.

Although the receptionist said Dr. Treon was "on time," we waited an hour or more.

When a clinical assistant called my name, I entered the clinic.

"Are you having any pain today?"

"That's right, I forgot: you always ask that question."

Vital signs were measured and recorded, then I rejoined Bill in the waiting area.

When Dr. Treon wandered through, he stopped to greet Bill and me.

As we hugged each other, the doctor eyed the white plastic presence on the magazine table. I'm pretty sure he was wondering what I'd cooked up now.

Eventually my name was called again. Bill, the bundle, and I were shown to the largest, nicest exam room—the same one in which we'd first met Dr. Treon on April 6th, 2005.

When the doctor joined us, we embraced again. Because the bundle took up so much space, and its curvaceous, chaotic form contrasted so blatantly with the right angles and orderliness of the room, and because it again caught Dr. Treon's eye, it practically insisted on attention. I removed its trash bag wrapping right away.

Dr. Treon's response was one of wonder and amazement. As I held it and explained it, I rotated the shelf and its offerings.

Invited to give the keynote address at an upcoming conference in Israel, Dr. Treon told us that "L'Cha'im" would come in handy, and he'd be practicing his pronunciation.

Dr. Treon asked how my energy level was.

"Fantastic. I feel the best I have in ten years."

He began to ask the usual litany of questions, but in a light voice.

"Any pain, night sweats..."

"No. No."

Installed high on a bookcase in Dr. Treon's office, "L'Cha'im 2005" catches people's attention. It's a humorous interpretation of the shelf outside the lab, where Zachary Hunter had asked Pat to park her Diet Coke bottle, and me to park my Propel bottle so long ago.

Saying Thank You

In late April of 2007, I spotted a small reddish circle high on my right arm, close to the shoulder. The next day, a cluster of tiny blisters inhabited the circle. This was clearly a case of "Do not pass go. Call Dr. Treon."

Over the phone, Dr. Treon diagnosed the outbreak of Herpes Zoster: shingles. He immediately prescribed Valtrex. How lucky! Thanks to my doctor's medical knowledge and quick action, the shingles remained confined to the site of its initial outbreak. Although the rash surface never spread, the subsurface virus radiated along neural pathways up to and through my shoulder, and down, to and through my arm, hands, and fingers.

A vicious virus, shingles can lie dormant for decades as a result of chicken pox. A person with an impaired immune system, like me, was particularly vulnerable.

The permeating pain became mind numbing and physically debilitating. Gabapentin and, once again, Prednisone, were prescribed. Gabapentin failed to decrease the pain. Dr. Treon substituted Lyrica. When that had no effect, I decided to skip it altogether, and suffer through the pain.

When Bill and Sara took a weekend trip to visit colleges, I attended a two-day seminar led by Dr. Wayne Dyer. His philosophy and meditation system had inspired me profoundly throughout the cancer ordeal, and served as a nurturing reservoir of optimism and empowerment. Honored as I was to be in Dr. Dyer's presence and learn from him in person, searing neurological pain split my attention between Dr. Dyer's words and its own ruthless web.

Pain notwithstanding, I attended both days of the seminar. During an intermission, conference participants crowded toward Dr. Dyer, his books in their hands, clamoring for his autograph. My desire was different. I sought contact, and connection. I managed to flow with the group until I reached Dr. Dyer. He seemed surprised and relieved that his autograph wasn't my goal. I introduced myself, offered a brief synopsis of my story, and expressed my gratitude to him. I thanked him for having contributed mightily to my re-gained good health and well-being.

When people are good to us, and do good things for us, I feel it's important to say "Thank You."

Breakthrough

Eventually, the shingles virus wore itself out, just as it had worn me out, and it left me alone. The next time Bill and I went to Dana-Farber for my three-month checkup, Dr. Treon told me that he'd be prescribing more Valtrex for me. Because my immune system had been shattered, and remained tattered, as a precaution against a recurrence of shingles he wanted me to take the antiviral medication every day, for the rest of my life. For the next year or so, a Valtrex pill was part of my day.

In November 2007, a group of paintings, spare in color, vibrant with life, signaled my return to work. The canvases share a luminous organic transparency. Paint, pencil, copper, enamel, and ink form the images.

The total number: Twelve.

Then, on August 18th, 2008, results from routine blood work showed a remarkable result. Dr. Treon was jubilant as he reported to me.

"IgM is 130. IFX—no monoclonal gammopathy. The CD4 has made a very nice recovery. It's 564. This is a good chunk of information. There's very important learning here."

The T cells were back! CD19 and normal B cells showed a good immune recovery, too.

"There's no need to continue taking Valtrex," he said.

Hallelujah! The complete immune system had regenerated! Although we had no way to gauge if all the new cells functioned with the full capacity of pre-alemtuzumab cells, we were beyond thrilled that they were back, and comfortable assuming that they all would do their jobs.

"This opens a debate," my doctor went on to say. "When do we start using the word cure?"

When do we get away from the mentality that this disease is "incurable?"

Generous, life-giving, wishing me well, my doctor's parting words that day: "Make us proud."

Hallelujah again! A Waldenstrom's Macroglobulinemia diagnosis need no longer be a life sentence or condemnation. There was healing, and there was hope.

Like the high tide in the ocean that lifts all boats, a breakthrough in the world of cancer lifts all hopes.

Cure

"Hi Karen Lee, it's Steve Treon calling. I saw you'd called earlier today and I presume it was about figuring out if the M spike results came back, and they're negative. And, once again, congratulations! I'm ecstatic, needless to say. If you have any questions feel free to call. All the best and have a good weekend. Bye-bye."

Late in the summer of 2008, Dr. Treon told me of the great strides, and significant progress he and his team were making. The mysteries of this complex blood cancer were being systematically unraveled. The researchers were zeroing in on its root causes.

"We will find a cure," I heard my doctor say. "We won't settle for anything less."

Epilogue

Like science and like art, the Twelve Weeks was at its core, a creative process. Both my personal world and the world of cancer research received a valuable legacy.

Fraught with challenges and uncertainties, the cancer experience made great demands of me. It required and inspired higher levels of truth, trust, and free fall. Hope took on new meaning. In many ways, the mental and spiritual evolution that cancer sparked continues to develop.

With meditation a twice-daily practice almost every day, my mind is calm and my thoughts clear. I've taken Reiki training and embrace new energy healing techniques as they cross my path. Music and the singing bowls are there when I need them.

With the good fortune to be pain-free and cancer-free, I've added some yoga and Gyrotonic exercise to swimming and walking. I respect and apply Nurse Laura's mantra: "Nutrition, Hydration, Rest."

When I felt myself drowning in quicksand, I was lucky to have "a different branch," in the forms of holistic healing techniques and a clinical trial, to reach for. As I made the mental transition from terror to hope, my family, friends, and medical team supported me. My vision to be cancer-free and healthy anchored my spirit through the traumas of disease, treatment, and recuperation.

About time, I treasure it, and for the most part, I live in the moment. My family is closer and more loving every day, friendships deepen and strengthen, and my heart holds unending love for all who helped me move from sickness back to health. Although I couldn't see the "Intangibles," I could feel them pulling for me.

Medical science continues to benefit from my experience. After the cancer was extinguished, my immune system completely regenerated, and now functions normally. My body experienced no residual damage and harbors no residual toxicity. The biology-based drug I received, and the results it achieved, remind us that the natural environment holds many gifts, and many secrets yet to be discovered, that can dramatically contribute to our collective well-being. In my case, the clinical trial had a remarkable outcome: the definition of Waldenstrom's Macroglobulinemia as "incurable" has been challenged.

An international disease, this lymphoma has been diagnosed in people on six of the seven continents. At the moment, only Antarctica is exempt. In terms of incidence per capita around the world, diagnoses of non-Hodgkins lymphomas, which includes Waldenstrom's Macroglobulinemia, are rapidly increasing. Experts believe lymphomas are partially due to genetic predisposition, and that environmental factors like pollution can trigger cancer in susceptible individuals.

In their ongoing work to identify the source of this disease and the safest, most effective way to attack it, Dr. Treon and his Mighty Team revisit my file for clues that will help point the way to a cure.

Many valubale lessons were learned from this clinical trial. They benefit current patients and provide insight concerning this and other therapies as physicians and scientists look to the future. As new drugs are tested in new clinical trials, more patients benefit from longer remissions, a better quality of life, and more time to spend with loved ones. In laboratories and clinics around the world, researchers and physicians predict that the number of complete remissions will increase. Perhaps the disease will become preventable.

As I observed in the infusion room, when anyone experiences some success, everyone experiences hope. It is my belief and expectation that Waldenstrom's Macroglobulinemia, and all other cancers, will become curable. I hold on to this hope.

Acknowledgments

The successful outcome of Twelve Weeks, both the medical process and the book, was a team effort. At just the right moments, people appeared with information, suggestions, and hope in many forms.

Family and friends cared for me and believed with me. Talented doctors, researchers, and healers provided expertise and spiritual strength. In his or her own way, everyone supported me and inspired me. As you read my story, you'll come to know them.

In making a book, encouragement matters. With patience and humor, Michele Baker, M.D. helped me re-enter the emotional world of cancer and stay on track writing about it. After hearing me speak and learning of my experience, David LeVine became my mentor and the book's champion.

A dedicated and talented group contributed to producing Twelve Weeks. Julie Sherman's patient, thoughtful work helped guide the manuscript's development. Stuart Horwitz provided the structural vision and the critical voice of the ideal editor. With enthusiasm and commitment, Karen Byrne's editorial voice and eagle eye brought fine-tuning to the text. George Bouret's photography captured the essence of the art. With enthusiasm for the verbal and the visual, Nick Stone deftly wove the elements together.

To each and all, my appreciation, my gratitude, and my love.